LAURA THALASSA

The QUEEN of All that DIES

BURNING EMBER PRESS

A Burning Ember Book
Published in the United States by Burning Ember Press, an imprint of Lavabrook Publishing Group.

For my mother,

the strongest woman I know

CHAPTER 1

SERENITY

I CAN BARELY remember a time before the war. The green, orderly lawns, the rows of houses, the neatly assigned shelves of food. That quest for perfection was the first thing to go when the king turned his attention to our land.

The first, but not the last.

War felled more than just order. We once knew casual compassion—politeness even. People smiled for the sake of smiling. Laughed because they couldn't contain their joy. One positive emotion begat another, and it spread like the most decadent disease.

And the colors. Every once in a while I still dream in such vivid colors. What I would give to live in such a bright place again.

The world we knew is nothing like the one I live in.

But none of this, none of it was so costly a price as the one we eventually paid. Somewhere along the way, my people lost the most precious thing of all.

Hope.

Well, most of us lost it. Most, but not all.

AN ALARM GOES off in the barracks, and I groan. My roommates—all seven of them—slide out of their beds before I do. But they hadn't stayed up late learning about international diplomacy.

I pull back my threadbare blanket and swing my legs out. As soon as my bare feet hit the cold concrete, I begin moving, grabbing my fatigues and changing into them. Most of the women next to me have already shoved theirs on and left. They're the smart ones. There might not be any breakfast by the time I get to the mess hall.

I sit on my bed and pull on my boots, wishing for the hundredth time that there was natural light in this place. For the last five years I've lived in this bunker nestled belowground. No matter how much I get used to this way of life, I can't adjust to this one thing.

Once my shoes are laced up, I jog out of my room and down to the cafeteria. Just as I suspected, I'm too late. The line winds out the door.

My stomach contracts painfully; it's a familiar ache. We're all underfed here. Most of the land above us has been razed, which makes food scarce. No one will admit it, but the war is coming to an end. It has to; our people are slowly starving to death.

Despite the long wait, I stand at the back of the line anyway, hoping there might be something left over by the time I reach the front. I can't bear the thought of waiting until dinner to eat.

I've been standing in line for almost fifteen minutes when a hand wraps around my arm and tugs me out of line.

"Wha—?" I glance up at Will, the general's son. He's handsome, has the dirtiest sense of humor, and he's responsible for getting me into trouble over the last five years. If circumstances were different, we might have dated, married, then had kids. But this isn't the world my grandparents grew up in.

"Did you have to pull me out of line?"

His face is serious, but his eyes shine excitedly. "The representatives want to see you—your father himself sent me here to get you."

Instantly my mood changes from annoyed to suspicious. "Why? What's going on?" The people near me glance in our direction.

Will's eyes flick to them before returning to me. "Not here, Serenity," he says quietly.

I look longingly at the cooks serving up oatmeal and accept the fact that I'm going to go hungry for the rest of the day.

I nod. "'Kay, I'll bite." I'm curious what put the twinkle in Will's eyes.

I follow him down the dimly lit halls until we arrive at the bunker's conference room. This is where the American representatives of the Western United Nations gather.

The WUN is a collection of countries that make up North and South America. It's a coalition that's been fighting the eastern hemisphere for almost fifteen years.

Not the eastern hemisphere, I think darkly. *King Montes Lazuli.*

When we stop outside the room, I can't help but swallow. The last time I was called in here on official business, the representatives had decided that I would begin training as the next emissary. My father currently holds the role. Poor Will has been training to become the next general for even longer than I have. I don't envy him, but I'm also guessing that no one envies me. If we lose the war, we'll likely be killed or imprisoned.

Not that the thought scares me. I'm already dying.

WILL KNOCKS ON the door, and a moment later my father opens it. He smiles, but there's a tension that pinches the corners of his eyes. "Serenity, glad you could join us," he says. He nods to Will and opens the door for us both to enter.

Unlike me, Will's now required to attend these meetings with the representatives. I consider it a blessing that I haven't yet been asked to sit in on them, but judging by the assessing looks I'm receiving as I step inside, I have a horrible feeling that is all about to change.

The two dozen men and women seated around the table are all that remains of our political leaders. King Lazuli has killed off most of the presidential line of succession. We who live in this bunker are all that's left.

"Serenity Freeman," General Chris Kline says. Will's father. "Good morning."

I incline my head, my hands clasped tightly together. "Morning."

Will places a hand on my back and leads me to a free seat next to my father. I can tell my dad's nervous by the tense set of his jaw.

I sit down, Will following suit. A quick glance at the faces around me tells me that no one here has gone to bed yet. My clasped hands squeeze even tighter together. Whatever is going on, it's big, and I'm somehow involved.

"The WUN is in danger of collapsing." The general just comes out and says it. I've always appreciated his bluntness, but now it makes my stomach clench. He's as good as told me that we're all dead men here. "The eastern hemisphere is much larger than we are; nuclear warfare has crippled our numbers and our economy. We're not going to last much longer."

All this information I'd pieced together on my own. I just don't understand why General Kline is telling me this.

I nod and glance at my father. He won't look at me.

"It's time to think about peace and what's best for our people."

My eyes widen. Now I think I do know what he's talking about. The representatives want to forge the terms of surrender.

A sick feeling twists my gut. I already know the general's next words before he says them.

"As the emissary of the WUN, your father is expected

to go to Geneva, where the peace talks are to be held." The general pauses. "And as your father's apprentice, we think it's best that you go along with him."

I swallow; my eyes sting. Our leaders always come back in body bags after visiting the king. And we can't do anything about it. The WUN has tried to assassinate him dozens of times, but somehow he always survives. The Undying King, as some call him.

My death sentence just got bumped a little sooner. As did my father's.

I look at my dad again, and I can see his eyes are red, his face anguished. I place a hand on his forearm and squeeze it. At least we'd be going in together. I prefer that to him going alone.

I turn back to General Kline. "I accept whatever duties are required of me."

A muscle in my father's forearm jerks beneath my hand. It's the only indication that this situation is tearing him up. I'm all he has left; he's all I have left. The thought of losing the last person in the world that loves you is terrifying. But no one in this room has the luxury of being selfish.

General Kline smiles grimly. "Good." He glances down at the paper in front of him. "You and your father will be representing the entire WUN."

What he means is that Canada and Central America are too splintered to send someone over. And the political infighting in South America makes them too fragmented to attempt this.

"We've already contacted our correspondences overseas

as well as the king's retinue," General Kline continues.

I curl my lip at the term *retinue*. The king has people who wait on him hand and foot while we starve.

"They are expecting our arrival in Geneva on Wednesday."

"So soon?" I manage to get out. That's three days from now.

The general's eyes move to mine, and they flash like my fear disappoints him. I can't help it. The king is the boogey man; no weapon scares me as much as that deceptively charming face of his.

"You will be filmed," he says, ignoring my question. "The world will be watching. This means you must tread lightly. If you do well, you'll boost the morale of our citizens. If you or your father are killed, it will prove to the world just how vulnerable we are."

His words make me lightheaded. I'd assumed that death was the worst outcome, but no. The worst outcome is that we never get the chance to work on a peace agreement between the two hemispheres. We've heard stories of the conquered lands. There's a reason we've waited this long to surrender.

"Ignore your normal routine starting today. Lisa will swing by your room in an hour to get you fitted for some appropriate garments. Tomorrow you'll be boarding the jet for Geneva. Try to get some rest before then."

This is what I've been preparing to do ever since I became my father's apprentice. Forge alliances. I've learned a lot of useful skills, but I've never had the opportunity to implement them as I do now. And now the fate of the entire western hemisphere depends on my father's and my ability to negotiate with the enemy.

CHAPTER 2

SERENITY

NINE YEARS AGO I watched my mother die. That was also the day I received the scar that runs from the corner of my eye down my cheek, a permanent tear for all the souls the war has claimed.

At the time the eastern hemisphere had just fallen and the new king had set his sights on the west. In the wake of oncoming war, my father started working nonstop, leaving my mother and me to keep each other company.

That Saturday morning was just like any other. I laid under our coffee table flipping through a magazine, while my mom sat on the couch reading.

The only indication that something was about to happen was the trembling ground beneath me. I heard Mom's mug rattle on the glass side table next to her.

My mother's gaze met mine. Even then we knew enough

about the war to immediately think the worst. But never had the enemy attacked civilians on our own soil.

A whine started up, distant at first. The sound got louder.

"Serenity, get down!" My mother lunged for me.

She wasn't fast enough.

The whine cut out, and for the briefest of moments, all was quiet. Then our front yard lit up, the windows shattered. A howling, fiery blast tore through the house, throwing my mother forward.

That was all I saw before the force of the explosion blasted the coffee table away from me and I tumbled, my body a ragdoll. Debris sliced against my skin, none so deep as the gash across my face.

Other than those cuts and what I later found out was a fractured wrist and several bruised ribs, I survived the explosion unscathed. Sheer providence kept me from further harm.

In the distance more bombs went off, the sound a whiplash to my ears. Each time they did, the ground shook violently. I whimpered at the pain in my arms and chest. But not even that could distract me from the sight ahead of me.

My mom's eyes had always gleamed like she had some secret to share.

Now they were vacant.

THERE'S A KNOCK on my door, and a moment later Lisa walks in.

"Hi sweetie," she says. The endearment always amuses me. As though I'm some innocent flower. I'm not.

"Hey Lisa." I can't muster much enthusiasm. Before the war, Lisa owned a wedding dress shop, so she's been the residential seamstress since her husband and the rest of her family moved in.

Her husband, like most of the men and women here, was an important figure when we still had a functioning government. My best guess is that he was a badass dude—the kind that can't actually tell you their profession because of national security. I see a lot of those types around here. The bunker only has a finite amount of space, so only the most essential men and women are allowed to live here with their families.

Lisa drops the pile of material she carried in onto my bed, and my eyes are immediately drawn to the vibrant colors I see. Bright red, gold, rose petal pink. Iridescent beads catch the light.

I finger a bit of lace that pokes out amongst the pile. "Please tell me these aren't my outfits." They're all beautiful, but the thought of wearing such flashy garments is horrifying.

She gives me a rueful smile. "Sorry babe, but orders are orders."

"And what orders are those?" Surely I'd have heard about this. I thought I'd be wearing drab suits just like the rest of the men and women that meet for diplomacy talks.

"To have all eyes on you."

My jaw slides open, and I look at her in disbelief. "Why would the WUN want that?" My father was the one they should have their eyes on. Not me.

Her eyes are sad. "Because you are young and attractive. It's easier to sympathize with someone who looks like you than someone like your father."

It makes sense. Of course it does. The representatives have to leverage whatever they can. Still I grind my teeth together. Those who watch the peace talks might sympathize more if I dress like this, but they will also see us as weak. No one is afraid of a pretty bauble, and that's just what I'll be.

"Time to remove your clothes, sweetie."

I shuck off my fatigues and stand in my bra and panties. Lisa doesn't say anything about the sick way my collarbones stick out or my flat, empty stomach, but her brows pull together while she takes down my measurements, as though it pains her to see me this way.

There was a time when obesity was the losing battle our people faced. Not so anymore. As soon as food became scarce, curves became coveted.

Lisa puts away the tape measurer and rifles through the clothing, removing garments that she knows she can't tailor to fit me.

"Where did you even get all of these?" I ask.

"They're not mine. These are property of the WUN— and no, I have no idea where and when they came by these."

I try some of the remaining garments on, and Lisa tugs and adjusts the material, writing down notes in her notepad on adjustments. After the better part of an hour, she packs up her stuff. "I'll finish these tonight and have them packed for you tomorrow," she says. "And I'm supposed to tell you that Jessica's pulled out of kitchen duty to cut your hair and show you a thing or two about makeup."

I almost groan at the thought. Getting a haircut is one thing, but makeup? I've never worn it. I'm going to look like a clown. All for a televised meeting that will be viewed mostly by the enemy.

Few people in the WUN will even be able to watch. The king destroyed a large portion of our electronics years ago, and he has since halted the sale and distribution of all devices manufactured in the Eastern Empire. We have only a limited number of functioning electronics left.

Lisa cups my face, bringing me back to the present. She stares at me for a long time, and I can tell she wants to say something profound. Her eyes are getting watery, and I'm getting distinctly uncomfortable.

All she ends up saying, however, is, "You've got this, sweetie."

I nod my head once, not trusting my own voice. Because the truth is, I don't. We don't. This is really, truly the beginning of the end.

MY ROOMMATES HAVE long since gone to bed when I sneak out of the barracks, my hair several inches shorter from Jessica's ministrations. At night the florescent lights that line the subterranean hallways are turned off to save energy, so I make my way through the compound based on touch and memory.

When I get to the storage cellar, most of the group is

already there, waiting for the meeting to begin.

Someone whistles. "Is that makeup, Serenity? And here we thought you were a dude this entire time."

I flip off David, the guy responsible for the comments. All he does is laugh.

Will nods to me and pats an empty crate next to him. I make my way through the cramped room to sit down. We wait five more minutes, and when no one else shows up, Will clears his throat. "This is the North American WUN command center. Let's commence the hundred and forty-third meeting of the Resistance." His voice is being recorded and streamed to other meetings occurring throughout the globe.

As the general's son, Will became the de facto correspondent with the Resistance. The group of us sitting here—all former soldiers and children of the various representatives—gather and relay information back to our leaders.

We make these meetings as clandestine as possible. While the WUN needs the information the Resistance feeds us, we don't want to be openly associated with them. While we share a common enemy, they're a terrorist organization.

"What are the casualty numbers this week?" Will asks first.

A crackly voice comes on over the Internet. "Ten thousand, three hundred and eleven globally—that's the official number. As usual, we have reason to believe there are several thousand more unreported casualties that have died from radiation sickness and biological warfare."

Next to Will, David jots these numbers down.

I rub my forehead. As much as I'm dreading the visit to Geneva, the WUN is at its breaking point. Our hemisphere's population is only a fraction of what it was before the war. It's not just fighting that's felling our numbers. People are sick.

Will's mouth is a thin line. "Any news on the enemy?"

"They're still holding the Panama Canal, and reports in the area say that they've taken over the hospitals and research clinics in the neighboring cities—just as they have in all other conquered territories."

"Have our spies figured out what the king's men are doing in these locations?"

"Same as all the others—a little of this and that. Stem cell research, the regeneration of cells, you know, the usual work up."

And we still had no idea what real medical developments the king was actually researching. He's managed to keep that under wraps for as long as we've been fighting this war.

"There was, however, one thing unusual about this takeover," the Resistance member says. "Many of the technicians the king let go were dazed."

"What do you mean by 'dazed'?" Will asks.

"They were confused. Couldn't answer our questions."

"Any ideas what might've happened to them?" I cut in.

The voice on the other end pauses. "None except the most general."

"And what would that be?" I press.

"They lost their memory."

THE NEXT DAY a knock on my door signals that it's time to go. I sit alone in the barracks, fingering my mother's necklace around my neck. I'm already wearing one of the dresses that Lisa tailored for me.

I despise the thing.

The door opens and Will pokes his head in. The sight of him brings me back to last night's conversation with the Resistance. The king's overtaken the Panama Canal; no wonder the WUN's folding. The war's ending soon if they've wrangled control of it.

And the hospitals ... everywhere the king goes, he infiltrates the labs first. Initially we'd thought it was to decimate any chance of medical relief—and yes, he does do that. But when stories of his unusual research trickled in, we began to take note.

"Mind if I come in?" Will asks. His eyes widen as they move over me.

I motion him inside, banishing thoughts of the king. "What are you doing here?" I ask once Will closes the door behind him.

"I wanted to say goodbye to you," he says. He shifts his weight, sliding his hands into his pockets. His eyes flick over me again. "You look really nice."

I snort. "Yeah, if by nice you mean I look like a giant peacock," I say, picking up a piece of the dress and letting it flutter back to my side.

Will sits down next to me. "You make it look good," he says, his eyes full of that same intensity I'd seen him wear earlier.

Suddenly I get the impression that this isn't just a

friendly goodbye. Will's not looking at me like I'm the soldier who fought alongside him. Nor is he looking at me like the friend who would stay up late talking about anything and everything that crossed our minds.

He's looking at me the way a lover should.

"Serenity, you're going to save our country," he says, clasping my hand.

I shake my head. "Don't put that on me, Will. We both know how this ends."

"No," he says, squeezing my hand tightly. "We don't. And the representatives wouldn't send you if they didn't think you'd sway the king."

The king. I'd have to speak with him, smile at him, pretend that he didn't destroy everything that I held dear.

"But more than that, you have to come back because I'll be waiting for you."

My throat constricts. I can't tell if it's from this strange ardor of his or that, in this moment, I realize I will never experience love. Not given my circumstances.

Will's expression softens. It's such a foreign emotion on him that I almost laugh.

And then he leans down and presses his lips to mine.

For a moment, I'm so shocked I do nothing but sit there. And then I recover and kiss him back. I would've thought my lips would be clumsy, but they're not, and the kiss ... the kiss is nice.

When it ends, I blink at him. Will has a whimsical look on his face. It relaxes his hard features, and it speeds up my heart to think that I'm responsible for it.

I take in his dark eyes. "I didn't know."

"Now you do." He's looking at me like he's waiting for something else. Something more.

I touch my fingers to my lips. "I wish things were different," I say, because it's the only thing I can.

The sharp lines return to his face. "So do I." He eyes the door across from us and clears his throat. "We should probably get going. I'm supposed to be escorting you out."

I nod and grab my bag. As I sling it over my shoulder, both Will and I hear the clank of metal inside it.

Will raises his eyebrows. "They're not going to let you take your gun."

"Then they're going to have to pry it away from my cold, dead hands." And I mean it. If I'm going to die on enemy soil—and I have no doubt that I am—I want the few beloved possessions close by. One of those is the gun my father gave me. Morbid, I know, but during the last ten years it's become a dear and trusted companion.

A smile spreads along Will's face. "I'm not sure even death could take that gun away from you." His smile slips as soon as he says the words, and I get the impression that he's vividly imagining it. My death.

"C'mon, let's go." Will takes my hand, threading his fingers through mine. This is the first time he's held my hand that I can remember. I can't help but think that it's too little too late.

I take one last look at the barracks as we slip out the door. The room is the closest thing I've had to a home for a long time now. But as I take in the narrow beds, the cement walls and floor, the basin all eight of us use to wash out hands and faces, I can't say I'm all that sorry to leave.

My heels clack as we walk through the bunker, drawing attention my way. The people we pass stop and stare. News has spread that I'm going to Geneva for the peace talks. I'm now the girl walking to her execution in a dress. But some look hopeful, and their hope gives me courage.

Will's palm slickens the closer we get to the stairwell, which will take us to the surface. As soon as we round the corner and see it, his hand tightens on mine.

"This is where I leave you," he says.

I nod. Swallow. No one goes outside unless ordered to. The radiation from the blasts is still too dangerously high. And if the radiation doesn't kill you, your fellow citizens might.

Will tugs on our clasped hands, pulling me to him. "Make it back here alive," he says. His lips brush my forehead. It's not a goodbye kiss, and I really appreciate that.

After a moment, he lets me go. I back up to the stairwell door, watching him. I feel hyper alive. It's the same feeling I have every time I fight on the battlefield. I can't figure out if it's the sudden, startling possibility of Will and me or the prospect of meeting the king that has me feeling this way, but it's not an unpleasant sensation.

"I'll try my best to come back alive," I say.

Will gives me a small smile. "I'm holding you to that, Serenity."

I CLIMB THE stairs for what seems like ages. When I finally reach the top, the floor closest to the surface, several people wait for me. Among them are the general and my father.

My father's eyebrows nudge up when he sees me. This is the first time I've ever looked remotely feminine.

"You look ... just like your mother," he manages to say. I blush at this—that's the best compliment my father could've given me.

General Kline grunts his approval. "Now that you're here, Serenity, it's time to get moving." As he speaks, the general begins leading the group to the garage, where all our vehicles are kept. "We're sending a dozen guards to go with you two," the general says to my father and me. "They are there to protect you should negotiations dissolve."

The general, my father, and I get into one of the military vehicles. The rest of our entourage piles into two other cars.

"I want you both to report to me every night," General Kline continues. "Be sure to watch your words. Let's assume the king can hear everything you say to me. You both know the code words."

In front of us the cement floor tilts up until it kisses the ceiling of the bunker. As I watch, the ceiling slides back, and the leaves that helped camouflage the hidden door fall into the bunker like confetti.

Natural light streams in, the first I've seen in months, and the sight of it takes my breath away. The washed out sky beyond is not the same blue that haunts my memories, but it's still one of the most beautiful sights I've seen in a long time.

Once the ceiling slides back far enough, our caravan

pulls out. My eyes drink in the war-scorched earth. Out here in the middle of nowhere, the damage isn't as apparent as it is in the heart of our once big cities, but if you stare long enough, you'll see it.

It's a five-minute drive to the hangar that houses our jet. Short enough that if the representatives ever needed to make a quick escape they could, but long enough that if the hangar were ever to be attacked, the bunker would remain unharmed.

We pull into it, and inside several aircraft wait. One sits in front of the rest, and several men and women already swarm around it, loading the jet, and checking up on its general maintenance.

"Ambassador Freeman," the general turns to my father, "this will work."

I see a muscle in my father's cheek flex, and something unspoken passes between the two of them. Whatever it is, it has my father angry.

Beyond us, the rest of our group is beginning to load themselves onboard the aircraft. I grab my bag, clenching my jaw at the airy way my dress swishes around my legs—as if I am some delicate thing that requires only the lightest of caresses and the softest material.

I stare at the jet that will take me away from this miserable land to one that's already fallen to the king. The same king that's taken everything from me. I'll come face to face with him. I take a deep breath.

Time to dance with the devil.

CHAPTER 3

SERENITY

EIGHT YEARS AGO my father put a gun in my hand for the first time.

That morning when I walked into the kitchen, he sat at our table sipping a cup of coffee, a wrapped box in front of him.

I halted at the sight of it.

"Thought I'd forgotten your birthday?" he asked, glancing up from his laptop.

I had. He hadn't mentioned it, and I hadn't bothered reminding him. He'd been so busy. So weary. It made me feel guilty any time I thought of mentioning it to him.

I continued to stare at the gift.

"Well?" He closed the computer screen and pushed it aside. "Are you going to open it?"

Tentatively I approached the kitchen table. "You didn't

have to get me a present," I said, even as I reached for the box.

He gave me a gentle smile, but something in his eyes warned me to curb my enthusiasm.

Carefully I peeled away the wrapping, savoring the fact that my father had remembered. Beneath it was a worn-out shoebox advertising men's loafers. I raised my eyebrows, earning me a chuckle.

"Open the lid, Serenity," my father said, leaning forward.

I lifted it like he asked, and balked at what rested inside.

"Go ahead and grab it—gently."

Reaching in, I touched the cold metal and wrapped my hands around the handle.

"Do you know what that is?" he asked me.

How could I not know? "It's a gun." I tried to curb my disappointment. I wouldn't be getting any new toys this year. Not on my father's watch.

"No," my father said. "That is a death sentence."

I stared at the weapon in my hand like it was a snake.

"I know you've seen the street gangs shooting up property for the hell of it," he continued, leaving his seat to kneel at my side. "That is not a toy. You point that gun, then you aim to kill."

My eyes widened at that. Of course I knew guns could kill, but my father was gifting me the weapon. As though he expected me to kill.

"Do you understand?" he asked.

I nodded.

"Good," he said. "Then get dressed. We're leaving in

an hour."

"Where are we going?" I asked him.

He flashed me a small, sly smile. "The shooting range."

NINE HOURS AFTER we left D.C., the flight begins its descent into what was once Switzerland.

My father takes my hand and squeezes it. He's not a man of many words, but throughout the flight he's been even quieter than usual.

"I never wanted this life for you," he says, looking at me.

I squeeze his hand back. "I know, Dad."

But he's not done. "You've had to grow up so damn fast. And now this. I've delivered you into the belly of the beast."

I look at him, really look at him. "You are all that I have left," I say. "I'd rather die here with you than live alone underground until the war ends." *And I'm captured.*

My father shakes his head. "You don't know what you're saying," he says. "You have your whole life ahead of you."

What he doesn't say is that my lifespan isn't all that much longer in the bunker than it is here. The real question is what would kill me first—starvation, capture, or my failing health.

"And what kind of life is that?" I ask.

He's quiet for a moment. "Will likes you. Has for a while. And I've seen the way you look at him when you think no one's watching."

My brow creases at this, and my cheeks flush. Out of all

the horrible things I've seen and done, why does this one embarrass me so much?

"Dad, that couldn't ever happen." Even as I say it, I wonder if it could. Will seemed interested in starting something.

My father sighs. "I just wish."

And that's all we do these days. Wish.

THE JET TOUCHES ground and I hold onto my seat as we bounce. Outside the sun is brighter than I've ever seen it, and the sky bluer. I don't know how it's possible that the world can look this lovely.

Outside the runway, a large crowd has gathered. My head pounds at the thought that they are waiting for my father and me.

I unbuckle my seatbelt as the aircraft coasts to a stop near the crowd. By the time my father and I stand, our guards are already waiting in the aisles, their faces grim. I know each and every one of them, which makes this whole situation worse. Now I have over a dozen people to worry over, to grieve for should anything go wrong.

One of them takes my bag from me, and now all I can do is twist my hands together.

Half our guards leave before we do. Then my father exits the jet. I linger back a moment, take a deep breath, then step out to face the enemy.

The air is cool, crisp, and the sun blinds my eyes. I blink against the glare as they adjust. Once they do, my breath catches. The crowd gathered cheers when they see us.

At first I can't figure out why they're cheering. And then I do. My father and I are going to discuss the terms of our surrender. The end of the war. In their eyes, they have won, we have lost, and the world might now return to the way it once was.

I descend down the stairs, keeping my attention focused on not falling in these heels.

On either side of me a camera crew films my entrance. The footage is likely being streamed across the Internet. Anyone who wants to view it can. Will is watching, I know he is, and that thought makes me raise my chin a little higher. I am a soldier, a survivor, and I represent the WUN.

A group of men wearing suits and earpieces waits for us in front of a car—our car. They look too clean, too slick, their hair combed and gelled into place, their suits tailored precisely to their body types. These must be the king's men. The king, I notice, isn't here. He's probably too busy figuring out how to best kill my people.

When we reach them, one steps away from the rest. "Ambassador Freeman, Serenity," he says, reaching a hand out to my father, then to me. I start at the sound of my name spoken from his lips. Of course they know who I am. "My name is Marco, and I am the liaison between you and the king."

I have to bite my tongue to keep from responding as I take his hand. Anything that comes out of my mouth right now will only make the situation worse. Instead I nod. Belatedly I realize that this makes me appear demure.

"Nice to meet you, Marco," my father says, smooth as

silk. My father's good at this, masking his true feelings behind a pleasant façade. Me, not so much.

THE DRIVE TO the king's estate, where we'll be staying, is long and quiet. This is the first time I've gotten a good look at the city I'll be staying in.

When we descended into Geneva, I couldn't see the extent of the damage done to the city. Now that I'm in the car, I can. Bullet holes in the walls, piles of rubble where buildings and walkways have crumbled, graffiti, boarded up windows.

Amidst the damage I can see the city's efforts to rebuild. Construction trucks, fresh dirt, piles of building materials. Geneva is already recovering.

I read in history books that this place used to be neutral territory, but it didn't change Switzerland's fate. Once the king sets his sights on a country, he'll do whatever he needs to secure it. This was what he did to peaceful countries; I'd seen firsthand what he did to rebellious ones.

The king's estate rises like a phoenix from the ashes. The walls gleam an unearthly white, the roofs the blue-green color of oxidized copper. The asshole has the audacity to flaunt his wealth in a broken city.

The hatred that smolders in my chest expands at the sight. It's a good thing the gun I smuggled in is currently packed away, else I might be tempted to reach for it and end the peace talks before they've begun.

I feel a hand cover mine. My father's looking at me with a warning in his eyes. I'm being too obvious about my emotions. I fix my expression into something bland and pleasant. At least the cameras aren't here to capture whatever it was my father saw flicker across my features.

"When we arrive," Marco says, breaking the silence, "I'll show you and your entourage to your rooms. King Lazuli is hosting a welcome party tonight. That's when you'll officially meet him. Tomorrow morning the peace talks will commence."

Our car passes through the gates and the security checkpoints. A row of Italian Cypress trees lines the drive. Beyond them is an expanse of green lawn. The symmetry and colors assault my eyes, and something sharp and painful lodges in my throat. A dim memory of how things used to be. The king's estate reminds me of life before war. But the beauty here is duplicitous; the king lives a fantasy. The city outside these gates—that's the unpleasant truth. The world is a mess, and no amount of paint and landscaping can cover that up.

Eventually the car comes to a halt in front of the estate. The doors open and someone reaches for my hand—like I need help exiting a car. Brushing aside the offer, I step out of the vehicle.

I gaze up at those white, white walls, and the only thing I can think of is that, somewhere inside, dwells the devil.

And tonight, I'll meet him.

CHAPTER 4

SERENITY

SEVEN YEARS AGO I killed a man. Four men, in fact. I was only twelve. My father was off at work, and I'd just gotten home from school when I was ambushed. Four men had followed me back to my house. I'd watched them hang back behind me, far away enough to appear as though they were casually strolling. But I'd seen them before, heard rumors about them. No one tells you that in war, sometimes the enemy is your neighbor.

So as soon as I entered my house, I moved into my room and opened the lockbox that held my gun. Just in time too.

The front door smashed open and the men were shouting, no doubt to work me up into a frenzy. And it worked. I screamed at the sound. My heart hammered in my chest.

The weapon was preloaded for an occasion just like

this. I clicked off the safety and knelt at the foot of my bed, breathing slowly to calm my racing heart. Gripping the gun with both hands, I aimed at the doorway to my room.

It only took them several more seconds to find me. As soon as the first man came within my line of sight, I pulled the trigger. The bullet hit him right in the middle of the chest. I'd mortally wounded him, but he wouldn't die instantly.

Two of his friends pressed into the doorway, their eyes wide. They were now more interested in what was going on than grabbing me. I shot both of them before they could react.

The fourth man must've seen his friends go down because I heard the pound of his footfalls moving away from my room.

If I didn't kill him now, he'd return for revenge. That was how this new world worked. I knew that even at age twelve.

By the time I'd left my room, the three other men lay on the ground moaning, the fourth man was already out my front door. I sprinted down the hall, past the living room, and followed him outside. As soon as I made it to the front yard I saw him running down my street. I knelt, took a calming breath, aimed, and fired.

His body jolted, then collapsed unnaturally.

By the time the ambulance arrived, all four were dead.

I got away with it too. The courts were too flooded with other cases to hear about the twelve-year-old girl who killed her would-be assaulters. The justice system proclaimed it self-defense, and the case was closed.

As EVENING DESCENDS in Geneva, I sit in front of the vanity in my new room. The yellow glow of the light makes my features soft. With my hair loosely curled and a touch of makeup on my face, I realize for the first time in maybe ever that I'm pretty. It's a shock, and not a pleasant one either.

In war, beauty is a curse—it catches your enemies' attention, and you don't want that. Better to blend in. But sitting here in my borrowed scarlet dress, blending in is the last thing I'll be doing.

My eyes move to the room behind my reflection. A four-poster bed large enough to swim in rests directly behind me, and next to it are shelves and shelves of books. The ceiling is a mosaic of painted tiles.

In this lavish place, I might not blend in, but it appears I might just fit in.

There's a knock on my door, and one of my guards pokes his head in. "Your father and Marco are waiting for you out here, Serenity," he says. Out there in the sitting room.

Back at home I slept in a room with seven other women; here I have an entire room to myself, my father has another, and the guards another; we all share a sitting room.

I stand up and take in my appearance one final time. My scar catches the light. I might look sweet as syrup, but here in the lion's den I won't hesitate to kill my enemies, diplomacy or not. We're still at war, after all.

Out in the sitting room my father chats amicably with Marco. I'm not fooled by it at all. My father's lethal ability is presentation. He can lie like he's telling the truth. And not just about the little things, either. He can pretend entire relationships into and out of existence. It's not a very honorable talent, but it's the least violent means to an end in war.

In order to convince your enemies you must convince yourself—believe your own lies for a moment. One of his primary rules of diplomacy.

Time to put it into practice. "Hello Marco," I say, cutting into their discussion.

Marco's eyes move from my father to me—or rather, my plunging neckline. "Miss Freeman." He nods. "How do you like your rooms?"

They are a constant reminder of your king's corruption, I think. Instead I say, "They leave little to be desired. Your king is very generous to host us here," I finish off the sentence with a brittle smile. I don't think I can make a long-term career of diplomacy; those words felt like poison coming out.

In contrast to my own disquiet, I can practically feel my father's approval across from me.

"Yes, he is," Marco agrees. "And speaking of the king, he's waiting to meet you in the grand ballroom."

My heart slams in my chest. The king who can't be killed. The king who's caused the death of millions. He's more legend than man. And he's one of the few things that scare me. Because I can't understand how someone can be that evil.

"Well then, what are we waiting for?" I ask, smiling amicably, as though I'm not screaming inside.

Marco assesses me. "What indeed?" he says. I don't like the way he looks at me, as though he's trying to understand my motives.

Marco leads us out of the room. Luckily no cameras wait for us here. Tomorrow I won't be so lucky; the estate will be crawling with them.

As soon as we're in the hallway, I thread my arm through my father's, and our guards fan out around us.

"You clean up well," I say to my father. He's wearing a suit, and it brings out his fine features—high brows, sharp cheekbones, tan skin, wavy hair the color of dusty wheat, bright blue eyes. The fatigues I'm so used to seeing him in wash out his features and make him look his age.

He glances at me. "Thanks—that'll be the only compliment I'll get all evening standing next to you." His eyes light with humor, and I flash him a genuine smile.

"Tell me that again when you're fighting off all the cougars later tonight."

My father chuckles, and for a moment I can pretend that we are not in our enemy's house.

The faint sound of music, conversation, and tinkling glass drifts from down the hall behind two large, closed doors. In front of them stand two of the king's guards. As soon as we approach the doors, the guards open them, and we enter the ballroom.

I blink, just to make sure I'm not seeing things. The room spread out below me is full of warm light, crystal chandeliers, and walls of mirrors. Everything else is covered in gold. People twirl on the dance floor while others talk off to the sides. Here it's as though the war never happened. Here violence, dirt, and death don't exist.

We must be as exotic to the people in this room as they are to me, because it takes mere seconds for the room to quiet. The momentousness of this situation slams into me then. The two of us represent an entire hemisphere of the world. We are the figureheads of the final territories still free of the king. Free, that is, until we leave—*if* we leave.

The cameras that I thought would be absent tonight are waiting for us. A film crew off to our left captures our entrance. At the bottom of the stairs before us another crew waits.

Next to me, Marco announces to the room, "The emissary of the Western United Nations, Ambassador Carl Freeman, and his daughter, Serenity Freeman."

My hand tightens around my father's arm as I stare out at the crowd spread out before me.

And then someone steps up to the base of the staircase. Someone who's haunted my nightmares since I was little. The face I saw when I killed.

King Montes Lazuli.

JUST WHEN I thought the evening was going to be another dull meet and greet, the WUN emissary walks in, and on his arm I see her.

The emissary's daughter. Serenity Freeman.

The world doesn't stop moving, the room doesn't go quiet, but I swear something inside me just broke and reformed the moment she turned her devlish eyes on me— and that's the only way to describe those eyes of hers. Devilish. She's a wicked soul, through and through.

Just like me.

She's unlike the women I'm used to. Her arms are sculpted, and her body is lean beneath her dress. It's an almost laughable contrast to the soft women that fill the rest of the room. I'm dying to lift her skirt, run my hands up those legs, and get to know just how toned the rest of her is.

As pretty as her body might be, it's not what's captivated me. I can't look away from her face. In another life it might've been sweet. But not in this one. A wicked scar slices down the side of it. It's the most obvious warning that she's a dangerous creature.

I wish I got off on fear and hate, because both are burning in her eyes the closer she gets to me. I've killed others for less than the expression I see in them, but this woman, she is someone who knows violence intimately. I'm almost positive that death doesn't scare her. But apparently I do.

And the strangest thought yet pops into my mind: I don't want this intriguing woman to fear me.

I know she's a trap. I know the WUN sent her here with her father because they're desperate, and they're hoping to bait me with a woman. Those clever fools probably never thought that what would attract me to her was everything that lay beneath that pretty skin of hers—the viscous, hardened soul that looks so similar to my own. She's the best challenge I've seen yet.

I need to get to know her. She might've just changed everything.

CHAPTER 5

SERENITY

SIX YEARS AGO Washington D.C. was leveled. It was sheer dumb luck that on that particular day, at that particular time, my father and I had driven to a shooting range on the outskirts of the city.

We stood outside, taking turns firing from one of the stalls. I steadied my stance and focused my aim when my peripherals caught sight of something they shouldn't have.

The blast rose into the sky, unfurling like some fiery flower. The sight was incomprehensible—too bright, too big, too breathtaking.

Too dreadful.

I tore my eyes away, and looked to my father. He was already yelling commands at me, but we both wore earmuffs, so they fell onto deaf ears. When he jerked his head towards the building that housed the indoor shooting range, however, I understood.

Flicking on my gun's safety, I shoved my weapon back into its holster just as my father grabbed my arm. Together we sprinted for the building; the few other people outside followed our lead.

I chanced a glance back. The explosion had expanded, and a thin white cloud haloed it. I knew in the pit of my stomach that we had until that cloud reached us to find safety.

My father and I ducked inside. He whipped off his headpiece and began shouting orders to the people loitering on the first floor. I didn't hear his words, but judging from the way men and women made for the stairs down to the basement, he'd said enough for them to seek shelter belowground.

He hadn't let go of me since we'd entered, and now he steered us to the same destination.

In the muffled silence I noticed all the little things that made the moment real: The way one man's jowls shook as he pushed his way past us. The coolness of the earth as we descended further into it. The controlled panic in my father's eyes, like fear sharpened his logical reasoning skills. It had. It's one of the many traits we share.

When we reached the basement, the stairway opened into a hallway. Tugging my arm, my father led me away from the crowd to the end of the corridor. We hooked a right, and my father pulled us into an empty office that had been left open.

He locked the door and overturned a nearby filing cabinet, further blockading it. Next, he flipped the desk. I began to tremble as my father directed me to a corner of the room, dragging the now sideways desk towards us until we were barricaded in.

Atomic bomb.

That was the first time I'd really put a name to what I saw. And it was all because of that damn desk, which looked so similar to the overturned coffee table I'd once read under all those years ago.

My father fit his earmuffs back on his head then wrapped his arms around me, and it was exactly the physical comfort I needed.

It didn't take much longer for the blast to hit us, though *hit* is the wrong word. It passed over us, tore through us. I threw my hands over my head as the blast slammed us into the desk. The explosion roared so loud that I heard it over my earmuffs. It was a monstrous symphony to the end of the world.

And then it was over—if you could say such a thing. The land we returned to hours later was not the same one we'd fled from. Gone was D.C., gone was the White House and every great monument I'd gazed upon with wondrous eyes. Gone was our home. Gone was my former life.

Later we discovered that all big cities across the western hemisphere had been hit. That day the nations that once were lay decimated.

No, the blast wasn't over. Far from it. If anything, it was just the beginning.

MY EYES LOCK with the king's, and I suppress a shudder.

He's even more handsome than the pictures I've seen of him. Black, wavy hair, olive skin, dark eyes, sensual lips. But it's more than just his features; it's how he wears them. Like he is something regal, something you want to draw closer to. It's not fair that evil can wear such an alluring mask.

His eyes move over me like a predator sizing up prey.

I make a noise at the back of my throat, and my father places a hand over mine. We can't talk here, not when the cameras are rolling.

I breathe in, then out. I can do this. For my country, I can. I step forward, and we descend down the staircase. I know my father can feel my trembling hands. It's a miracle that my legs are holding me up at all. The entire time the king stares at me. Not my father. Me.

It takes all my energy to keep moving and look calm. In reality, I can't hear anything over the pounding of my pulse and the ringing inside my head. Not until we reach the bottom, until I stare into the king's deep brown eyes. Then the moment comes into hyper focus.

The king peels his eyes away from me to greet my father. "Ambassador Freeman," he says, "it is my pleasure to host you here for the peace talks." It's frightening to see that the king shares my father's talent for camouflaging himself to fit his audience. The king doesn't need peace talks to get what he wants, but he plays along, lying effortlessly through his teeth.

I drop my hold on my father's arm, and he takes the king's outstretched hand as cameras go off. "King Lazuli, it's an honor to finally meet you," my father says. "I hope that our two great hemispheres can come together to foster future peace." My father lies just as effortlessly as he stares the monster in the eyes and shakes his hand.

Now it's my turn.

The king turns his attention away from my father, and my stomach contracts painfully. This is the man who killed my mom. The man who leveled my city and all my friends living in it. He's the man who I've seen shot on national television, yet still he lives.

Unlike his response to my father, I can see the king's genuine interest in me. His eyes look lit from behind. "Ambassador Freeman, I presume that this is your daughter, Serenity Freeman?" the king asks.

Next to me my father's body goes rigid, and I know he senses the king's interest in me. "She is," my father says.

The king gives me a slow, sly grin and grabs my hand. I fight the overwhelming impulse to yank it free, cock my fist, and smash it into his face. Instead I bare my teeth as the cameras go off. I know it looks more like a snarl than a smile, but it's the best I can do at the moment.

King Lazuli brings my hand up to his lips, and I close my eyes to block out the sight of his mouth against my skin. I only open them once he pulls my hand away from his lips. "It's a pleasure to meet you Serenity."

He means it. Heaven help me, I've caught the attention of the king.

"King Lazuli," I choke out. I can feel tears burning my eyes, blurring my vision. I can't cry, not on television.

"Montes," he corrects me quietly. His eyes flick to my father's. "I believe the negotiations in the upcoming days will go quite well. I have a feeling for these things." The king is still holding my hand, and I feel him squeeze it.

None of this gets past my father, who nods once, his mouth a grim line.

The king's eyes move to mine and drink me in before returning to my father. "Mind if I whisk your daughter away for a dance?" the king asks.

My eyes widen. *No.* No, no, no. I don't know how to dance, but that's not even the issue here. The thought of spending any more time in the king's presence has me nauseous. I'm either going to get sick, or, more likely, I'm going to try to kill him.

"Not at all," my father says, his words clipped.

"Fantastic." The king flashes him a smile, and his attention returns to me. He raises an eyebrow. "Shall we?" he asks, as though I've already agreed to it.

"Only if you ask nicely." The words are out before I can attempt to censor myself. I shut my mouth before I can say more.

Those around us fall quiet. Out of the corner of my eye I can see the camera crew, my guards, and the king's retinue shifting nervously, their eyes darting between us. I don't know what reaction they're waiting for, but it's not this.

The king cocks his head, a small smile growing across his face. He raises an eyebrow. "Would you like to dance with me, Serenity?"

"I'd love to." I bite the words out because I have to say them.

Once I accept, the budding tension releases.

"So would I," he says, and again I can see he's being genuine. He gives the hand he's still holding a tug, and I'm gently whisked away.

I can tell everyone there is already aware of us—or him, more precisely, though I can feel curious eyes on me. As soon as we walk onto the dance floor, the king tugs me close. Too close. I can see the rough skin of his jaw, the gentle wave of his hair, the flecks of gold in his brown eyes.

His hand presses into the small of my back, and we begin to move. After glancing at other couples, I move my free hand to his shoulder like the other women do. The footwork, however, completely confuses me.

"I don't know how to dance," I say.

"Then it's a good thing I'm leading," the king responds, his expression amused. He glances down at my chest. "Beautiful necklace," he says, though I know it's just an excuse to stare at my chest.

"It was my mother's."

"Mmm," he says, and that's the end of that.

"She's dead."

"I'm sorry to hear that."

"No you're not." I can't get my mouth to shut up. Not right now when I'm caught in the arms of my mother's killer. "She died when your army dropped a bomb near our home."

Now I've caught his attention. His eyes narrow, but he doesn't look angry. More like I intrigue him.

"It was the same day that I received the scar on my face," I continue.

The king's gaze moves to my scar. "It seems I've caused you a lot of pain. I'm sorry for that."

I smile sardonically. "Save your lies for someone who will believe them."

The king's grip on my hand tightens. I'm in dangerous waters. "What makes you think I'm lying?"

"A man who was truly sorry would never have dropped the bomb to begin with." My breath catches as soon as the words leave my mouth. Have I gone too far?

The king scrutinizes me, and then ever so slowly, a smile appears. "I could have you killed for what you've said to me."

Fear grips my heart, but I call his bluff. "You won't."

He spins me. "Oh, and why is that?" he asks, raising an eyebrow.

"Because I amuse you." It's hard to admit that all I'm good for here is his entertainment.

His gaze drinks me in, and he presses me closer to him. "You do. Keep it up and the WUN might not face total annihilation."

I raise my eyebrows. "The truth suits you well." Even if it is psychotic. But I'd prefer hearing the ugly truth than a pretty lie.

My dress swishes around me as we twirl. It's not lost on me that that's what I am right now—a pretty lie, a soldier disguised as a lady.

"*You* suit me well," he says, his gaze sweeping over me. It sickens me that he seems to approve of what he sees.

My fingers dig into the muscles of his shoulder. "Sorry, but I don't mix business and pleasure."

"There's always time for firsts," he responds.

I'd gut him before that ever happened. I thin my eyes as I study him. "And why would I do that? I've considered you my enemy all my life."

The king smiles at me, thoroughly enjoying himself. "I don't really care about your personal problems." He's clearly warmed up to telling the truth.

"I can't imagine why you've been single this whole time," I say sarcastically. The song we're dancing to ends and a new one starts up.

His lips quirk. "Why get married when there are so many beautiful women who already want to be with me?"

I close my eyes and breathe through my nose. "Maybe you should go back to lying."

"Hmm," he muses, eyeing me, "the lady doesn't mind talking about destruction and death, but throw in a little sex and she gets demure."

My face flushes before I can help it, and the king chuckles. "My, my, have you never ... ?" He gazes at me curiously. "How old *are* you?"

Even through my burning cheeks I give him a nasty look. "Nineteen."

"Nineteen? And you've never been romantic? Did you just get out of an ugly phase?"

Despite his offensive words, I flash him my first real smile of the evening. "I was too busy killing your men to bother with love."

Now he looks mad. It's nice to know that the king might actually care about the death of his soldiers. "Watch your words," he snaps.

I decide to back off. If I anger King Lazuli too much, my father and I could easily find ourselves on the wrong end of a gun.

He watches me, and I can practically see the anger flow away from his face, replaced with that predatory look I saw when I first locked eyes with him. "You were a soldier?" he asks.

"Yes."

"But not anymore?"

"I will always be a soldier," I say, "but right now I fight with my tongue rather than my fists."

He gives me a slow smile. "Perhaps we can put that tongue to other uses."

"Then perhaps I will resort to fighting with my fists."

"I welcome the challenge." In his eyes is a promise that he'll make good on.

Tonight I'm sleeping with my gun.

I RIP MY dress off and run my tongue over my teeth as soon as I enter my bedroom. The representatives knew. They *knew* there would be a chance that dolled up I might catch the king's attention. Of course. All other tactics hadn't worked with him. Everyone else came back in a body bag. Why not give it a shot and tempt the king with flesh? It was the oldest trick in the fucking book. And it worked.

I tear the rest of the clothes off of my body and change into a pair of pajamas.

"Serenity?" my father calls from the sitting room.

"What?" I ask as I untuck my hair from my shirt. My

voice is angry.

He fills up the doorway to my room and takes me in. Neither of us needs to say anything—and we wouldn't dare anyway, the room had to be bugged. But he doesn't need to. His anguished expression tells me how he feels about our current situation.

"I'm sorry." He shakes his head.

"Why did no one tell me?" Even as I say this, I wonder if that's what had my father tense around the general when we left. He might've known then what I'd only just figured out.

I can't bring myself to be mad at him. We were all just pawns at this point.

My father pinches the bridge of his nose. "It was never official. You're a soldier and a future emissary. We wanted you to do what you do best—represent the WUN."

I read into what he can't say under the king's roof: acting was never my strength. I can barely hold my tongue; pretending to like the vilest man I know is beyond my abilities.

"We should check in with General Kline right now," he says.

I nod, my hands balling into fists. "I'd love to talk with him."

"Serenity." My father's voice carries a warning.

I sigh. "Let's just get this over with." I had a bad case of jetlag, and I wanted to get some sleep before tomorrow's peace talks.

I follow my father into his room, where his laptop rests on a side desk. I grab a nearby chair and pull it alongside my father's.

Once we're situated in front of the computer, my father calls up the representatives. They answer almost immediately.

"Ambassador Freeman and Serenity Freeman checking in," my father says.

On the other side of the screen I can see the bunker's conference room and the representatives sitting around the table. Now that I'm here inside the king's house, in this place filled with glittery objects and natural light, the conference room looks especially bleak.

"Good to hear from you Carl," the general says. "How's it going?"

My father's eyes slide to mine. "Fine so far. Have you been watching the footage?"

"Yes. Is Serenity there?"

My father turns the laptop so that my face takes up the screen. "General Kline." I nod to him.

"Serenity, aside from that comment you made during your introductions, you seem to be doing well making the king's acquaintance."

There are so many things that I want to shout at the general, none of which I can voice, one because he's still the leader of my country, and two, because I have to assume we're being recorded.

So instead I say, "Surprised? I was too." I lower my voice. "You've thrown me to the wolves, General." That's the closest thing I can come to the truth, that I'm here to persuade the king through more carnal means.

"Serenity, nations rely on your actions. Now is not the

time for weakness." General Kline's practically chastising me.

My throat works. "He killed her." My father reaches over and squeezes my shoulder, his subtle way of telling me to shut up, that I've said too much. But the king already knows what I've just spoken out loud—that I blame him for my mother's death.

"And you've killed mothers, fathers, sons and daughters. War has taken something from everyone, Serenity. We can end that. You can end that."

His words sober me up. He's right, of course. The only difference between the king and I is that the king's body count is much higher, and for most of his kills he never had to dirty his hands.

My gaze moves from the general to his son who sits further down the table. "I'm sorry, Will," I say. His face is too grainy to make out, but I'm sure the expression he wears is not a pleasant one.

"There's nothing to apologize for," he says. "Negotiate an agreement and make it back here safely. That's all I want."

My throat constricts and I nod. Now that the cat's out of the bag, I know what I must do.

I'm going to have to charm the king into giving the WUN what it needs.

CHAPTER 6

SERENITY

FIVE YEARS AGO my father and I moved into the bunker. By that time we were in a full-scale war with the eastern hemisphere, and the king had started picking off those political leaders not already dead. Located several miles outside of D.C., the bunker was an asylum for what was left of our government officials and their families.

It also offered some measureable protection against the high radiation levels caused by the nuclear blasts. Not that it mattered. The radiation was in the water, in the earth and the food supply. We'd lived with it long enough; the damage was already done.

The day my father and I moved in, when I first saw the beds that lined a single room, my chest tightened. I realized that the world I thought I knew had been gone for a while now and somewhere along the way *people* had become synonymous with *threat*.

My wariness eventually wore off, and my next reaction was excitement. I might make *friends*. I had to dust that word off; I'd shelved it from my vocabulary for so long.

The bunker, however, came with its own sacrifices. No natural light filtered into our new home, and I had once been a self-proclaimed child of the sun. An unpleasant schedule came to rule my days. And social interactions were difficult to maneuver; I found I was way more skilled at making enemies than I was friends.

Still, I was safe, surrounded by people that didn't antagonize me, and I had reliable food and shelter. For the first time in a long time, I felt hopeful.

"I HATE DRESSES," I mumble as one of my guards zips me up.

He snickers.

"Shut up. It's not funny." I can't breathe in this thing.

"Freeman in a dress? Hell yeah it is," my guard says.

I throw him a look just as Marco knocks on the door to our suite.

The guard squeezes my shoulder. "Own those negotiations," he whispers.

I leave my room as my father opens the door. "Morning Marco," he says, grabbing his briefcase.

Marco nods to him. "Ready to go?"

My father looks over to where I stand.

"I'm ready," I say, now that my wispy dress is on. I glance back at my room. My gun lies underneath the pillows on my bed. It's hard to walk into the peace talks in my flimsy outfit without my usual protection.

"'Kay, then let's do this," my father says.

We follow Marco out into the hall, our guards shadowing us. At least they are allowed to carry holstered weapons. I've seen most of them in action, so I trust their skills.

We move to the other end of the king's mansion, where the negotiations are to take place. I fist my hands in the black folds of my dress. I've learned a lot about diplomacy from my father, but I've never been able to apply any of my lessons. I know how negotiations with an enemy state work in theory, but not in practice, and I fear that something I say or do might cause irreversible damage.

I can identify the conference room from all the way down the hall. Cameramen and film crews cluster around the door. Flashes of light are already going off, which makes me think that the king must have arrived before us.

My heart pounds a little faster at the thought. Last night felt like we danced on the edge of a knife. One wrong move and I'd cut myself.

Despite the obvious danger that comes from dealing with the king, yesterday he hadn't struck me as particularly ... evil. Nor, for that matter, did he seem immortal, though he did appear to be younger than his true age. If I had to guess, I'd say the king is in his mid thirties. King Lazuli, however, has been conquering countries for nearly thirty years.

My thoughts are interrupted by a flash of light, and then the camera crews are on us, snapping shots and filming our entrance.

Unlike the conference room back in the bunker, this one is full of light and gilded surfaces. It is a room that a king does business in, and the sight of it reminds me all over again just why I despise the man who rules over half the world.

King Lazuli waits for us inside the room. His eyes find mine almost immediately. Once they do, they don't bother looking away.

In that moment I can feel in my bones that my father and I are merely toys here for the king's entertainment. Nothing more. We have no real power, so the king is allowed the luxury of gazing at the emissary's daughter and ignoring everyone else in the room.

I can still see flashes of light from my peripherals, but my attention focuses on the table. Someone's set placards in front of each seat. I look for my name, not surprised to find it placed next to the king's chair.

"How ... convenient," I murmur quietly as I pass him.

King Lazuli pulls out my chair and leans in. "Convenient—yes, I do believe that word sums up our relationship."

I didn't notice it last night, but there's a subtle lilt to his words. English is not his first language. I wonder what is.

"We have no relationship," I whisper back to him. Luckily, there's too much going on around us for our conversation to gather unwanted attention.

His eyes linger on my face, moving to my scar, then my lips. "You won't be saying that by the time you leave."

I hold his gaze and suppress a shiver. As much as I want to fight his words, I fear they're true.

MY FATHER TAKES a seat across from me. His eyes move between the two of us, but other than that, there's no indication that the seating arrangement bothers him. I'm not deceived. He hates the king more than even I do.

Someone places a document in front of me. It takes me a minute to realize this is a peace treaty, a tentative contract drawn up listing the conditions that need to be met in order for the war to end.

King Lazuli's arm brushes mine from where he sits to my right. My eyes flick to him, but he's not paying attention to me. "Ambassador Freeman, Serenity," the king says, nodding to each of us, "in front of you is a draft of the terms of your surrender."

I see flashes of light go off as each media outlet allowed in here captures the beginning of the negotiations. Each one distracts me from the matter at hand.

My father pulls out the document the WUN crafted up that catalogues our terms of surrender. After reading it on the flight over, I can rattle off the essentials: Our people must be provided with medical relief, first and foremost. Then steps must be taken to clean the environment—too much radiation has seeped into the earth and the running water. It's in our food, and until we can expel it, people are going to keep getting cancer.

Once those two requirements are met, then our secondary measures are to boost the economy and reestablish the social order that existed before the war.

The king takes the document from my father and flips through it. Suddenly he laughs. "You think I'm going to let your country revert back to the materialistic, wasteful state it was in before the war?" he says, his eyes moving over the page before lifting to meet my father's gaze. The irony of his statement isn't lost on me, here in this opulent palace of his.

Across the table, my father relaxes into his seat, looking at ease when I'm sure that's the last thing he feels. "The WUN is not suggesting that. We merely wish to get our economy back on its feet."

The king's eyes flash. "Your hemisphere will never be where it once was."

THE NEGOTIATIONS DRAW on for a long time even after the king makes it known that he wants to cripple our economy. I shiver at the thought. Though pretty much anything would be an improvement from the current state of the western hemisphere, I know from history that there'd be long-term problems if the king decided to purposefully weaken our economy.

I page through the king's document in front of me. Most passages are long-winded discussions of the terms of the agreement. I keep looking for the medical relief the king would provide for our people, but I can't find any mention of it.

"Where can I find the terms of medical relief you'll provide the WUN?" I finally ask, turning to the king.

He swivels his body to face me. "There are none," he says.

I blink at him a few times. "None?"

"None."

I stand suddenly. "You'd leave our people to suffer? To die?" I don't know what I'm doing. It feels as though someone's squeezing my lungs because I can't seem to get enough air.

The king leans back in his seat. "Only some of them." He gives me a challenging look.

My anger obscures my vision. I ball my hands into fists. "This isn't a game!"

Silence.

No one moves.

And then a whole lot of things happen at once. The king stands, and judging by the vein throbbing at his temple, he's pissed. Behind me several people push forward, and my guards press in close.

King Lazuli leans in, his eyes flashing dangerously. "Yes, Serenity, this is a game. One you've already lost."

I'M ESCORTED FROM the negotiations for the rest of the day. The king's guards take me back to my room. They linger outside it, standing guard in case I try to leave.

Now that the anger has dulled somewhat, embarrassment and guilt quickly follow. I can't act like that, even if I think I'm defending the WUN. No one's going to thank me if the negotiations dissolve because of my emotional outbursts.

I hear the door to our suite open and, a few seconds later, a knock on my door. My heart hammers away in my chest. I stand, and my muscles tense. Knowing my father, he's not going to yell, and his quiet disappointment is so much worse to bear.

The door opens, but instead of my father, King Lazuli stands in the doorway.

My eyes widen. "What are you doing here?" My earlier anger hasn't simmered back to the surface yet. I'm too surprised.

He closes the door behind him and strolls into my room, taking a look around. "How are you liking the palace so far?" he asks.

I raise my eyebrows. "It's fine."

"*Fine?*" It's his turn to raise his eyebrows. "Surely it's more than just fine."

Now my anger's returning, like a dear old friend. "Okay, it's more than fine. It's absolutely repulsive that you can live around such opulence when the rest of this city is so broken. I'm sickened to hear you deny my people basic medical relief while you host dinner parties inside your palace."

The king approaches me. "There it is. The truth: you hate everything about me."

I suck in a sharp breath of air. "*Yes,*" I breathe.

King Lazuli holds the crook of his arm out. "Walk with me."

I take a step back, eyeing his arm like it's poisonous. I just admitted to the king of the eastern hemisphere that I hated him.

When he sees my hesitation, he says, "I don't bite."

"No," I say, "you kill."

"So do you, soldier."

We stare at each other a moment. Not one fiber of

my being wants to touch him, but I remember General Kline's words yesterday. I need to play my part.

Reluctantly I slide my fingers through the crook of King Lazuli's arm, and he leads me out of my room.

"Where's my father?" I ask as soon as we pass his empty room.

"He's still in discussions with my aides."

"And you're skipping out to what—give me a tour of your mansion?"

The king glances down at me, a small smile playing on his lips. "Something like that."

I frown at his expression and a sick sensation coils through my stomach. I can practically smell the desire wafting off of him.

The thought makes me want to puke. I've been rude to him since we met. I stood up to him; I admitted that I hated him. He must truly be psychotic if that excites rather than angers him.

He leads me outside to the gardens. "How lovely," I say, "you pay someone to cut your hedges into cute little animals. I'm so impressed."

His lips twitch. "I'm pleased to hear you like them so much. I'll have the gardeners shape another just for you. Perhaps a gun? Or are you more of a hand grenade lady?"

"How about you simply uproot the hedge you plan on shaping and watch it slowly die? That would be a more accurate representation of me and my people."

The king sighs. "You do not know the first thing about power."

"And you don't know the first thing about compassion," I bite out.

To our right, a large alcove has been cut into the hedge that borders the gardens. Inside it sits a marble sculpture. The king pushes me into the alcove.

My back bumps into the nearly solid surface of the hedge as the king presses his body against mine. "You think you know something about compassion? A soldier trained to kill?"

"Yes," I say.

"Then prove it."

I raise my eyebrow, still pinned between him and the hedge. Despite his closeness and his heated emotions, I'm not scared. I know how to take him down if I need to, and I trust him more when he's not so composed.

"How exactly would you suggest I prove it?"

His gaze flicks to my mouth. "Kiss me."

My breath hitches. "I think you've confused passion with *compassion*."

"No, I haven't." His eyes glitter, and I have to remind myself that he's a sick human being, because right now all I'm noticing are his expressive eyes and sensual mouth. "Compassion is showing kindness towards the man who killed your mother."

"You want to see compassion? Fine." I take the hand pressed against my shoulders and kiss his knuckles. "I've now kissed the hand of my mother's killer."

Before he has time to react to my chaste kiss, I bring my other hand up and slap him.

His head whips to the side. "I'm also a vindictive bitch," I say.

Slowly he moves his face back to where it was. There's a dull pink handprint across his cheek. His eyes flash, and I'm already learning that this is when he's at his most dangerous. "And I don't play fair," he admits.

The words are hardly out of his mouth when he closes the distance between us and his mouth captures mine.

There's nothing sweet or diplomatic about this kiss. His lips move roughly against my own, and his hand runs down the length of my side, as if even a kiss isn't enough to satiate him.

I will my mind to go blank before I kiss him back. I press my eyes tightly closed as I force myself to wind my arms around his neck and lean into him.

As soon as he feels me respond, the kiss deepens. His lips part my own and his tongue presses against mine.

Oh God, I don't think I can do this. It's too much. I turn my head to the side to break off the kiss.

I swallow down my bile. "Enough," I say, my voice hoarse.

He steps away from me, and I pull in a deep breath of air. The king's staring at my lips, as though looking at them long enough might cause them to resume their former activity.

I gaze at him, feeling like a cornered creature. This is when *I'm* my most dangerous. He must sense it as well because he steps aside. I brush past him, and he catches my wrist. "I want to see you tonight." His meaning is clear.

"No," I say.

"Yes."

"Not until you offer full medical relief to the WUN

with no strings attached." It's a ballsy move, manipulating him like this. But this is why the WUN sent me.

"I could simply have you killed if you don't agree."

"Then kill me," I say, tugging on my wrist. I am more than ready to leave the king and his empty threats. Chances are, he will eventually kill me, but not like this.

He doesn't let go of me. "I'll think about it," he finally says, and I know he's referring to the medical relief and not having me killed.

"And all I'll do is *think* about visiting you until you make your decision," I say.

The king tugs my wrist hard enough for me to stumble into him. "Stop toying with me," he growls against my ear, his voice low and lethal.

I pull away from him. "Unlike you, I don't play games, *Montes.*"

His eyes trail down my face to my lips. "And I get what I want. Always."

I yank my wrist out of his grip and back away from him. I can see the cold calculation in his eyes.

"There's always time for firsts," I say, and then I walk away.

"WHAT WERE YOU *thinking?*" Unlike my father, General Kline yells when he's angry.

Next to me, my father broods. When he returned an hour ago, he looked at me and shook his head. That's all it took for me to break down and apologize. I wanted him to be proud of me, not disappointed.

General Kline, on the other hand, could kiss my ass.

I flash him a vicious smile and hold up my index finger, signaling him to give me a moment. Seizing a nearby pen and sheet of paper, I scrawl a note on it.

The king came to my room after that incident, we went for a walk, and he kissed me. I've promised to do more if he negotiates medical relief into the peace agreement.

My cheeks burn as I hold the paper up to the camera, and my father looks away.

I've already told my dad about my little walk in the gardens. I can't imagine what he's feeling. Of the two of us, his is the worse task. He has to pretend to negotiate with a dictator while allowing that same man to take advantage of his daughter. At least I have some agency in the matter. He has none.

I pull the sheet away from the screen and hand it to my father, who will have to burn it later. This is the securest way to communicate.

The conference room in the bunker is quiet. I'm sure the situation doesn't sit well with anyone in there. I feel like a harlot, trading sex for promises.

The general bends over the table and scribbles something onto a sheet of paper before approaching the screen.

Good job, Serenity. Hold him to that and leave the rest to your father for now. If you try to leverage anything else, he's going to figure out what's going on.

As if the king hasn't already. It didn't take a rocket scientist to deduce what my role here was. I'm just surprised that it's actually been working so far.

The general removes the note from the screen and returns to his seat a short distance away. "From now on, control yourself during negotiations," he says gruffly.

I work my jaw, but nod.

Behind me, I hear a distant knock on the door. My dad and I glance at each other.

"I'll get it," I say.

I push out of my chair and leave my father's room, making sure to close the door behind me. I pass through the apartment's common area and open the front door.

Marco stands on the other side. "The king requests your presence at dinner," he says, giving me a sullen look. The feeling's mutual.

"Request denied," I say, closing the door.

Marco's foot shoots out and catches the door before it can latch shut. "You can't deny the king's request."

"Well, I am." I give Marco's foot a good kick. He yelps and pulls it back, and I slam the door shut.

"What was that about?" my dad asks when I return to the room.

"The king requested my presence at dinner."

"And?" my father asks.

There's loud knocking on the other side of the suite door.

"I politely declined."

My father raises an eyebrow while the representatives watch from the other side of the screen. "Are you going to answer the door?" he asks.

"No."

My father lets a small smile slip out, just enough to tell me that I'm humoring him.

The general clears his throat. "You should go to dinner with him."

"Well, I don't want to."

"That's not a good enough reason, Serenity," the general says.

I lean in close to the screen. "You want me to use my womanly wiles to secure a favorable peace agreement? That's exactly what I'm doing," I say. "Let me do my job." The truth is that I'm not trying to play hard to get—I don't know the first thing about attraction. I simply can't stand the thought of being close to the king right now.

THE FOLLOWING MORNING I'm back in the conference room, sitting across from my father while we wait for the king.

The king pushes open the conference room doors. He holds onto two documents; one he drops in front of my father, the other he drops in front of me.

He leans in next to my ear. "I expect to see you in my room, tonight," he whispers.

I stiffen, watching him as he takes a seat next to me. His leg brushes against mine, and I flinch from the contact. Across from me my father's eyes move between the two of us.

"Here is a revised peace treaty that has been adjusted based on yesterday's discussions," the king says.

My father and I flip through the document, and I can't help the way my hands shake, crinkling the paper. I already know what I'm going to find before I read it.

"Medical relief?" My father says, looking up from the document in front of him. His voice carries both confusion and hope.

"Serenity happens to be very persuasive," the king says, glancing at me. My stomach clenches at his heated look. I try to tell myself that I'm merely nauseous at the thought of what's coming tonight. But it's more than just that. It's that in some dark corner of my mind, the thought of being alone with the king excites me.

I close my eyes and breathe in and out. When I open them, my father's gaze rests on mine for a moment. Just long enough for me to read the sheer panic in his own.

"YOU DON'T HAVE to do it, Serenity," my father says. He's sitting on a side chair in my room, his hands clasped so tightly together that his knuckles are a bluish white color. I'm flipping through the dresses I temporarily own.

"Dad," I throw him a glance, "you and I both know that's not an option." There's no telling what the king would do if I backed out after he'd held up his end.

My father scrubs his face and pushes himself out of the chair. "Come here," he says, opening his arms.

I stop rifling through my clothes to look at him. His face is weary—old. And as he stands there with open arms, I realize that he might need my comfort more than I need his.

I walk into his embrace and he envelops me in a hug. He speaks into my hair. "I'm not okay with this." His hold on me tightens. "I've been ordered—" My father's voice catches. "I've been ordered to let this happen."

"I know." I'd assumed as much. The general is the mastermind behind this idiotic plan. It doesn't matter how much my father disagrees with it, if General Kline ordered it, he's duty bound to follow through. As am I.

He holds me for a long time, and I'm hesitant to pull away before he does. I'm afraid of what I'll see on his face.

"You'll never know how proud I am of you."

I give a humorless laugh. "There's nothing honorable about what I'm doing."

My dad draws back to look at me. If he cried while he held me, all traces of his tears are gone. "Your life has never been easy, Serenity. The world has always demanded something from you—war is a series of hard choices—but you haven't let it break you. Not even now, when this is being asked of you. No father could be prouder of his daughter."

I blink back tears and swallow. "Thank you," I say quietly.

THIS EVENING, WHEN Marco knocks on our suite's door, I'm armed for battle. I have a plan that will keep the monster at bay.

I open the door. "The king requests—"

"Yeah, yeah, I know," I say. "Let's go." I push past Marco. The guards won't come with me tonight, not for this sort of thing.

Marco jogs up to me. "You're going the wrong way Miss Freeman," he says, catching my arm and spinning me around.

"Oh." I let him lead me in the opposite direction, and I smooth down the fabric of the lacey plum colored dress I wear. For the millionth time I wish I was wearing my fatigues. The tight bodice and high heels limit my movement.

We tread down the halls, and I memorize every twist and turn Marco makes. I'll need to since I doubt the king will escort me back to my room before he gets what he wants.

Every so often someone passes by me in the hallways. Their eyes dart to mine, then away. I sometimes receive this reaction from people who notice my scar. Tonight, however, I wonder if this has more to do with the filmed negotiations. I never considered the fact that people might recognize me once the footage hit the Internet, but they must.

Marco and I climb a set of stairs and turn down a hall. I can tell we're nearing the king's private rooms. There's a stillness about my surroundings that the rest of the mansion lacks.

I follow Marco up to a door and wait while he knocks. A servant opens the door and ushers us in. A quick glance around the room tells me that this is a private dining room. The lights have been dimmed, and a small round table has been set for two.

Romantic. I believe that's how one would describe the

setting. Unease gathers in the pit of my stomach.

The king steps into the room from some side chamber, fiddling with a cufflink of his suit. When he catches my eye, I see him pause. His eyes move over me, his gaze searing. I can tell he doesn't want to simply have his way with me, and that realization surprises me.

"Thank you, Marco," the king says, "you may go now."

Marco inclines his head and backs away. I watch him leave us. Only once the door clicks shut, do I turn to face the king.

He's studying me. "Are you happy?"

"About what?" I ask.

"Your precious medical relief."

"I'll be happy once I see the finished peace agreement with the medical relief included. Until then, I remain skeptical." The king could always withdraw that clause of the treaty once he gets what he wants from me. That's why I'm going to have to make sure he doesn't.

"You don't trust me?"

I guffaw. "I don't have the luxury. In my world trust will land you a knife in your back and an early grave."

"So cynical," the king says, tsk-ing. He approaches me. "Why didn't you come to dinner last night?" he asks. His eyes gleam. He's not a man to take rejection well.

"I thought we just went over my opinion on trust."

King Lazuli cups my face and tilts my head up. His thumb strokes my jawline as his eyes dance over my lips. It takes most of my self-control to let him do this. Even this small touch feels extraordinarily intimate. "You don't trust yourself with me?" he asks.

"*Especially* not with you," I say, holding his gaze. My pulse is in my ears.

He drops his hand and moves away from me, a smile playing along his lips. "Hungry?" he asks, indicating the table.

I'm not, but pretending to eat is better than the alternative. I nod. "Starving."

I make my way over to the table, where King Lazuli pulls out a chair for me. I give him a strange look as I take it.

"Are you not used to a man pulling out your chair for you?" he asks.

"Where I live, a man would sooner mug me than pull out a chair for me." It's not completely true. I wouldn't get mugged in the bunker. But out on the streets where resources are scarce? Absolutely.

The king frowns at this. "Once this war is over, I will teach your country's men how to treat women."

I can't help it, I laugh. There are so many things wrong with his statement. "One, King Lazuli—"

"Montes," he corrects me, walking around the table and taking a seat across from me.

"—the men of my country aren't savages by nature. *Your* war has made savages of us all, me included." Of course the megalomaniac across from me would twist a problem he created into some form of cultural sexism. "And two, you are the last person on earth who should speak of how to treat women."

I went too far. I can see it in the way the vein at the king's temple throbs. We stare at each other for a few long seconds, and I can practically see the king's internal debate. In the past he's killed off everyone who speaks out against him, but clearly he's hesitant to do that to me, now that he's gotten me in his private rooms. But how to handle the situation?

The moment is interrupted by what appears to be the king's personal chef. She sets a covered plate in front of each of us, and then removes the metal lids. "Filet mignon served with a red wine sauce, fried gnocchi, and caramelized shallots. Paired with a cabernet sauvignon."

I stare at the plate in front of me. I don't recognize any of the food items the chef just rattled off, and I can only identify the reddish-brown lump on my plate as meat. But from the smell wafting off the food, it will taste delicious.

The chef pours a small serving of wine into the king's glass, and I watch, fascinated, as the king swirls the liquid, smells it, and tips a portion back into his mouth. After a moment, he nods, and the chef pours more wine into the king's glass, and then mine.

"You make food look like an art form," I say.

"That's because it can be," the king responds.

I shake my head and glance down at my meal. He will never understand how insulting this is to a girl who is always underfed.

"Go ahead," he says, "try it."

I lift my knife and fork and try a bite of the meat. I have to close my eyes as I eat it. I'm not sure I've ever tasted anything so delicious.

I hear the king chuckle across from me and my eyes snap open. "Now try the wine." His voice lilts, reminding me that he's just as exotic to me as his lifestyle is.

I reach for my glass. I've only had sips of alcohol up until now. Not too many people in the bunker bother with the stuff, but I've tasted it enough to expect the strange flavor that hits my taste buds. What I don't expect is the warm richness of the liquid. It heats up my throat, and then my stomach. I didn't know any substance could do such a thing.

"It's good," I say reluctantly, and then I take another drink. And another.

"Just good?" There's a twinkle in the king's eyes. "That's the best you can do?"

"Yes."

The room gets quiet, and I know that we're both remembering my earlier words. I wonder why he hasn't brought them up again.

"Tell me about yourself," I finally say, because I can't think of a more open-ended question to distract us.

The king raises his eyebrows. "What is it you want to know?" he asks.

I shrug. "Whatever it is you want to tell me."

"I'm an only child," he starts.

"Me too," I say, taking another swig of my wine.

He nods. "My mother passed away when I was eight, and my father passed away when I was twenty-two."

"I'm sorry," I say, and I mean it. Regardless of who the king is, I can empathize with the pain of losing a parent.

"Thank you," he says, holding my gaze. In that second, my pulse speeds up. I'm a fly caught in a spider's web, a moth drawn to flame. He's pain and death, yet I'm falling into those dark eyes of his. Perhaps he truly is something supernatural if he can coax this response from me.

King Lazuli glances away. "I enjoy playing football—soccer—I sing in the shower—"

I raise my eyebrows. "You sing in the shower?"

The grin that spreads along his face is pure sin. "I can always give you a demonstration, but you'd be required to join me."

"I think I'll pass." I reach for my full glass of wine and take another drink. I glance at it once I pull it away from my mouth. I could've sworn I'd almost finished the wine. Those servants of his should double as spies; they're shadows, slipping in and out of the room, refilling drinks, removing silverware—essentially seeing to our every need.

"How about you?" the king asks, tipping his own glass back.

I chew the inside of my cheek and stare at my wine. "I live in a room with seven other women. This trip is the first time I've seen natural light in months, but what I miss the most about the sky are the stars—oh, and I love to swim, even though I haven't been able to for several years."

The king holds my gaze. "Would you like to?"

"Like to what?" I ask, drinking more wine.

"Go for a swim. I have a pool."

My eyes widen, though I shouldn't be surprised to learn about this. "I don't have a swimsuit," I say. What I don't mention is that it seems wrong to enjoy myself when so many others can't.

He waves away my concern. "That's not an issue. Marco can get you one." The king stands up. "Give me a moment." He walks out of the room, presumably to talk to one of his servants.

As soon as he's gone, I eye the door. I could slip out now and return to my room. Where would that leave me, though? No, I need to stick around a little longer.

At least my plan is unfolding as I wanted it to. So long as I keep the king talking I don't have to do anything physical with him. But more importantly, if the king sees me as more than just a pretty face with an attitude, I'll have more leverage.

The king comes back in the room. "Grab your glass of wine," he says, seizing his own glass and the wine bottle that sits next to it.

I glance at our half-eaten plates. "What about the food?"

"It'll be here when we come back."

I know he says that for my benefit. I doubt the king would eat a reheated meal. But he's probably learned enough about me to know that I'd balk at wasting it.

He takes my hand and leads me to the door. I stare at our joined hands. The backside of his is tan, and I don't know why that particular detail makes me wistful, but it does.

Ashamedly, I savor the warm press of his palm. I can tell that he's used to being touched by the way his focus is on other things. And now, horror of horrors, it sinks in that I actually like skin contact with the king.

"What are you thinking about?" he asks.

"Nothing." I respond too fast, and the king's lips twitch. "Why do you ask?"

"You had a small smile on your face for a minute there.

It was nice."

I look away, mortified that the king caught me smiling while I was thinking about him. Scratch that, I was embarrassed that the king caused me to smile in the first place.

"And the lady shuts down yet again. I should add smiles and compliments to the growing list of things that make you uneasy," King Lazuli says.

"You are what makes me uneasy," I say.

His grip on my hand tightens. "I know." He looks down at me, and I see the desire in his eyes.

I swallow. Tonight is going to be long.

I HOLD MY towel tightly to myself when I leave the bathroom. It's a good thing the alcohol is really starting to hit my system and lower my inhibitions. Otherwise there's no way I'd have the courage to do what I'm doing now.

King Lazuli waits for me in the room that houses his pool, wearing a swimsuit that leaves little to the imagination. I suck in my cheeks. I'd expected the king to have thin, doughy arms and a shapeless stomach under all those suits of his. I hadn't expected him to be toned like a soldier.

Our eyes meet across the room. "Are you going to take off your towel?" he asks.

"As soon as I get more wine." I probably shouldn't drink more. I'm already starting to feel a little queasy from the alcohol and overly rich food.

The king grabs my glass from where it rests on the edge of the pool next to the wine bottle, and he brings it over to me. "How about a trade: your glass of wine for the towel."

Instead of answering him, I take the wine in his hand, down it in two long gulps, and then let go of my towel.

It drops to the ground, and I'm left standing in only a black bikini. The king takes a step back, his expressive eyes brighter than usual. I know what he sees—a lean body toned by war. He might even see some of my fainter scars.

I never thought there was anything particularly beautiful about my body. It is useful, and in my war-torn country, that's the best I can ask for.

Only now, as Montes's gaze drinks me in, I realize he's savoring me like he does his wine. Like I am something rare and refined and he wants to take his time enjoying me. The thought makes me aware of every inch of exposed skin.

He takes my empty glass and sets it on a nearby ledge, his eyes serious. I sway a little on my feet as I watch him; the alcohol is already affecting me.

When the king turns back to me, he bends and scoops my feet out from beneath me.

"What are you doing?" I gasp out.

"What do think I'm doing?" he asks, carrying me to the shallow edge of the pool, where steps trail down into the water.

Alcohol swirls in my stomach, and I'm not sure whether I like the heady way it makes me feel. It's causing me to notice the way the king's dark hair curls at the base of his neck, and the golden skin that covers his strong muscles.

My body dips, and I hear the first splash of water as the king steps into the pool. He gazes down at me, and I catch my breath.

I'd never much cared for those epic love stories I'd heard growing up—Romeo and Juliet, Tristan and Isolde, Helen and Paris. All couples who'd placed love above all else; I thought the whole lot of them were idiots. But the way the king is looking at me ... now I can see why so many loved those stories. There is something to forbidden passion. One heated look has me feeling like I'm on the edge of a precipice, waiting to jump.

My body dips again as we descend down the last two steps. The water kisses the bare skin of my back, but I'm still staring at the king, and he me.

I blink rapidly. I'm here to seduce the king, not to actually feel something for him. I need to remember that at all times.

To distract myself, I focus on my surroundings. The white walls dance with the strange patterns the water makes. "This place is beautiful." I forget for a minute that this beauty represents everything I despise about the king. Right now I'm able to let go of some of my hate.

"If you think this is beautiful, you should see the pool at my official headquarters."

"Is that an offer?" I joke, still staring at the beautiful light that dances above us.

"It is."

My gaze snaps back to the king. "You should seriously leave the lying for the cameras," I say.

We move into deeper water. "I'm not lying," he says, his eyes trained on me.

I blink at him. He's serious. "Why would you invite

me?" I ask.

"Because I enjoy your company." His statement is proof that he's out of his mind. I've been nothing but mean and malicious to him.

"I hate you, remember?" With all the alcohol thrumming through my system, I can't put emotion behind the words.

"I'm starting to think you don't, though." His eyes laugh at me.

I push myself out of his arms, enjoying the way the water ripples over my skin. I do hate the king, just not right now. In the morning I will.

I hope.

I swim over to where the wine bottle sits. "I think I need more alcohol for this conversation." I'm actually feeling plenty buzzed as it is, but I do need to change the subject before the king corners me into agreeing to the visit.

Just as I reach for the bottle, I see movement out of the corner of my eye. I jolt at the sight of King Lazuli. I hadn't heard him swim up next to me.

He grabs the wine bottle and moves it out of my reach. "I think you've had enough for now, Serenity." I shiver at the way he says my name. "Me on the other hand ..." He flashes me a wicked smile before he tips the bottle back and takes a drink from it.

My abs clench at the sight of him. If I didn't know better, I'd say I was feeling lustful. He sets the bottle down, and when his eyes meet mine, heat pools low in my stomach.

"Let's play a game," I say quickly. He raises an eyebrow.

"I'll ask you a question, and you can choose to answer it, but if you decide not to, you're going to have to take a sip of wine." That'll loosen his lips.

The grin he gives me is full of mischief. "I'll play your little game, but only if I'm allowed to ask questions as well."

I nod. "Okay." I can live with that. "I'll start you off with an easy one: what's your favorite color?"

"Blue. What's yours?" he asks.

"I'll answer that only if it's your official question."

"It is."

I watch the way the light from the water dances over his skin. I want to hold onto this moment, where we are no longer enemies. Merely a man and a woman discovering each other.

"Yellow." The color of the sun and the stars, the color of happiness.

"*Yellow?*" The king's eyebrows nudge up.

"What, you thought I'd like the color of spilled blood or something?"

He tips his head back as he weighs my words. "Yeah, I kind of did."

"Next question: where are you from?" I ask, thinking about the roll of his words.

He pauses, watching me with an amused smile on his face. "I was born in the country formerly known as France."

The water laps against us as I file away this new bit of information.

"Are you enjoying yourself at the moment?" the king

asks.

I search Montes's eyes. I could lie, make up an answer, or I could also pass. I do neither.

"I don't know," I answer honestly. "Maybe."

"Maybe," King Lazuli repeats. "I'll take it."

I glance out the window, where I can make out the moon. "How old are you, really?" I ask.

The king grabs the bottle of wine and drinks rather than answering.

"How old were you the first time you killed someone?" he asks.

"Twelve. And I killed four someones that first time."

"Four." He's looking at me like he's having trouble believing me. "What—?"

I hold up a hand. "My turn, remember?"

His eyes drop to my lips and he nods.

"Have you ever personally killed anyone?" I ask.

"No."

His answer doesn't surprise me. The king strikes me as the kind of man who doesn't care about other's suffering so long as he doesn't have to see it. He survives his cruelty only because he removes himself from it. I think in some ways I might be the more brutal of the two of us.

"Why did you kill those four men?" he asks me. I knew he was going to ask me this.

"They were going to rape me," I say. I look away from him as I remember.

So much is left out of my statement. How brain and bone flecked the floor like confetti. How one of them took an agonizing ten minutes to die. The entire time he begged me with the ruin of his mouth to put him out of his misery.

When I look at Montes again, his face is studiously blank, like he's trying to hide his reaction. I realize then that my life might shock the king as much as his life has shocked me. I still can't comprehend the sheer quantity of lives he's taken through his wars, but maybe he is also having a hard time believing that I can kill so easily.

"Tell me how a decent man can be okay with leading a war," I say.

"That's not a question, and I'm not a decent man," he says.

"You're right, I forgot for a moment."

The king presses in close to me so that my back is up against the wall of the pool. His hands rest against the tiled edge, trapping me between them. "Told you," he says, his voice gravelly.

"Told me what?"

"I don't think you really hate me."

"That's just wishful thinking on your part," I say, but silently I worry that he's right, that a few hours with him have weakened my long-held beliefs.

"Okay," I say, changing the topic, "if you don't answer the question I just asked you—"

"Statement," King Lazuli corrects.

"—then you can at least answer this one: why do you like me?"

A sinful smile spreads along the king's lips, and he shifts his body so that his slick skin rubs against mine. "You're clearly new at this," he says. I bristle at his words.

80

"Attraction and chemistry don't follow any logical rules. You're not the prettiest girl I've ever met, nor the smartest, nor the funniest."

I narrow my eyes at him.

"But you are the girl I've altered a peace treaty for, and you are the girl I'm spending the evening with."

"You're evil and deceptive," I say.

"And you're a kindred spirit."

That stops me. It stops me completely. I've never thought of it that way. That the two of us might be the same. The more I think about it, the more frightening similarities there are between us.

The king shifts against me, drawing my attention to the sculpted muscles of his chest and the arms that pin me to the wall. My eyes trail up and rest on his mouth.

The slow burn of the alcohol allows me to focus on only one thing at a time, and right now I'm focusing on those lips.

I blink slowly, the wine churning unpleasantly in my stomach.

"Are you going to let me kiss you?" the king asks.

"Does my answer even matter?" I flick my gaze up to his.

"No, not when you're looking at me like that. But I still want to hear you to say it."

"I won't. Not for you." Admitting I want him to kiss me feels too much like I'm betraying my nation.

He moves his left hand from where it rests to lift one of my legs. He wraps it around his waist. I swallow and fight the urge to close my eyes against the feel of his fingertips on the sensitive skin there.

He's challenging me to stop him with his eyes. I don't.

The king sets his hand back against the edge of the pool and removes his right hand to wrap my other leg around him.

My gaze moves between his eyes, his dark, fathomless eyes. "You can't make someone love you," I say.

"I don't need you to love me."

I'm sure that buried beneath all the king's narcissism and conceit, there's a man that wants companionship, affection—acceptance. That's what all humans want. But perhaps I give the king too much credit.

He leans in slowly, watching me, daring me. At the last minute I turn my head away from him.

"You don't get to have me," I say. "Not after you've taken everything from me." I don't know when the evening became so serious, and now the wine has loosened my lips. I'm saying things I shouldn't be saying. Not if I'm supposed to be seducing my way into an advantageous peace treaty.

"Is that a challenge?" King Lazuli's gaze dips to my breasts, and his knee rubs the fabric of my bikini bottoms against me. He knows what he's doing—I'll give him that.

"No, I'm just stating a fact." I have to coax my voice to sound normal.

"Just like you hating me is also you stating a fact."

"Exactly."

"Good," he says. "Now I know that you have absolutely no idea what a fact is."

My mouth drops open, and he uses that opportunity to

82

lean all the way in and kiss me.

He was right earlier when he said he didn't play fair. His lips press hotly against mine, and his tongue caresses the inside of my mouth. I use my own tongue to shove his out, but this is where I make a critical mistake. Kisses are just as much a battle as they are a joining of desires, and in my ignorance I've unknowingly deepened the kiss.

The king reciprocates with force, his tongue scorching my mouth. I've never been kissed this way before, like I'm some desperate desire of the king's. He rubs himself against me, and I can feel him harden.

No. This can't go any further.

I push him away from me, and I scramble to get out of the pool. My exit is not very graceful, but that's the last thing on my mind.

I'm breathing heavily when I turn to face the king. He's treading water, studying me with a predatory look in his eyes. Or maybe it's lust I'm seeing. It doesn't matter.

"Scared?" he asks, taunting me.

"Yes." I sway on my feet, feeling lightheaded.

His tone changes. "Are you okay?"

I shake my head. The wine's no longer a pleasant buzz, but something more insidious. I feel my stomach cramp and nausea rise. "I think I drank too much."

I stumble over to one of the nearby chairs and lean my head between my legs. This position doesn't feel so bad.

When I feel a hand on my arm, I look up and see the king crouched in front of me. I must be losing my senses; I didn't hear him exit the pool and approach.

His gaze looks concerned. "We should probably get you

to bed."

I nod and get up, grabbing a towel and wrapping it around myself.

The king escorts me back to my room, which surprises me. I'd assumed he'd send Marco or one of his other men to accompany me. Or that he'd lead me to his quarters. I can't make sense of the king when he does something even slightly honorable.

Once we stop outside my room, the king brushes a kiss across my lips. "Feel better," he says. And then he's gone.

CHAPTER 7

SERENITY

FOUR YEARS AGO the western hemisphere went dark.

I was doing rounds when it happened. I sat in the back of a military issued vehicle, a gun slung across my body.

An older bunker member—a retired colonel—sat up front, driving the car around the perimeter. It had been a quiet night. Usually at least one incident cropped up during my shifts, but tonight I seemed to be getting a break. My gaze drifted up to the night sky. I searched for my favorite constellations, but light pollution from the nearby city of Annapolis obscured them.

My eyes had only just begun to travel back to my surroundings when the sky lit up. It flashed, blindingly bright, turning night into day. Then the light shrank away.

Another bomb.

"Shit."

Less than a minute later I heard the blast. It sounded like the devil was shouting, like he was going to consume me and the earth. The wave of energy hit me, throwing me back into the bed of the vehicle. Beneath me the earth shivered, and the car engine faltered, the front lights flickering before it decided it wasn't going to die after all.

And then there was silence. Ominous silence.

"What in the fucking hell ... ? Serenity, you okay?" the colonel shouted back to me.

"I'm fine," I said, pushing myself upright.

By chance my gaze fell on Annapolis. The city, which only a moment ago had been ablaze in light, was dark.

I beat the colonel to the radio. "A bomb's been dropped. Repeat: a bomb's been dropped."

I was so shaken that it took me a moment to realize the message hadn't gone through; the radio was off. I went to click it on, only to find that it had already been on. I glanced back up at where Annapolis should be. Now it was shrouded in shadow.

Later I learned that King Lazuli had detonated several nuclear bombs high above the WUN's territories. The explosions had released EMP pulses that took out all electronics that weren't heavily shielded from them.

Most electricity. Many cars. Virtually all mobile devices. Nearly every computer. All snuffed out. Only the bunker and a few other heavily fortified locations—most belowground—survived the EMP pulse unscathed.

The rest of the WUN got set back decades that day.

BRIGHT RAYS OF sunlight wake me. I wince at the sight of them and rub my eyes. My head pounds once, then a few seconds later it pounds again, and again. A horrible headache blossoms, worsening with each passing second. All I want is to fall back asleep, but the churning pain in my stomach has me throwing off my covers and running for the bathroom.

I lift the lid of the toilet and vomit. My stomach spasms while I bend over, letting me know it's only just warming up. I spend the next thirty minutes huddled around the porcelain bowl, retching until there is nothing left in my stomach. I flush it all down, pretending that last night's wine is responsible for the crimson tint of the water.

I feel weak, and my head is screaming at me. I might as well have drunk poison last night; it would have the same effect on me. I push myself to my feet and lean over the sink to catch my breath. I wonder briefly if the king also feels this way.

My skin heats at the thought of him. Last night I got to know him too well. We shared secrets, drank wine, kissed.

Oh God, I'm going to see him soon.

And that's when I notice it. The strange silence of my suite. Surely my father would've poked his head in by now. I haven't seen him since I left last night.

I pad back into my room and take another look out my window. It's late morning, but that can't be right, not unless ...

A sick feeling that has nothing to do with my hangover washes over me. Did I sleep through the negotiations?

I cross the room and fling open my door. In the common area a lone WUN soldier waits.

He sees my face. "The king requested that the remainder of the negotiations be done without your attendance," he explains.

"What? Why would he do that?" I ask, furrowing my brows. My worry is quickly morphing into a more familiar emotion. Anger.

The guard shrugs. "You're probably doing your job a little too well."

I give the soldier a sharp look, and he holds up his hands.

"All I'm saying is that the king probably wants to make sure he's still in control of the situation. Having you there might affect his decisions."

Because one really shouldn't mix business and pleasure. And last night I established that I was here for the king's pleasure.

The guard is still talking, but I can't hear him over the noise in my head. I leave him, slamming the door to my room a little harder than I had intended.

I clench my hands. I want to scream—no I want to hurt something. I want to slam my fist against skin until it bruises.

The king wasn't drunk like I was last night. No, he's been busy orchestrating a plan of his own. One where he makes no consolations to the WUN, or to me, or to my father.

Just like I had hoped last night, my hatred is back; however, what stokes it is not my country's wrath, but my own.

I've only been awake an hour when I hear a knock on the door. The WUN soldier answers it before I do.

"The king wishes to deliver a present to Miss Freeman," I hear someone say on the other side of the door.

That's all I need to hear. "Don't bother taking the gift," I yell at the soldier. "I won't accept it."

My guard shrugs to the person standing in the hallway. "Sorry sir, orders are orders," he says before closing the door.

Once it clicks shut, the guard shakes his head and glances at me, a twinkle of respect in his eye. "The king's about to learn just what a ballbuster you are."

"The king's a fucking prick."

The guard snorts. "Tell me something I don't know."

I'm staring out my window, bathed under the dwindling sunlight, when I hear my father enter the suite. As soon as I do, I rush out of my room, ignoring the faint pound of my fading headache.

My father rubs his eyes, his face weary.

"That bastard," I say.

"Serenity, watch your language," he says.

The irony is that I've been ruder to the king's face than this.

"What happened?" I ask.

My father takes a seat on one of the couches in the common area and drops a package he came into the room carrying. "Other than the medical relief you managed to wrangle from him, King Lazuli's not budging on most of

89

his conditions—and they're the important ones."

"He kicked me out of the peace talks," I say quietly.

My father meets my eyes. "I know," he says, his voice resigned. Of course my father knows.

As we stare at each other, I feel another strange pang of sympathy for the man in front of me. The situation is unfolding how he feared it would.

"I'm sorry," I say.

"You shouldn't be the one apologizing," my dad says.

But that's exactly why I'm apologizing—because he blames himself. My father has a whole lot of insight, yet none of it could prevent what's happened. What a burden it must be to perceive the future yet be unable to change it.

His eyes shift to the package at his feet. "You have a present from the king."

"He can take his present and shove it up—"

"*Serenity.*"

"Yeah, yeah," I grumble. I grab the package and walk it into my room. Once I'm alone, I rip open the cardboard box. Inside is a pale yellow dress, and resting on top of it is a necklace made of yellow diamonds. Yellow, because it's my favorite color.

I work my jaw at the sight. How many stomachs could these items feed? How much medical relief could they afford? Everything that comes from the king is blood money.

My hands shake when I pick up the card resting on top of the pale fabric. The note is simple.

Forgive me, and feel better.

I crumple up his note. Forgive me my ass. The king is not sorry. But he will be.

MARCO RAPS ON our suite five separate times before I decide to meet the king. He has my father to thank for that.

The entire time my father sits in the corner of the room, peace treaty on his lap, his hands threaded through his hair. He hasn't turned the page since the knocking began.

Marco bangs on the door once more, and my father stands suddenly. Throwing the document on a nearby table, he strides towards the door.

"Dad, what are you doing?" I say, standing up from my own seat.

"I'm going to tell Marco that you will not see the king."

Crap. I hadn't meant for this.

"Wait, no." I cut him off, and stop him with a hand. "Dad, it's fine."

"It's not fine, and I can't watch this."

If my father intercedes now, it could be game over. Scenarios dance through my mind, none of them good. The ripple effects could be disastrous. I can't let that happen.

"Please, Dad. Sit down. I'll answer the door."

"I can't ask this of you," he says. "None of us can."

My throat works at his admission. "It's alright. This arrangement isn't forever. Just please, go sit back down."

My father stares at me for a long time, his nostrils flaring. For a man who's good at masking his emotions, he's not doing so well at the moment.

Finally he nods and walks back to his seat, his movements mechanical.

Hurrying to the door, I grab the handle and fling it open before I can reconsider my actions.

"Evening Marco," I say when I step out into the hallway.

"The king requests—"

"I know," I say, pushing past him.

"He wants you to wear your gift," Marco says to my back.

"And I want to live in a world where I don't have to worry about radiation poisoning, but neither is going to happen anytime soon."

I can hear Marco's huff, but he's smart enough to realize a lost cause when he sees one.

This evening Marco leads me to a different area of the mansion. We stop in front of a solid wood door and Marco knocks twice.

"Come in Marco." I can hear the king's muffled voice on the other side of the door.

Marco twists the handle and ushers me inside. The king's back is to me and he's staring at the walls of the room.

I suck in a breath of air. The walls are covered with maps of every nation on earth. Strings crisscross the images, connecting one section of land to another. Pins hold the strings down, and beneath a few of these pins are images. Most are of people whose faces have been crossed out; only a precious few remain unscathed. My earlier nausea rises.

"Feeling better, Serenity?"

"Fuck off."

The king turns to face me, his expression unreadable. "You're not wearing my gift."

"You can't bribe me into liking you."

The king's eyes flick to Marco. "You can go."

Behind me Marco's footfalls fade, and a moment later the door clicks shut. There's no one else in this room but the two of us. No guards, no servants. Like the pool last night, it's just the two of us.

"I can't have you clouding my judgment during negotiations," he explains without me asking.

My hands fist. "Right. Because how awful would it be to compromise for once in your life?"

"I haven't spent the last decade waging war with your country to finally compromise."

"No," I agree, "you haven't."

The king glances away from me at the maps that line the walls. "I'm not an idiot," he says, not looking at me. "I know the WUN sent you here to seduce me."

My body goes rigid. I have no idea why his confession shocks me; it doesn't take a scientist to put two and two together.

He laughs, the sound hollow. "The problem is, it worked." His eyes move over me, and something in them softens for a moment before he shutters the expression.

"Uh huh."

His lips curl into a smirk. "You find that hard to believe?" he asks. I'd say that he was mocking me, except his eyes are too serious.

I fold my arms over my chest. Of course I do. "Why are you telling me this?" I ask.

"To warn you."

"Warn me about what?"

"I get what I want. Always."

"You keep telling me that, yet I haven't seen any proof."

"You want proof?" he says. His eyes are calculating, and the smile dancing on his lips is sly. He's no longer the man I talked to yesterday; he's the man who's been taking over the world for the last three decades.

I take a step back. I shouldn't have spoken just now; my words were careless, and around the king, careless words could mean the difference between life and death.

I shake my head and close my eyes. "No, I don't want proof. I just want this to end." I open my eyes. "I don't want to see any more crossed out faces on those maps of yours." I jut my chin to the wall behind him. "I don't want to be hungry all the time. I don't want to see the hollow-eyed looks of the people I live alongside."

"I can give you that," he says, slowly walking towards me, not stopping until the two of us are dangerously close.

"Of course you can—but you won't."

"That's because no one's offered me the correct price yet." He says it like this is a simple matter of haggling.

I throw my arms up. "You can't expect the WUN to willingly cripple our future economy for you."

The king eliminates the last bit of space between us and fingers a lock of my hair. "That's not the price I was referring to." Almost lackadaisically, his eyes move from my hair and land on my face.

And now I get it. I take a step back, then another. I furrow my eyebrows; I think I'm going to be sick. "No."

"Why not?"

"Even if I believed that was a legitimate trade—which we both know it isn't—no."

"You could end this all now, and you refuse to agree to it?"

"You're asking me to make a deal with the devil."

"You and I both know you already signed your soul away a long time ago, Serenity."

"Because of you and your stupid war. I already told you last night, you don't get to have me."

The king prowls towards me, closing the distance between us once more. "I'm not just talking about sex," he says.

But sex would be included in the arrangement. "I'd rather die than do anything with you."

"If it's death you wish, we can arrange that."

The king reaches out to touch my arm, and I slap his hand away. "Don't. Touch. Me." I'm shaking; this was never supposed to happen. I'm getting played by the king, and I don't know how to get myself out of this situation.

King Lazuli sticks his hands in his pockets and leans in conspiratorially. "You know the thing about strategy? It takes knowing when to act and when to be patient."

I take a good look at him. King Lazuli's been waging this war for almost thirty years, yet he looks to be little older than thirty himself. I've seen footage of him shot, blown-up, and stabbed, yet he hasn't died. He's unnatural in more ways than one.

"If you try to force me into this plan of yours, I will find out your secrets," I say, "and once I do, I will kill you." I stare at him long enough for him to see the vehemence behind my words. And then I turn and walk away from the king and the sick tapestry that hangs along the walls of the room.

I'm almost to the door when he speaks. "I plan on making you love me before that happens."

CHAPTER 8

SERENITY

THREE YEARS AGO I saw combat for the first time.

I was allowed to fight despite being underage. Many of us were. The war had raged on long enough that the military would take almost all willing and able-bodied soldiers—even underage ones, so long as they were over the age of fourteen and their guardian agreed to it. My father had consented—albeit, reluctantly—and so had Will's.

Will and I, members of the same platoon, had been stationed in New York, near where New York City once stood. The two of us hunkered down outside the skeletons of former buildings, our breaths clouding in the chilly night air. Our battalion had reappropriated the ruins and turned them into makeshift barracks.

"We're missing all the action," Will complained, picking up a pebble and chucking it at an abandoned car across the street.

Because we were younger. Our military might recruit minors, but they tended to shelter them from action if they could.

Several minutes later one of the other members of our company whistled from a block away. "The king's men are dropping out of the sky!"

I glanced above me and sure enough, the dim outline of parachutes obscured the patches of the sky. There looked to be dozens of them.

"Oh shit," Will said.

My heart slammed inside my ribcage. We were being ambushed. I grabbed my mother's necklace and kissed it for good luck. I'd killed before, but never under such treacherous circumstances.

Shots pinged in the distance—likely other soldiers from our company trying to shoot the king's men out of the air. From what I could tell, it had no effect.

Will raised his weapon.

"Don't shoot," I said, staring up at the sky.

"Why not?" He lined up his gun's sights.

"We don't have enough bullets to waste." Not when our targets were too far away to aim with accuracy.

"So you think we should wait?" He sounded incredulous.

"Mmhm." My hands trembled.

Will shook his head but lowered his gun. "This better be a good idea, 'cause I feel like we're missing a perfect opportunity."

"Just wait for them to get within range."

He huffed, his way of agreeing without conceding his point.

It took an agonizing five minutes for the enemy to get close enough to shoot. When a man managed to land on our block, Will and I jogged over to him as the soldier extricated himself from his harness.

"I got this one," Will said, aiming his weapon.

I nodded next to him, my gun also trained on the enemy soldier.

Will hesitated, readjusted his grip, then hesitated some more.

"What are you waiting for?" I whispered.

"Nothing."

I cast a look over at Will. His hands fidgeted, his eyes were wild.

He'd never killed a man. I'd assumed he had. We lived in the kind of world where violence was inevitable.

The soldier was now glancing up at us as he frantically fiddled with the straps of his parachute. In several more seconds we'd lose the advantage we now had.

Next to me Will shifted his weight, his hands adjusting and readjusting their grip on his weapon. He wasn't going to finish the enemy in time.

Steadying my breath, I aimed my weapon and fired.

The bullet took the soldier right between the eyes—a quick, painless death. That was as compassionate as I was going to get out here, given the circumstances.

For ten long seconds neither of us moved.

Will finally lowered his gun. "I froze up." I could hear the embarrassment in his voice.

"Nothing to be ashamed of."

I pushed down my nausea. By now I'd learned that it wasn't physical. It was more of a soul-sickness. Another piece of my humanity chipped away.

"*You* were able to kill him," Will said.

You, a girl. That's what he meant. Like owning a vagina made me inferior in some fundamental way.

I gave Will a long look, then shook my head and began walking towards the body. I expected most of the teen boys in my platoon to be sexist, but not Will.

"I'm sorry," he said to my back.

I waved him off. "You'll get another chance to kill tonight. I'm sure it'll help your wounded ego recover."

Will did in fact kill for the first time that evening. And when he saw the woman's lifeless eyes, he vomited all over my shoes. The machismo act fell away after that. It didn't stop either of us from continuing to slaughter enemy soldiers, but by the end of the night, Will was no longer so eager to take lives.

Once upon a time, we were innocent. And then we were not.

THE NEXT FEW days at the king's estate are strangely quiet. Our time here is almost up. Not much progress has been made between my father and the king as far as negotiations go. My father enters our suite each day weary and beaten down. The WUN is not in a position to make an advantageous agreement, and the king is making that clearer now more than ever.

If we can't reach an agreement in the next two days, when our flight is scheduled to leave, the king will continue to wage war on us until we're forced to surrender, and then the WUN will have to agree with whatever demands he asks.

The twisted king hasn't tried to see me since our brief interaction in his map room, yet our last visit managed to spook me. I can't tell how much of what he said was true and how much of it was a lie. The king is a tactical mastermind, that much I know. So I can trust that whatever he decides will be solely in his best interest. I'll get used, and so will the WUN.

And now I have to see him in less than an hour. King Lazuli's hosting some bigwig dinner, and we're the guests of honor. It'll be the first time I'm in front of the cameras again since I was banned from the peace talks.

I carefully apply the makeup I was packed with. I've probably spent more time on this trip poking myself in the eye with the eyeliner pen than I have learning the ins and outs of the king's proposed peace treaty. And I've spent hours poring over that thing.

I turn away from the mirror and glance at the far corner of my room where I shoved the king's gifts. I don't want to put the gown or the jewelry on; to me it symbolizes all the broken families and defeated nations he's claimed.

But so close to when we have to leave, my mind is haunted by the possibility that I could do something for the WUN. Tonight.

I retrieve the king's gifts from the corner. I give the pale yellow dress a dirty look. Somehow the king managed to spoil my favorite color. I remove the towel wrapped around my torso and pull the gown on.

Once I do, I frown. My entire back is exposed. The rest of the dress falls suggestively over my curves. It fits me perfectly.

I grab the diamond necklace that goes along with the dress, and before I can think too much about it, I clasp it around my neck. It feels like a manacle.

I finish applying makeup and arrange my hair so that it lies in loose curls over my shoulders, and then I leave my room. I look nothing like the elegant women I've seen here, with their perfectly coiffed hair and painted faces, and for that I'm glad. I can still recognize myself in the mirror.

Outside my room, my father speaks animatedly with one of our guards. Gone is the devastated man who considered defying orders for me.

A wry smile passes over his face when he catches sight of me. "You almost pull off the sweet and innocent look," he says. "Almost."

"What ruins it? My scar?" I ask. I grin back at him.

"Nope—it's all in the eyes and the jaw. And that smile doesn't help. You look like you want to gut someone." Now my dad's grinning.

"You can dress up a pig, but it's still a pig."

My dad comes over to me and grasps my hand. "Not a pig," he says, staring me in the eye, "a soldier."

MY FATHER AND I follow Marcus to the banquet hall, our

guards shadowing our procession. Inside, people haven't yet sat down to eat. Instead they mill about the room, sipping on champagne and chatting with one another.

The room stirs as we enter. You'd think that the king's stuck-up friends would get used to the sight of us, but they haven't. Nor have the camera crews. I notice that most of their lenses zoom in on me. I guess their audiences are more interested in my (lack of) involvement in the peace talks than they are of my father's or the king's.

My father leans into me. "You need to interact with these people tonight. Talk, be friendly, and try not to scare anyone too much. I'm leaving you to mingle."

He must see the fear in my eyes as he pulls away because he pats my shoulder. "Make me proud."

I give him a look that tells him what I think about that statement. He grins at me and winks before moving away from me to talk with an elderly man—the former prime minister of what used to be England.

My skin prickles; I can sense the king watching me. I turn and lock eyes with him. He swirls the wine in his glass as he assesses me. His eyes meander down my body and back up, and as he does so, an approving smile spreads across his face.

I suppress a shiver at his gaze. I imagine this is how he looks at unconquered territories.

The camera crews crowd me, despite the WUN soldiers standing guard. I keep my expression bland so the world doesn't see the terror coursing through me. The king has always been my boogeyman, but boogeymen aren't supposed to be real. They're the things of nightmares, the things your parents kiss away.

But he's real. And he wants me. And the entire western hemisphere might benefit if I simply face my fears.

The plan I've toyed with for the last several days comes to fruition. I will do this, even if it's as scary as running headlong into battle.

I roll my neck like I do before I work out and push my shoulders back. I'm going to give the cameramen one hell of a show.

I stride towards the king, who stands on the other side of the room. I let my body sway a little more than usual, just to pull eyes to me.

Up until now, all anyone knows about the king and me are rumors—if that. I'm about to blow those rumors open.

I can hear the uncertain shuffle of my guards keeping formation around me and the eager clamor of camera crews. They're like carrion circling a wounded creature—they can practically sense a story about to happen.

I'm gathering stares; I can feel the way they crawl along my skin. The king looks amused—no, transfixed—as I make a beeline for him. He too knows something is about to happen.

The crowd parts for me, and the buzzing chatter in the room dies down. I close the remaining distance between the two of us until I'm standing in front of him.

"Miss me?" I ask.

King Lazuli's face is serious, but his eyes smile. He's definitely enjoying the show.

"I haven't missed anything more," he responds smoothly, like the slick politician he is.

"Then why haven't you kissed me yet?" Now the room goes quiet.

This, this is a gamble. On the one hand, the king might reject me in front of a crowded room—scratch that, in front of the entire world. That I can handle; I haven't believed he's been sincere about his feelings for me since the day we met. And if he does reject me, the WUN will have definitive proof that the king's just toying with all of us.

On the other hand, if he goes along with this, the world will anticipate favorable negotiations with the WUN—if he's openly friendly with the emissary's daughter, he's surely friendly with the nations she represents. My hope is that it will increase the odds of an advantageous peace treaty for us.

This possibility scares the crap out of me. It means more contact with the king. Intimate contact.

Montes raises his eyebrows, his eyes twinkling like mad. This whole exchange delights him. He takes the final step that removes all the distance between the two of us, and I feel the press of his tux against my chest.

A roguish grin lights up his face. He slides a hand along my jaw and cups the back of my head. My heart speeds up, and I can't tell whether fear or a thread of desire is responsible for it.

His cool breath fans across my face. "Just remember tomorrow that you started this," he says quietly.

I don't know what to make of his words, but then I don't need to. His lips are on mine, and they move softly, sweetly against my mouth. I kiss him back, parting my lips and running my tongue over his.

The murmurs around us quiet, and in the silence that follows I can hear the frantic shuffling of camera crews that want to capture what could be a pivotal moment in the negotiations.

But even that is background noise compared to being completely and totally enveloped by the king. His fingertips touch my cheeks with the lightest of pressure. There's a kindness to the touch, and I have the oddest urge to weep that someone can be this gentle to another human being. That it's the king who caresses me like this ... I can't rectify my conflicted emotions.

One of King Lazuli's hands moves to the small of my back, holding me close, his thumb stroking the bare skin there. I move my own hand so that it cups his jaw, and I'm shocked by its roughness. Shocked perhaps because he feels more like a man than a nightmare.

Our poolside evening together bubbles to the surface of my thoughts. He was a different person then, and right now, while his lips move against mine, he's that same person. The thought makes me forget that I'm in the arms of the enemy, and that my country might consider me a traitor for my current actions—actions I make on its behalf.

The kiss ends, and the king draws away slowly, his eyes lingering on my lips. Desire and a trace of something else flare up in his eyes.

Around us the room is silent. I can feel half a dozen cameras focused on me and the king. I'm sure several are capturing my father's expression as well, but I'm too busy staring down Montes to care much about that.

Whatever this is, it's no deception on the king's part.

It's something far, far worse.

Someone whistles on the other side of the room, and then I hear the tinkling of silverware on glass. More join in; some people even tap the side of their glasses with a knife.

I look from them to the king, my brow furrowed.

"They want us to kiss again."

I feel my cheeks heat. My courage is all used up. King Lazuli dips down and brushes his lips against mine. My mouth responds, moving languidly over his, even though the entire situation freaks me out. At least we've definitely given the world a show.

This time when the king pulls away, his lips skim over my cheek to my ear. "You're cute when you blush."

My nostrils flare in annoyance, but I compose my face before anyone takes notice. The king's hands linger, one in particular gets comfortable around my waist.

His eyes drop to my gown. "You look gorgeous—the dress fits you perfectly."

The mention of this hateful gown reminds me that the king is more than just silky words and soft caresses. He's the enemy.

I give him a tight smile since I can't be openly rude to him while so much attention is on us.

King Lazuli seems to understand this, and a sly grin spreads across his face. "Like the color?"

"Uh huh." I clench my jaw so much it hurts.

The people who cluster around the king have focused their attention on me, and I know my pleasant exterior is cracking. I entwine my fingers around the king's, and pry his hand from my waist.

"Mind if I steal the king for a moment?" I ask the crowd.

The group shakes their heads and shrugs. "Thanks—I promise I'll only be a moment." I drag the king away from the crowd, not that he seems to mind it in the least. The camera crews start to follow us, so I turn and give them all a death glare. It's enough for them to keep their distance. For now. I know I've caused too much of a scene for them to stay away long.

Once I get the king a safe distance away from the crowd, I drop the act. "I'll do it."

"Oh? And what exactly is it that you'll do?" the king asks.

I narrow my eyes. "Whatever it is you want with me."

I can see the king's breath catch. He's getting exactly what he wants, just like he promised me he would.

"But—" I say, "I have a condition."

The king raises his eyebrows and waits for me to continue.

"You need to compromise with the WUN—don't cripple their economy, don't withhold needed funds. Give my homeland enough benefits to get them back on their feet."

"You do realize that's incredibly vague," the king says. What he doesn't say is that in his world, ambiguity is an exploitable weakness.

I touch his arm; I'm going to have to get used to his touch if I go through with this. He glances down at where my hand rests, then back to my face. His eyes are vulnerable.

"I'm asking you to be honorable," I say. I give him a long look, and I see some of his humanity seep into those bright eyes. "Please, you don't need to blackmail me or the western hemisphere to get what you want. I'm coming to you freely."

The king cups my chin, and I see real tenderness there. "I'll come up with a final agreement, but your father will have to approve of it for us to have a deal."

A deal. That's what this is. I nod.

He bows his head and steals a kiss from me. "Good. Then I look forward to a long and prosperous future for all parties involved."

I did it. I just sacrificed myself for my nation.

CHAPTER 9

SERENITY

TWO YEARS AGO I became my father's apprentice.

He hadn't always been our land's only emissary. I hear we used to have many. Men and women appointed by the government to engage in diplomacy with foreign nations.

When the Western United Nations was formed, this branch of the government was refashioned. A single position—that of WUN emissary—was created. It proved to be a fatal one. Half a dozen men and women died before my father, who'd once served as the Secretary of State, had been elected into the role.

He managed to hold onto the position and his life, mostly because he hadn't set foot onto the Eastern Hemisphere.

There should've been another round of elections since my father took the title of emissary. He should've abdicated the role to another official, along with all the other representatives that lived in the bunker. But once the western hemisphere went dark, our electoral system disintegrated almost overnight. In it's absence we had to revert to an archaic system of power: bequeathing titles from parent to child. And now my father was passing the position onto me.

I knew all of this the evening he called me into his office. I'd seen and lived so much that this shouldn't have scared me. But it did.

Once I shut the door behind me, my father glanced up from his papers. "Do you know why you're here?"

I gave him a sharp nod. "You want to teach me how to be an emissary."

My father scrubbed his face. "I don't want to do this—that you've got wrong. But neither of us have much of a choice."

"Dad, I'm no good at diplomacy."

He cracked a smile. "You're my daughter. You're good at everything."

I rolled my eyes. "You're a little biased."

"And you're a little humble."

His words were proof I'd never have his sharp tongue. He always knew the right thing to say to diffuse a situation. I was more likely to punch someone in the face than I was reasoning with them.

That first lesson was brief, unlike the hundreds to come. By the end of it, my father left me with one final bit of information. "Serenity?"

My hand was already on the door. I turned back to face

him.

The wrinkles around his eyes and mouth deepened. "As an emissary, if an accord is ever to be reached between us and the Eastern Empire, you will likely be a key player in it."

I swallowed and nodded. I now carried a heavy responsibility.

"Do you know what that means?"

I waited for him to finish.

His gaze lingered on me a long time before he finally answered his own question. "One day you'll meet the king."

That day had come.

THE ROOM IS quiet as my father contacts the representatives. I barely made eye contact with him after my kiss with the king. I couldn't. The whole situation still gives me the heebie jeebies.

My dad, for his part, seems to be at a loss for words. So we wait in silence, until the representatives flash onto the screen. We do the usual greeting, and then there's a pause.

"Serenity," General Kline says, "you gave the world quite the show. The Internet's blowing up with it."

What he doesn't say is that everyone's calling me a traitor, a whore—whatever unoriginal names they can come up with. There will be no honor to my sacrifice. Women who have filled the role of temptress have always been looked down upon.

"I got King Lazuli to make another agreement," I snap, my voice bitter.

My father turns to me, surprised.

"Tomorrow," I say to the general, "if there's a semi-decent bone in the king's body, the WUN should have a fair and equitable peace treaty."

All's quiet for a moment, and then my father speaks. "What did you agree to, Serenity?" he asks, worry tingeing his voice. The rest of the representatives wait for my answer.

I glance down at my hands. "I don't exactly know."

I'M NOT SURPRISED when I hear knocking on the suite door. I glance at my father's closed off room. He's locked himself away in there since our talk with the representatives. His excuse is that he's relaying updates to those nations who couldn't send their own emissaries. I know better. I heard his muffled weeps. He can't stand the situation, so he's hiding from it.

Now the room's ominously quiet. My father knows what waits for me in the hallway, just as I do, and he's decided to ignore it.

If only I had that luxury.

Be brave, Serenity, I tell myself, because no one else is here to comfort me in this moment.

I rise from my seat, setting aside the WUN's proposal, and answer the door.

Marco stands outside. "The king requests—"

"Yeah, yeah." I could go the rest of my life without hearing these official missives. Particularly when they involve illicit business. I step out of my room and follow Marco through the palace. We pass the king's private dining room and continue on, eventually stopping in front of an ornately carved door.

Marco opens it. "This is where I leave you."

If I speak, he'll surely hear my fright, so I nod instead and step inside the room. I glance behind me in time to see the door close and Marco's form vanish from sight. It might as well have been the iron bars of a cell slamming shut.

I am trapped.

I turn my attention to my surroundings. I'm inside the king's richly decorated sitting room. It's beautiful and lacks for nothing, save the king.

I step up to a window. Below me, lamps cast the king's estate in shades of amber and orange. The city beyond lies in darkness. My hands slide along the windowsill. The greatest irony here is that the king lives in the light, the innocents in the dark. The king belongs to those shadows that lurk outside the light. As do I.

"You're still in my dress."

I swivel around, startled to find the man himself leaning against an open doorway, hands tucked in his pockets. He still wears his dinner attire, only now his suit jacket is gone, and the cuffs of his sleeves have been rolled up past his elbows. Aside from his swimsuit, this is the most casual I've ever seen him.

"I knew you'd come for me," I respond, touching my sternum in a poorly masked attempt to hide my cleavage.

It only serves to draw the king's attention to my chest.

There they linger. Seconds tick by, and neither of us moves. I don't know what's passing through his mind, but terror and excitement consume mine. I'm incapable of moving, even if I tried.

The king's gaze flicks back up to mine, his dark eyes intense in the low lighting. Pushing away from the wall, he prowls forward. The trance is broken. Something's changed, and things I know nothing of are about to happen. With each step the king takes, I can see a little more of that fire burning in his eyes.

What have I agreed to?

Taking my hand, Montes leads me to a fainting couch. I allow him to guide my body onto it. The entire time I watch him like he might tear my throat out if I look away or move too quickly.

The king kneels next to me, a hand dropping to one of my ankles. It slips under the silky seam of my skirt and glides up my calf. Over my knee.

My heart's in my throat; I can feel it pounding there, cutting off my breath.

Up his hand delves, over my thigh. Then stops.

"You're shaking."

I close my eyes. His words carry no inflection, so I can't tell whether he considers this a good or bad thing. I have no idea what the hell I'm supposed to be doing either, but chances are, if I take an active role in whatever's going on, I will end up attacking him, the Undying King. That can't happen.

That won't happen.

I lick my dry lips. "I've never ... done this."

"This?" the king repeats like he's confused. His fingers brush between my legs.

The small burst of pleasure tightens my stomach, and I glare at him. "Yes, *that*."

His hands slide out from under my skirt. "What *have* you done?" Curiosity smolders in his eyes.

"I've been kissed."

"That's it?" Again, his words are inflectionless. He lays a hand on my hipbone

"That's it."

He swears under his breath, his grip tightening. I can tell conflicting desires war within him because he's looking through me more than at me. I also know the moment they resolve themselves.

He hesitates, then rises to his feet. "Leave."

I don't move. This is not how it's supposed to play out.

"Move, Serenity, before I change my mind."

Slowly I stand. The fear is fading, replaced by confusion. I consider the man in front of me. Logic is telling me that he's letting me go because of some moral compass he carries. My emotions are telling me any moral compass he possesses is so warped and eroded he wouldn't know a good deed from a bad one.

"I'm giving you tonight," he says, not looking at me. "Enjoy the company of your father. Tomorrow, you'll be at my side, not his."

CHAPTER 10

SERENITY

A YEAR AGO I discovered I was dying.

First my appetite diminished. I'd skip breakfast because in the morning I couldn't keep even the tasteless oatmeal down. Better to leave the food for people whose bodies wouldn't reject it.

Life continued that way for a couple months—long enough for people to notice. Long enough for them to assume I was pregnant despite the fact that I'd never even been kissed. Will took a lot of heat for that. But when months passed and no baby came, people forgot.

All save for me.

The nausea fled as quickly as it came. For a while I could pretend my health issues away, until one morning when my nausea returned. I made it to the bathroom in time, only what I retched up wasn't simply food and bile.

Blood tinted my vomit red.

I breathed heavily as I stared down at the irrefutable evidence that I was sick. I never told my father. I never told Will.

The sickness never fully went away.

THE NEXT MORNING, I watch my father leave the room, worry creasing my brows. I hardly slept last night, I was so worried about what today's outcome would be. I half waited for the knock of the king; I'd assumed that he'd change his mind and collect on my side of the deal before he approached my father today.

But the knock never comes. Strange enough, my worries morph from what the king will do with me once the treaty's signed to what will happen if the king decides that whatever I have to offer isn't good enough.

The WUN soldiers watch me as I pace. When their stares become too disconcerting, I move to my bedroom and begin to organize my dresses by color, then make my bed. It takes twenty minutes in all, and it does nothing to calm my nerves, so I stretch and do several sets of pushups and sit-ups.

Once I have a nice sheen of sweat along my body, I hop into the shower, letting the water calm me. But even that can't relax me, not when I start to feel guilty about wasting clean water while my friends in the bunker share a dismal basin's worth each day.

I dry off and change, pulling on one of the more bearable dresses I've been packed. Today I was supposed to board a flight with my father. Now, in between fretting over what waits me after the sun sets, I wonder how I will possibly let the man who raised me go.

I've just finished applying mascara when the door to our suite is thrown open and my father storms in. "Grab your things, Serenity."

"What?"

"We need to go, *now*."

I switch to soldier mode. "What do I need?"

"Shoes you can run in and anything you can't live without. You have three minutes."

I don't waste another second. I grab the gun my father gave me long ago and load it before turning the safety on and shoving it down the bodice of my dress. It's not the safest place to carry a loaded gun, but my guess is that being unarmed in the king's palace at the moment is even less safe.

I pull on my combat boots, wondering just what words were exchanged between my father and the king. Clearly, the king hadn't made good on his promise to be honorable. Otherwise, my father wouldn't be acting this way.

I don't have time to change out of the ridiculous dress I'm wearing, but I rip off most of the skirt so that I can run better. The sound of tearing fabric is unbelievably satisfying.

As I finish getting ready, I can hear the WUN soldiers gearing up around me. There's a buzzing excitement in the air, the thrill that comes before battle.

"We're going out the rear windows," my father says, "and then we're going to cross the gardens and exit through the back of the estate, where a car will be waiting to take us to our jet."

My eyes widen. I hope I'm one day half as good as my father at these things. He's had our escape plan prepared way ahead of time.

My father glances at his watch. "Okay soldiers, your three minutes are up. Let's move to the back of the room."

The words are barely out of his mouth when there's a pounding on the door. I glance at my father.

"Don't answer that," he says, his voice deadly serious.

"Wasn't planning on it."

The pounding gets louder, and then I hear a key inserted into the lock. My eyes go wide as I look at my father. The soldiers fan out around us, covering us just as the door opens and Marco comes in with a dozen palace guards.

What could've possibly gone on during negotiations?

"Ambassador Freeman," Marco says, "the king has ordered me to retrieve your daughter."

My heart pounds at the mention of my name.

"I did not agree to the terms of the revised peace treaty, so he does not have that kind of authority over her," my father says.

I glance between Marco and my father. He didn't agree to the king's proposal. Why?

"You can agree to the peace treaty or not," Marco says. "Either way, the king is not going to let Serenity leave here."

I hone my attention on Marco. The king thinks he can keep me around despite the negotiations. Of course, this is his back up strategy to make sure he gets what he wants.

"Dad, what were the terms of the peace agreement?" This is the question I've been dying to know.

My father doesn't answer, but Marco does. "Money, medical relief, a series of programs to revitalize your hemisphere's shithole economy." I hear the acid in Marco's voice. I always had the feeling that below Marco's smooth exterior there was a dick of epic proportions. Now I'm finally meeting him. "The king would freely give all of this so long as you stayed here with him."

My gaze moves from Marco to my father. "Is that true?" I ask.

My father's focus is on Marco, but he nods in answer.

"Dad, if it's true, then why didn't you agree to the king's terms?"

Now my father looks at me. "I won't sign away your life, Serenity. I've already made too many personal sacrifices; I will not make this one."

What my father says brings tears to my eyes. He's choosing me over a nation—over an entire hemisphere. It's the most foolish decision he's ever made, but it's also the moment I feel the sheer force of my father's love for me. He won't let the boogeyman touch me.

"That's your official decision?" Marco asks.

"It is."

"We have to take Serenity," Marco says. "And we will use force." At his words, the WUN soldiers cluster around my father and me, but it doesn't make me feel safe. The king's soldiers outnumber ours, and they're better equipped. Not to mention that I no longer have a clean shot with them blocking me.

My father grabs my hand and pulls me behind him. Unlike me, my father's tall stature doesn't shield him from our enemies. Not completely.

"Dad—" I whisper.

"You're going to have to go through me," my father says to Marco, ignoring me.

My hand twitches and I barely breathe. Something's about to happen, and now I can't see anything beyond the cocoon of bodies surrounding me. Around us WUN soldiers are casting my father sideways glances. Right now he's the commanding officer, and they're waiting for him to make the call. I already know he won't be the first one to spill blood.

"So be it," Marco says.

Before I can so much as grab for my gun, someone fires a shot, and then another. Blood and bone spray down on me, and then my father is falling, my father who's now missing the back of his head.

I can't hear anything, the shots are still ringing in my ears. But I know I'm screaming, and now I've crumpled to the ground, holding my father's broken body to me.

My father, who taught me how to ride a bike, how to shoot a gun, how to be a diplomat and a decent human being. My father, my last remaining family.

My father.

My father. Murdered in front of my eyes.

Around me, I can sense movement, and I hear more gunshots go off. I stand, letting my father's slick body slide off my arms.

I've heard stories before about how grief can turn into bloodlust, but I've never experienced it before. Not until this moment. It builds like poison in my veins, converting my expanding grief into something violent.

Now I am a force of nature; I am the embodiment of rage. Enemy soldiers are coming at me, and I force my elbow into the neck of one and the solar plexus of another. I grab the gun from my bodice, and I begin shooting the enemy alongside my guards. Headshots. All of them.

I'm still screaming, and I can feel blood and tears dripping down my face. I know I look ferocious, and this gives me pleasure. Their fear and their pain give me pleasure.

I keep firing, even as more guards rush in. Amidst the chaos I see Marco run for the door.

I lift my gun, aim, and fire at him. The bullet grazes his arm, and then he's gone. I've missed my opportunity.

The king's soldiers, who are streaming into the suite, aren't shooting at me. They should be. They're not going to take me alive. I'm leaving this place one way or another. If it's in a casket, so be it.

"Soldiers!" I yell to what's left of my men. Five are still standing. That's all that's left. "Get to the window. We're getting out of here!" I can barely hear my own voice from all the gunfire. I signal to the back of the room just in case their hearing is as bad as mine.

The WUN soldiers move to the window, and I'm taking out the king's men one at a time. I back up to the rear of the room, shoving my now-empty gun back into my bodice and snagging another two from the bodies at my feet.

I throw a leg over the open window. I'm the last one out. We're on the second story, so I have to jump. I glance down and see one of the WUN soldiers waiting to catch me, the other four guarding the soldier's back. Beyond them I can see to the end of the king's property and the road beyond. That's where the car my father spoke of should be waiting.

A hand wraps around my arm. I don't think; I bring my arm up and shoot to kill. The king's soldier falls away, but more come after me. They'll shoot my guards if I don't do something first.

I aim and fire. One, two, three, four go down before the gun clicks. I drop it and grab another from the carnage. I shoot three more men and drop the weapon. I pick up two more guns before I'm able to focus on jumping down. This is all the ammunition I'll have between here and scheduled pick up, so I'll have to restrain myself from shooting anything that moves.

I make eye contact with the soldier waiting for me below, and then I jump, my arms pointing to the sky since I'm carrying two loaded weapons. He catches me, easing my impact.

"Let's go!" I shout.

The soldiers surround me, and we sprint through the king's stupid gardens. I pass the alcove he pushed me into, and I have to suppress the desire to shoot the balls off the marble statue that rests within it.

The quiet is eerie, and I know not to be deceived by it. The king's guards are regrouping, setting something up. I pray to any god willing to listen that our ride will still be waiting for us, that we'll get past the king's people, and that we can get the hell off this godforsaken land.

The gardens taper off, and beyond them is open grass. The trees and hedges have hidden us from view until now, but that's about to change.

I don't need to tell the soldiers this; they've noticed. Our collective speed picks up. We exit the gardens, and I spot the wrought iron fence running along the back of the king's estate.

A shot rings out and blood sprays as a soldier ahead of me takes a bullet to the head. What remains of his body collapses, and I have to jump over him to keep from tripping. There's nothing we can do for him at this point.

"Sniper!" I shout. The remaining soldiers and I scatter, running wildly left and right. I've trained with these people; we work soundlessly as a unit. Only now I'm their commander. Because my father …

My eyes move over the fence, until I spot a car waiting about a hundred yards down to my left. I whistle and point to my men. Their movements are still wild, but they're moving towards it. I hear the sound of another gunshot, and the soldier running ahead of me falls.

I snarl and glance over at the mansion. It's impossible to see a sniper from here, so I can't do anything about it. But someone does catch my eye.

The king, standing on his back balcony. He's too far away to shoot as well, otherwise I would. He's also too far away for me to make out his expression. I hope he's hurting, I hope he knows I slaughtered his men, and I hope today causes him unending grief, like it will for me.

I know it won't.

I turn away from him and focus on the fence and the car, some heavy SUV with tinted windows. Another shot rings out, and I hear it ping against the car's armor. At this point, I can only hope it didn't destroy anything vital, or else we're out of an escape.

Ahead of me, someone—probably our ride—has cut away two of the wrought iron fence posts, leaving an opening wide enough for a person to slip through. The soldiers exit through it and jump into the car.

I'm the last out, and I follow my soldiers into the back of the SUV.

Our driver, a burly, bearded man, guns the engine and peels down the road, constantly checking his rearview and side view mirrors.

We skid around the corner, the car fishtailing, then we're accelerating until my surroundings blur. Three official-looking cars pull onto the road behind us. I glance at our driver. He doesn't look nervous. No, he smiles when he notices the vehicles. If I didn't know better, I'd say he's just as bloodthirsty as I am.

I hear a distant, high-pitched whine, and then the first car behind us explodes in a burst of flame. The sound of crumbling metal follows a second later, presumably as the two cars following the first crash into it. Someone laid in wait for those cars. And someone shot them with a grenade launcher.

Our driver whoops and slams his palm triumphantly on the driving wheel. "That's how it's fucking done!"

Rather than join in, I feel myself weaken as I release the

last of my adrenaline. I lean back in my seat. "Who are you?" I ask.

The man pauses a beat. "I am a part of the Resistance."

He eyes me in the rearview mirror. "And judging by the fact that you have more blood on you than a butcher, I'm guessing that you aren't as traitorous as everyone's making you out to be."

I look out the window. My hands are shaking. Soon the rest of my body will follow suit, and then I'll have to truly feel again. Once that happens I'm going to wish I were dead. As it is, my head pounds as it tries to disassociate itself from all that just happened.

My father's dead.

His body lies in enemy territory.

I bury the emotion that's rising. Just because I'm not running and shooting at the moment doesn't mean I'm safe. I can't allow myself to fall apart now, not when I have three WUN soldiers whose lives I can still save.

I digest this. "Thank you," I finally say, "for risking your life to get us out of there."

The man grunts in response. "Did you kill him?"

I don't need any clarification to know whom he's asking about. "No," I say darkly.

Silence falls over the car, and for several minutes there's a strange kind of calm. It's not real, not when the blood of a dozen different men drips down my body and I tightly clench two guns in my hands, safeties off. Not when the car we're in is careening through the city of Geneva, zipping around other vehicles and pedestrians.

The sound of blades slicing the air catches our attention, and our driver swears. "That was faster than I expected," he says, looking up at the sky. I follow his gaze, and I see a helicopter heading our way.

Our driver makes another quick turn. "I'm going to pull into a garage in about thirty seconds. Once I do, get ready to jump out. You'll be entering a nondescript blue car, which I'll pull up next to. Got it?"

"Yes," I say. The men next to me grunt. They're even quieter than me.

The SUV fishtails as our driver takes a turn at breakneck speeds. The chopper makes a beeline for our car.

"You must've been some kisser," our driver mutters under his breath.

The wheels of our car squeal as our driver makes the tight turn into the parking garage to our left. As soon as we enter, the car accelerates to the other end of the structure, where a beat-up blue car idles.

Our driver slams on the brakes once we're almost upon it, and the WUN soldiers and I pile out of the vehicle.

"Thank you," I say over my shoulder, my voice hoarse. I push down the emotions. I need to hold out just a little longer.

Our driver nods. "Stay safe."

THE HELICOPTER DOESN'T notice the dingy blue car that leaves the garage. Instead its attention is focused on the black SUV we were in a minute ago.

I swallow down my worry for our previous driver as I watch his car careen down in the opposite direction, drawing attention away from us. As soon as the king's men realize I'm not in the car, his life will be in danger.

The rest of our drive is quiet, and the trip stretches on and on. I have no idea where we're going or what we'll find when we finally stop. To be honest, I don't really care at this point.

We move out of the city and pass through several more. As I stare out at the foreign landscape, a hand lands on my shoulder and then one of the soldiers pulls me into his arms and squeezes me tight. Only then do I realize I'm crying. I press my face into his chest, and heave great sobs.

So many people died today—some at the hands of the king's men, some at the hands of me and mine. So much death. The emotions are welling up; I can hear the keening sound work its way up my throat.

The soldier rubs my back. He's older—closer to my father's age than my own—which only makes the ache inside me hurt more acutely. His actions are so much worse than the usual tough guy act soldiers love to play, because at least aloofness separates us from the pain. This is the exact opposite. I can't avoid, can't suppress, can't hide from it anymore.

I sob harder into the soldier's chest as the events replay over and over through my mind. I feel anger, pain, regret, and pity. Gruesome images play alongside sweet memories. I'm being torn apart and restitched into something awful.

"Shhh, it's going to be alright," he says.

But it won't be. Not ever.

CHAPTER 11

SERENITY

I STAND IN front of the jet's staircase. The engines are still slowing down, and the pilot won't let me exit the aircraft until they come to a complete stop. It's a comical precaution in light of all I've been through in the last twenty-four hours.

Outside I can hear the crowd of WUN citizens waiting. Whereas my send off had been rushed and private, my arrival looks to be a bit more public and celebratory. The crowd sounds excited, but it's unclear what they know. Do they think a peace agreement has been reached? Do they know one was never signed? Do they know my father is dead?

I glance down at my blood-soaked body. The men I was with wouldn't let me and the other soldiers change or wash off. The world would need proof of what occurred in Geneva for the story to be as believable as possible.

And what then? Even if the image of me covered in blood sparked one last great push to fight against the king, we are doomed to lose the war.

The pilot's attendant shoos me away from the door so she can lower the staircase. My heart pounds in my chest. I know I'm about to cause a riot, and I'll be expected to talk. After all, I am now the WUN's emissary. The thought has me choking back a sob.

The attendant clears her throat to get my attention. I can tell she doesn't want to touch me—not that I blame her. "Whenever you're ready, you can go."

I look behind me at the three WUN soldiers, all that's left of our original entourage. Just like me, they are still covered with gore.

The soldier who comforted me hours ago now nods to me. I take a breath and walk out of the jet.

I screamed and cried my last tears several hours ago. I've got a good hour or two of respite before the grief swallows me up all over again.

Now is not the time for weakness. Now is the time to show my strength. So I square my shoulders; I need to send the message that I am not scared. If the king is my country's worst nightmare, I'll be his.

I step into the doorway and stare out at the crowd that waits. Once people catch a glimpse of me, they go quiet. The posters some hold wilt in their hands. Whatever their expectations were, it's clear that this is not it.

I descend down the stairs and touch my country's soil for the first time since I left. It's the first time I've ever set foot in my homeland without my father.

People holding cameras rush at me. I already knew this would happen. The woman locking lips with the king two nights ago is now covered in dried blood; this is as sensational as it gets.

My eyes find the representatives. They're all here, along with Will. They've decided to temporarily lift their safety precautions and leave the bunker all to welcome my father and me back.

I breathe heavily through my nose and walk to them, ignoring the WUN soldiers holding the crowd at bay and the ancient-looking cameras that follow my every movement.

I'm not a part of this moment; I'm seeing this all through a long, dark tunnel. The representatives' stoic expressions, the horrified screams of the crowd, which are now mixing with the increasing cheers by those who thirst for enemy blood.

Will looks shell-shocked. I can't get over how strange the sight is when he's usually so unruffled.

The general pushes his way to me. "What happened?" His brows are furrowed, and his nostrils flare. He can smell the death on me.

I lean in to him. "I'm only going to retell the story once," I say. "If you want this to go down in WUN history, you're going to have to give me a microphone and make a show of it."

He looks me over, his face grim, and he nods to the side. "We already have a makeshift stage ready." I glance to where he indicates. Sure enough, there's a small podium set up, probably meant for my father. But now it's there for me.

"Are you sure you want to record this?" the general asks. "It could be used against you once the war is over."

"I will be killed for my crimes, regardless," I say. This is the sick truth I've known since I could think properly on the flight over. There's no other alternative for what I've done.

The general stares at me for a long moment; I can see the morbid curiosity behind his eyes. "This footage is not going to appear to the public until we've okay-ed it—*if* we okay it," the general says.

"I understand." I approach the stage with the general at my side. Will appears on my other side, hovering but not touching me. I can see his concern etched into his crinkled brow. Underneath it I see fear, but I can't tell if it's fear for me or fear of me.

When the crowd sees what I'm doing, they creep closer to the stage.

I stop when I reach the podium. The microphone— probably one of the few still in existence on this side of the world—is angled for someone much taller than me— my father. That's why the king's men shot him in the head—because he was that much taller than everyone else.

I try to blink away the memory of my father cradled in my arms, but when I look down, I see his blood—now dried—still discoloring the skin of my forearms.

The crowd is staring; everyone's waiting for me. Time to get this over with.

I take the microphone from where it rests. "Over a dozen men and women of the WUN left for Geneva—only four of us have returned." I pause to collect myself. "This blood," I hold out my arm, "is the blood of my father, who was shot before my eyes because he would not agree to the king's peace treaty. We know this is how the king deals with dissension.

"This is also the blood of our fallen soldiers, who died trying to help me escape." I pace the stage. "And it is the blood of my enemies, whom I killed when they tried to capture me."

The crowd roars. Without meaning to, I've worked them up into some kind of frenzy.

Fatigue sets in. I haven't eaten or slept since we fled. "I want peace, and I was willing to pay the highest price— my own freedom." The crowd quiets. "If you watched the negotiations, then you saw me with the king. You saw me kiss the king. You saw a traitorous woman doing what traitorous women always do, right?" There are uncomfortable murmurs in the crowd.

"Wrong," I say. "The king has killed every one of my family members. He's taken my friends and family from me. I hate him with every fiber of my being.

"The king wanted me—so much so that he changed his peace treaty on my behalf. He thought he'd keep me in Geneva with him. And when my father refused to let that happen ..." I close my eyes and breathe slowly, "the king had him killed."

There's angry murmuring. People are confused, and I don't have it in me to clarify the situation more. In fact, I don't have much of anything left in me, period.

I place the mike back where I found it and walk off the stage. There. I've done it. Said what I needed to say. And now I can quietly fall apart.

THE REST OF the day blurs. Will is beside me for most of it, except while I bathe. I'm actually afforded a real bath, not just a basin of water and a washcloth like usual. It has nothing on the king's showers, and it's still not enough to wash off all the blood, but it is familiar. And familiar is what I need at the moment.

Since I returned to the bunker, the representatives—minus me and Will—have been locked inside that room of theirs, no doubt trying to figure out what to make of this mess.

Once I finish bathing, I return to my room. Will's already there, waiting for me. I walk right into his arms and allow myself this closeness. I rub my face into the rough material that covers his chest, enjoying the feel of a body.

The sensation reminds me of the king's skin pressed against mine. The dark promise in his gaze.

I pinch my eyes shut. The last thing I want is to remember him fondly.

Will's arms encircle mine, and we stay like that for a long time, saying nothing. I can feel Will shaking; the situation bothers him too.

I finally pull away from him. "I need to sleep."

"I'll stay with you," he says.

I shake my head. "No. I want to be alone."

Will frowns. "You'll be okay?"

No. "I promise." I give him a small smile to further convince him.

He looks torn.

"Seriously Will," I say, "the representatives need you more than I do."

He flinches at my words; I hadn't meant them to sting.

"Please," I say, "find out what's going on with them so you can tell me when I wake up." Which might be never.

Reluctantly he nods. "If you need me, you know where to find me," he says. He hesitates, and I can see he's trying to figure out whether he should kiss me.

"Go," I say, giving him a push; I don't want anyone's lips on mine in a long, long time.

I DON'T KNOW how many hours I lie there, locked somewhere between sleep and wakefulness. Long enough to hear my roommates come in and whisper to one another as they get ready for bed. Long enough to hear them leave sometime later, and long enough for several people to crack open the door and poke their heads in only to quickly retract them and leave.

At some point I realize I'm no longer sleepy, merely weary. I haven't eaten in a while, though someone has left a plate of food and a glass of water next to my bed. A sick part of me wants to never again eat. I want to waste away until I join my parents in death.

Eventually someone comes in, and they don't leave. I feel a hand shake my shoulder. "Serenity, wake up," Will says from behind me.

I'm too tired to even tell him to go away, so I merely lay there.

"Serenity, the representatives need you. They've made contact with the king."

I BURST INTO the conference room, feeling more alive than I have for the last day or two. The king's face is plastered on the enormous screen. He looks tired, his eyes sad.

"You haven't eaten," he says. I don't know how he can tell over the screen.

The representatives glance between Montes and me. They know that something happened between us, but they don't know what.

Behind me Will puts his hand on my shoulder. The king's eyes flicker at the movement.

I shrug Will's hand off and approach the camera set up in our conference room, just so that the king can see my anguish more clearly.

"Why?" I whisper.

He watches me with solemn eyes but stays silent.

"I was willing to do what you asked, so why did you have to take the one person that mattered to me?"

His face is stoic.

"Why?" I ask again, this time louder.

When he doesn't answer, I scream like a wild animal. "Answer me!" I shriek. Hot tears snake down my cheek.

Instead of doing just that, the king's attention returns to the general. "Do we have an agreement?"

I follow the king's gaze to the general. "An agreement?"

I ask. How could the WUN and the king agree to anything at a time like this?

I glance at Will. Only now do I notice that his eyes are red rimmed. My gaze darts back to the general, who's rubbing his eyes. He drops his hand and looks at me for a moment before returning his attention to the screen.

"We do."

My heart patters away in my chest.

The king's eyes find mine, and he stares at me for several seconds before moving his gaze over the room. "Congratulations ladies and gentlemen. The war is officially over."

MY MOUTH IS gaping long after the king's image disappears. The room's quiet, abnormally so.

I'm the first to speak. "What just happened?"

My eyes land first on Will, who looks like he's only barely holding it together. Then they move over each of the representatives. None of them will meet my gaze.

My breathing speeds up, and at the back of my mind I worry that I might pass out from anxiety. I'm weak enough that it's a distinct possibility.

"Why won't any of you look me in the eye?" My voice rises.

No one responds.

"What. Just. Happened?" My voice cracks.

Still no response. I put a hand to my head; I'm feeling faint.

"Sit down, Serenity."

"No," I snap. "Not until someone tells me what's going on."

A muscle in the general's jaw twitches. "The king approached us with a peace agreement."

"And you accepted it. In the wake of what happened, you still accepted it." I am a hair's breadth away from losing it.

"The king gave us everything we wanted and then some," he says.

"Uh huh." I can feel more hot tears cascading down my face. People are shifting nervously in their seats. The last time they saw me, I was covered in blood. I'm a wolf amongst a flock of sheep.

"Serenity," the general says, "this peace agreement will save the lives of millions. It's better than anything your father saw up until the day of his death."

I let out a strangled cry at the mention of my father. "Why didn't you include me in the decision making?"

"You weren't in a sound state of mind."

I nod, because he's right. I choke down my pride and vindictiveness. The representatives did what they had to do to ensure the well being of the western hemisphere.

"Tell her," Will says.

I look away from the general to his son. Will's hands are balled into fists, and he's crying as well. Only now do I realize that there might be a reason Will hasn't tried to comfort me like he would've a day ago. There might be a reason why the representatives can't look me in the eye and why there's an agreement at all in light of recent events.

"What is it?" I ask, returning my gaze to the general. Dread coils at the pit of my stomach.

The muscle in General Kline's cheek jumps again. "The king had one condition in the agreement."

"No," I whisper. The king wouldn't—the representatives wouldn't. There must be one decent person amongst the remaining leaders of the world.

The general's face is grim. "In return for peace, we're to deliver you to the king."

CHAPTER 12

SERENITY

I STARE AT the general for a moment, not allowing myself to comprehend his words. And then they sink in. Bile rises up my throat, and I barely have time to grab a nearby trashcan before I retch.

Someone places a hand on my shoulder, but I shrug it off. I wipe my mouth with the back of my hand and straighten.

The general's still speaking, but I'm no longer listening. I feel my legs buckle, and then Will is there, scooping me up and carrying me back to my room.

My entire body shakes.

I can't go back.

"Serenity, he's not going to kill you," Will says as he lays me on my bed. He crouches next to it so that we're at eye level. His gaze moves to my lips; he looks pained. "The king's not going to kill you—or imprison you." He takes a deep breath. "They've been talking about the possibility of a wedding."

I go still. "A wedding?"

Will nods, and I can see his throat work. He closes his eyes and I see his body shudder.

"I have to marry the king?"

Will opens his eyes. "That's what it sounds like."

"I have to marry my father's killer?"

His face crumbles and he looks away. "It's better than death or imprisonment," he says, his voice rough.

"Get out."

"What?"

"*Get out!*" I scream.

Slowly Will gets up and backs away from me. "I'll make this right, Serenity. I swear it."

I pretend I don't hear his words. I'm tired of promises. Of vendettas. Of posturing. Of politics and death.

Once he leaves the room, I curl into a ball and pretend nothing exists at all.

I STAY IN bed for another two days, shaking, sometimes rocking myself. Eventually I eat the food that someone's left for me, one small bite at a time. My stomach contracts painfully as each piece of food enters, and I have to fight off my rising sickness. I drink some water, if only to get rid of my splitting headache.

By the end of two days, the most painful emotions have dissolved away. I still feel like one giant, open wound, but

I can think through it. I can be rational. Somewhat.

So I get up, wash myself, get dressed, and head to the conference room. Not surprisingly, when I get there, the representatives are in session. I've rarely seen them outside this room.

The group quiets when they see me. "I'm here to cooperate," I say, striding into the room. "I'll do what you want for the good of the country. What do you need of me?"

For a moment no one speaks. For all their smooth words, I've managed to silence these politicians several times over the last few days. Then the general approaches me, and in a rare show of emotion, he envelops me in a hug.

"You are the daughter I never had," he whispers into my ear. His voice is gruff. "I'd hoped you'd make my son happy one day."

I wince at his words. He doesn't know that he's making this so much worse for me.

He pulls away. "Has Will told you anything about what's going on?"

I glance about the room. I don't see the general's son; I wonder if he's been playing hooky just like I have.

"Only that I might be ..." my throat works, "*marrying the king*." The words burn coming out. "Whose idea was that?" I ask.

The general's lip curls with disdain, and he shakes his head. "His," he says.

After I killed the king's men, I'd assumed that if he ever got his hands on me, he'd execute me, regardless of his feelings. In the end, that's what war is, a string of revenge killings.

But his men hadn't tried to kill me, and they'd had many opportunities during my escape. He always wanted me alive.

I wonder if the peace agreement the representatives agreed to was the same one the king presented my father. If it was, then the man that raised me would've died in vain. I suppress my shudder.

The general clears his throat. "The king has a jet here waiting for you."

I raised my eyebrows. "Why didn't anyone wake me?"

"He gave us orders to leave you be until you were ready."

I'm struck by two things the general has said. One, the general is taking orders from the king. For as long as I've known the general, he's been the de facto leader of the WUN. It's strange to see him abdicate his leadership role.

And two, I'm stunned that the king gave those particular orders. Had circumstances been different, I'd say it was kind of him. But I've come to learn that this is the king's style—to cut you up then kiss the wounds he inflicted.

"Now that you're here," the general continues, "we will contact the king's retinue and let them know you're awake. They'll probably have you board the flight as soon as possible once this happens; they are going to assume you're unwilling and dangerous."

I nod.

"Once you arrive at the king's palace, he's planning on announcing the end of the war and your engagement."

I scowl at this; the thought of being engaged to him causes me physical discomfort.

144

"It sounds like there are already wedding preparations in the works," the general says. "It'll be filmed and aired over the Internet—the thought is that the wedding will symbolize the marriage of two hemispheres. It's quite brilliant, actually—it should go a long way to encourage peace."

"*Don't*," I say. My breaths are coming out quick and ragged. I can't bear to hear more on the subject.

The general puts a hand on my shoulder. "You'll be okay, Serenity. The asshole actually seems to care about you."

My eyes flick to the king. "Don't lie to yourself, General. I'm marrying a monster."

WILL AND THE general lead me up to the surface. They're the only ones I allow to accompany me. We reach the top of the final set of stairs, and I stare at the door to the garage. On the other side of it, the king's men wait for me. These are my last moments with the people I know.

I reach for the door and pause. "What will happen once I'm gone?" I ask the general. I've wanted to know the answer to this question since I left my bed. I knew my fate, but I knew nothing about what would happen to the WUN and its former political leaders.

The general gives me a sidelong glance. "The western hemisphere, under the governance of the king, will begin to receive medical relief in those areas that need it the most. There will also be additional efforts to cleanse the land of the radiation that's gotten into the soil. After that, the king's focus will then be rebuilding our economy."

I fidget. "What will happen to you and Will and the rest of the representatives?" I ask.

"The king has granted us amnesty and allowed us to continue to govern these territories under the supervision of his men."

I raise my eyebrows. "That's ... really good news." We'd always planned on being executed if we lost the war. I'm still not convinced that won't happen. After all, there are no checks on the king's power.

The general nods. "It is. The peace agreement is better than we'd ever anticipated—or hoped for."

I shift my weight. We've come back to the elephant in the room—that I'm leaving because of the agreement.

The general must realize how callous his words sound—spoken to the one person who will lose everything—since he takes a step back. He looks between Will and me. "I should let you two have your own goodbye." The general salutes me. An unbidden tear drips from my eye as I give him a small smile and salute him back.

Will and I watch him leave, neither of us willing to speak until his footsteps completely fade.

Will steps in close to me and cups my cheek. "It was never supposed to be like this," he says.

I wrap my hand around his wrist and lean into his hand. "A lot of things were never supposed to happen like they did." I close my eyes. I might never see Will again. That thought constricts my heart, and I have to force the thought from my mind. My body can't take much more emotional pain.

He leans his head against mine; I can tell by his ragged breathing that he's trying to keep it together for my sake.

"If this is the last moment we get, I want to make the most of it," I say. One final memory of the man and the life that will never be mine.

Will nods against me, his hand sliding to the back of my head. He presses his lips to mine, and our mouths move urgently. I'm memorizing the taste of him even as I'm saying goodbye.

When his lips finally leave mine, they move to my ear. "You have to kill him, Serenity."

My body goes rigid against him. "You work for the king; you can't say things like that anymore," I whisper.

"The Resistance—those people who saved you—they will spread to the western hemisphere. Once they do, I'm planning on joining," he says.

"And what do you hope to accomplish?" I ask. The war is over; we lost. The best any of us can do now is make the situation as bearable as possible. I'm not sure that killing the king would actually make the world better, or if it would just open the position to all the other power-hungry people out there.

"No one man should have that much power," Will says.

Silently, I agree with him, but it doesn't change the fact that the king might be the world's best chance at getting back on its feet. More fighting will only prolong our suffering.

"And what happens once he's dead, huh?" I ask. "They'll kill me too."

Will shakes his head. "No, they won't. We have the

footage of your arrival still, remember?"

My skin prickles. I don't know whether this discussion fills me with fear or excitement, but I do feel my mortality in that moment. I'm certain I'll die before my time—not that I'd ever believed otherwise.

I back away from him and grab the handle of the door. "I'll think about what you've said."

"Do."

"Bye Will."

He tips his head. "Goodbye my future queen."

As soon as the aircraft leaves the ground, the king's men relax. Not completely, but they're not encircling me the same way they had been when they picked me up in the bunker's garage.

One of them has my gun; he took it off of me when they patted me down for weapons. I keep my eye on him. I will kill for that gun. It's the last piece of my father I have.

I glance out my window and watch my homeland get smaller and smaller. This high in the sky, the land looks beautiful. You wouldn't know that the earth is poisoned with radiation, and its people are desperate, scavenging things.

I don't know when I'll be back here, if ever. It feels like a final goodbye. There's nothing much that I'm leaving—a few final friends, my past, my old way of life.

I can feel the wary stares of the king's men. Their animosity practically rolls off of them; I meet their gazes and give them each a slow, predatory smile. It pleases me to see the lines on their faces deepen. They've either seen me kill their comrades, or they've been warned.

It takes me a few minutes to realize that I'm causing them pain to feel better about my own. Once I do, I close my eyes and lean my head against the window and let myself nod off to sleep.

THE SENSATION OF falling wakes me up. I look out my window and see the rosy light of dawn as the jet makes its descent. When I look down at the scenery, I suppress a gasp. Small islands dot the blue expanse of ocean.

"Where are we?"

No one answers me. Big surprise.

As the aircraft descends and we draw closer to the small islands, the scenery comes into focus. It's not quite arid, but not quite tropical either.

A larger landmass looms in the horizon. I know in my gut this is my destination. The jet passes over it and circles back. I can see a small airstrip ahead of us. And then we're landing.

Once the aircraft coasts to a stop, I stand, ignoring the way the guards tense as they fall into form around me. The sick part of me enjoys how skittish they are.

The engine dies, and the jet's stairway is lowered. The guards ahead of me begin to move, and I follow them out. This is the second time I've arrived on enemy soil. And it is still that. To everyone else, the war might've ended, but it never will for me. Not so long as I live with the king.

This moment reminds me of a story my dad told me a

long time ago. There was once an ancient battle, fought for ten years. The Trojan War. At the close of it, the Greeks, on the edge of defeat, surrendered and left in their place a huge wooden horse—a gift to their victorious enemies, the Trojans. Little did the Trojans know that waiting inside the wooden beast were Greek soldiers.

The Trojans brought the horse into their walls and celebrated their victory long into the night. Once the Trojan citizens had all drunk themselves into a stupor and gone to bed, the Greek soldiers left the horse and slaughtered the enemy. They won the war this way.

The king has only demonstrated his excellent talent for destroying things, but scant few at rebuilding the world. And now that the war is over, he's let the enemy into his house.

Perhaps Will is right and the king needs to be destroyed once and for all. I smile grimly. Perhaps I will be his Trojan horse.

CHAPTER 13

SERENITY

A SMALL GROUP of people wait for my arrival off to the left of the jet. Judging by how small the crowd is, I'm guessing the king has kept quiet about my bloody escape. I wouldn't be surprised if the world thought I'd never left the king's side.

The guards lead me towards a limo. As they do, my eyes drift back to the small gathering that watches me. The crowd shifts, and my steps falter. The king stands in the middle of them, dressed impeccably in a suit. Our eyes lock, and a small sound escapes from me. The sight of him splits open the wound I've been carrying inside myself.

I veer towards him. My guards are on me in an instant. Their hands wrap around my arms and pull me back. I push against them, my legs buckling.

The king approaches me slowly, his face unreadable.

"*Why can't you just leave me alone?*" I scream.

The king stares unwaveringly at me, but I could've sworn for a moment something like shame passed through those dark eyes of his.

"You killed him!" His face blurs as tears form. Emotionally, I've regressed back to the day I escaped. "You can't have me Montes! Not ever!"

"My king," a voice near me says, "should we administer the sedative?"

"I will never forgive you!" I shriek. "You hear me? Never!"

"I think that would be best." The king's voice glides over me like the smoothest silk. He's not even listening.

Someone extends my arm, and I buck against them. They drop their hands, and I elbow the guard behind me. He makes an *oomph* noise, and his grip loosens. I use the opportunity to wrench my arm free, and I slug the guard closest to me.

That's as far as I get. The rest of the king's guards close in and grab me, lowering my body to the ground. I thrash against them, but it's useless. They pin me down.

I'm sobbing horrible, heart-wrenching cries.

"Serenity, it's going to be okay," the king says from above me. I can feel his hands brushing my hair from my face.

I want to slap them away. I want to tell him to stop being nice when he's so evil. Instead I continue to sob.

I feel cool wetness rub against the crook of my arm, and then a slight sting. It doesn't take long for the numbness to overwhelm the pain.

I open my eyes. "Why?" I ask the king weakly.

But I never get my answer. The king's form blurs and fades with the last of the pain.

WHEN I WAKE up, I'm on a bed. I blink as I sit up, noticing the satiny comforter beneath me.

Where am I?

I glance around and jolt when my eyes land on the king. He sits in the chair next to my bed, pinching his lower lip in contemplation.

Looking at him hurts—he reminds me too much of all that's broken within me—but I can't tear my gaze from him.

"Hello Serenity," he finally says.

"Montes."

"Feeling better?"

I guffaw. "Like you care."

"You're right," he says, "I don't." He says the words so cavalierly, but his face betrays him. He's lying, and I really wish I couldn't tell. It's harder to despise him when he acts human.

"I want my gun," I say.

"And why would I give you that gun? You're difficult enough as it is."

His condescension is barely tolerable. "It's one of my only possessions. I want it."

The king tilts his head. "That's the gun that killed several of my men, isn't it?"

I say nothing.

"I've gotten a good look at it," he continues. "It's old but well cared for. Obviously it's important to you. Perhaps it was a gift from someone who once loved you?" He's openly taunting me and coming dangerously close to the truth.

Without realizing it, I've fisted my hands. I want to hit him. It's taking most of my self-control not to. I can see what he's doing

"You're a sociopath," I whisper.

"And you're a kindred spirit."

He's said that before. "I am nothing like you," I snap.

"You're right," he says. "I've never killed over a dozen people and then worn their blood like a trophy for an entire day."

I'm on my feet in an instant, and so is he. "I watched my father die that day, shot dead on your orders," I hiss. "I held his body in my arms as he bled out on me. So yes, I took pleasure in killing those men that harmed him."

The king steps closer to me. "I never ordered your father to be killed."

His words are a slap in the face. Still, "It's too little too late, Montes."

"No, it's not. The war is over."

"Ours isn't."

He works his jaw. "The wedding is at the end of the week," he says. "It's happening whether you want it to or not."

I slam my hand down on the bedside table next to me. "Goddamnit, Montes, you can't control everything—that's not how the world works."

"It's how my world works."

"And that's why you're going to end up alone." Preferably under six feet of soil.

"You need to learn about forgiveness."

I flash him a vicious smile. "Or else what? You'll kill me? Your threats hold no power over me. I've already lost everything I care about."

"Or else you'll never be happy," he says.

"I wouldn't recognize happiness if it stood right in front of me," I say.

"Clearly," the king says.

I narrow my eyes at him as he walks to the door. He pauses when he grabs the handle. "We're announcing the end of the war and the wedding this evening," he says. "A lot rests on how convincing you are. So if you don't know what happy is, I'd suggest you learn to fake it fast."

I DON'T KNOW what day it is, or what time it is, and I can't decide if I am jet lagged, or if my tiredness stems from my emotional and physical exhaustion. I stay in the room the king left me in. For all I know, I'm on some sort of house arrest.

Not that I mind. A servant comes in several hours after the king left, bearing food. I try to eat some and vomit it back up. I've gone too long without eating.

It's as I flush the toilet and clean myself up that I realize I want to live. In spite of the wedding, in spite of my father's death, in spite of every other fucked-up part of my life, I'm not ready to fold my hand. So I walk back to my food and eat it agonizingly slow, taking long breaks between bites to let my stomach settle.

I take a shower, and for once I let myself enjoy the way the water pelts my skin and force myself not to feel guilty that so many others don't have this luxury. I am in the unique position to change that—to change the entire world if I so desire. I am going to be the king's wife. The queen. Now that I've stopped running from the idea, I realize the doors it opens.

CHAPTER 14

SERENITY

MISERABLE. I AM absolutely miserable.

"Emerald green or orchid pink?" my wardrobe manager—*wardrobe manager*—asks me, holding up each dress.

"Neither."

She nods absently, as if that is the conclusion she's come to as well. "Yes, these colors are too casual—we want something that's hopeful yet regal." She stares at me for a beat, and then her eyes widen and she snaps her fingers.

I'm in the ninth circle of hell.

"I just had a thought. I'll be right back!"

"Can't wait," I mutter.

The hairstylist standing behind me yanks my hair, and my head snaps back. "Ow!"

"S-sorry, My Lady," the woman stammers. She sounds frightened, and she has good reason to be. I'm already rethinking this whole will-to-live bit if it includes being manhandled.

"Don't call me that," I growl out.

She nods her head and bites the inside of her cheek.

I'm being too abrasive, as usual. This is why friendship never came easily to me.

I reach up and place a hand on her arm. "I'm sorry," I say, gentler this time, "I'm just not used to people touching me." Or caring about my appearance at all.

In fact, over the last few hours I've repeatedly fantasized about grabbing my father's gun and ending all our lives. And then I'd remember that my gun was confiscated. Probably for the best.

My wardrobe manager comes waddling back into the bathroom with a shimmery golden dress draped over her arms. "Is it not perfect?" she says, holding the thing up so I can get a good look at it.

The thing is absolutely hideous; all that gold is giving me a headache. If I had a choice, I wouldn't be caught dead in the garment, but the same could be said for any dress I've crossed paths with. At this point, the sooner I agree to wear a dress, the sooner this will be over.

"There are no words," I say.

The wardrobe manager flashes me an eager smile. "I was hoping you'd say that. The king's going to have a hard time keeping his hands off you once he sees you in this."

I manage a weak smile. "Lucky me."

SHORTLY AFTER I'VE finished getting ready and my stylists

have slipped out the door, I hear a knock. I grab the handle and open the door. On the other side King Lazuli waits.

His eyes widen when he sees me, and I watch as they slowly drink me in. When his gaze makes its way to my face, his eyes change from something hungry to something regretful. I recoil at the sight, and he pretends he didn't notice my reaction. We just managed to have an entire conversation solely based on body language.

"What, no guards?" I ask, noticing that he came to my room alone. It isn't the first time either. Earlier this morning he came alone as well, which means despite all he's done to me, there's a level of trust there. That, or he really can't be killed.

He takes my hand and kisses it. When he returns it to my side he says, "I hope you've been practicing how to pretend to be happy."

"Your beloved empire will be fine. I can be convincing when I want to be."

The king's eyes search mine. "I know."

He places his hand on my lower back, and I suppress a shiver. I'm not supposed to feel like this. I'm not supposed to react to his touch after everything.

"Ready?"

I take a breath and nod. "Let's do this."

The king leads me through his palace. This place is different from his mansion in Geneva. Both are grand and feel like stuffy royalty, but the king's palace here is larger and it seems more lived in than his other house. But like the mansion in Geneva, the floor plan here is hopelessly confusing.

"Where are we?" I ask.

"In the hallway," the king says.

I roll my eyes, and he laughs when he sees my expression. I realize too late that to him, exasperation is a better emotion that hate, fear, or sadness. And it is. It means that I can feel something towards him that's softer than what I have felt since I arrived.

"You know what I mean," I say.

The king's lips curve upwards at my interest. He should know that his reaction is only annoying me further. "We're in the Mediterranean—but you'll have to figure out what island we're on."

I file this information away and try not to think about how far away we are from my homeland. I'm dying to ask about the WUN, but I keep my mouth shut. I'm going to have to ease my way into a position of trust. For now I'll be the agreeable fiancée.

"How many houses do you own?"

"We," he says.

I flash him a questioning look.

"*We* have many houses. By the end of the week they'll be yours as well as mine."

My eyes widen, and then I glance away. I can't wrap my mind around all the implications of being married to this man.

Married.

To my parents' killer.

Suddenly the food I ate earlier doesn't seem like it's content to stay in my stomach. I stop walking and breathe slowly.

The king leans in so that he can peer into my eyes. "Are you alright?"

I hold up a finger, and he patiently waits. The nausea passes, and I begin walking again.

"What was that?" he asks.

"It's my body's reaction to you."

"I'm glad I leave you short of breath."

"Don't flatter yourself; I was trying not to barf."

The king's concern fades into an amused smile. We walk in silence after that, but with each passing second I feel the heat of King Lazuli's hand spread through me.

It angers me that my body reacts this way. Hell, it angers me even more that the king considers every emotion of mine that's not hate or pain a small victory..

He leads me outside to a limo. Photographers and cameramen swarm around us almost immediately, and again my stomach roils, this time from claustrophobia. A chauffeur holds the door open for the king and me, and I all but dive into it. I thought the publicity we'd received before was bad, but it seems I'd only received a taste of it in Geneva.

The king follows me into the car, I'm sure taking in my wide eyes. "I hope this is not you being convincing, because you're horrible at it," he says.

"Shut up."

Again, the king smirks, and I want to throttle him. Even if there wasn't this terrible baggage between us, there'd still be something about him that gets under my skin.

As soon as we pull away from the palace, I roll down the

window. I can feel the king's eyes on me, but I ignore him. Once the window's all the way down, I stick my head out, then the rest of my torso.

For a single blissful second the air sings in my ears and streams through my hair. Then I feel a firm pair of hands wrap around my waist and yank me inside. I yelp and tumble into the king's arms.

"Are you trying to kill yourself?" the king asks, raising his voice. I can see that vein in his temple begin to throb.

"You caught me," I say sarcastically, "I was trying for death by moving vehicle."

"Be serious," he commands.

I raise my eyebrows. "Is that the tone you use on all your subjects? Because frankly, it—" My voice cuts off when the king leans forward and runs a hand through my hair.

He's fixing my hair. I don't know why this action of his catches me so completely off guard, but it does. Maybe because the gesture is affectionate, especially when I notice the slight quiver of his hands.

"Did you really think I was trying to kill myself?" I ask.

His hands pause, and they loosely cup my hair and my chin. "What do you think?" He stares at me, and I see concern in them.

"I'm thinking that there are far more effective ways of killing myself than jumping out of a moving car through the window." Seriously. I'd just use the door.

"Your father died a week ago."

I flinch at his words. Why would he bring that up?

"You had to be sedated when you arrived," King Lazuli continues. "I'm going to assume the worst until you prove otherwise."

I frown at him and push his hands away. "Well, I'm not planning on killing myself, so your concern is not needed."

The king doesn't leave my side. Instead he reaches around me and rolls up the window, and I feel my skin sear in every place his body presses against mine. The window seals shut, yet he doesn't move away. My eyes crawl over his arm to his shoulder, to his square jaw, to his mouth. There they pause, and then I meet his gaze.

My breath catches as we stare at each other.

He's the enemy.

It's too bad my body doesn't think so. It's ready to say *que sera sera* and forget the past.

The king leans in slowly, giving me plenty of time to pull away. There's no reason to fight him now that I'm forced to marry him, but that's not why I hold my ground. No, if I'm honest, it's because I want to feel something other than pain and hate.

He stops short of my mouth, though. Reaching up a hand, he traces the scar that drags down my face. "I'm sorry."

"No, you're not," I say.

"This time I really am."

A lump forms in my throat. "Don't say that." *Or else there will be no one left for me to hate but myself.*

He drops his hand, and something tugs at my heart. Regret? Yearning? I can't tell, but it's an emotion I don't want to feel.

"Where's my father's body?" I ask. It's been on my

mind lately. I'm not sentimental over death; I've seen it, seen the way a soul leaves a person's eyes. The body is just a vessel—once whatever animates it is gone, it's just flesh. Still, I can't help but want to put my father's body to rest.

"It's being kept in a morgue in Geneva." The king's expression is cautious. He's watching me like I might snap. This conversation brings up all that's passed between us.

"Geneva?" I say, my throat hoarse. That is a punch to the gut. "I want his body returned to our homeland."

"I can arrange that," he says.

I stare at him for a beat, then nod once.

We sit in uneasy silence for the remainder of the drive. When the car finally stops and I look out the window, my heart drops through my chest. There are hundreds of people streaming into what looks like an amphitheater. This is really happening.

"Are you sure you're ready for this?" the king asks.

"Like I have a choice."

His leg brushes mine as he moves towards the doors. "Good point." His eyes slink over me. "I forgot to tell you—you look lovely."

Lovely. I want to laugh at his words. "You shouldn't have bothered with the compliment," I say "I'm many things, and the least impressive of them is lovely." I push past him just as someone opens the car door.

Lovely. What a load of bullshit.

CHAPTER 15

SERENITY

THE KING'S BEEN onstage for only a couple minutes when he calls me out. His voice booms out on the loudspeakers. "I have some important news I want to share with the world, and I want Serenity Freeman to help me announce it."

I know what's coming next, and I think the audience does as well. There's a buzz throughout the crowd. As I walk out onto the stage, I plaster on a smile and act as though my legs aren't wobbling beneath the dress I wear. Around so many people, my brain's having trouble processing what Montes is saying.

I come up next to him and stare out into the crowd. My smile wavers as I take in the hundreds—no, thousands—of occupied seats. A strong hand takes my own. I look down at the hand then back up at the man who holds it. He is the king of the entire world. He's a man who can't die. A man who doesn't age. He's a man who's made my life a living hell since the war began, and he's the man I'm forced to marry.

"The Western United Nations and the Eastern Empire have come to a peace agreement. The war is over."

I've never heard this many people cheer in such a confined space, but it seems to resonate through my bones. I smile at the sound, and it's genuine. Peace, at last.

The cheering goes on for a minute, maybe more, before the crowd is quieted and the king resumes his speech. "Now that there is peace between the two hemispheres, we can begin to look forward to the future."

The king turns his focus on me, and my heart drums faster. "There is no one I'd rather spend it with than the woman standing next to me." The look in his eyes is genuine; he's good. He's almost convinced me.

And then he does something I really wasn't expecting. He gets down on one knee. My heart is hammering away in my chest, and I'm sure if a camera got close enough, they'd capture the whites of my eyes on film. I'm about to take a step back when I pause.

You need to convince them.

He pulls out a small box and opens it, revealing a ring inside. "Serenity Freeman, will you marry me?" he asks, smiling. His eyes are vulnerable.

In a room full of thousands of people, it's absolutely silent.

I put a hand to my heart. Beneath my skin I can feel it pound. "Yes," I whisper. Only my whisper blasts across the sound systems thanks to the mike hooked up to me.

The crowd roars their applause, and the king's face breaks into a blinding smile, one that brightens his entire face and reaches his eyes. There's genuine happiness there, and I wonder if I might be the only person in the world that's not pleased by the situation. I think of Will.

No, I'm not the only one.

Taking my hand, the king removes the ring from its case and slides it onto my finger. It's a band made up of yellow diamonds. I can't decide whether it's the ugliest or prettiest thing I've ever seen.

The king stands, and without giving me a warning, he cups my face and his lips touch mine. I freeze for a split second, my mind and body conflicted, before I move my lips against his and return the kiss. I can feel a low burn starting at the bottom of my stomach and work its way through my limbs.

I touch a hand to his cheek and stroke the rough skin there. My abs clench. Aching want. Guilt. Divided loyalties.

The crowd continues to cheer, although now some whistles join the noise. It unsettles me that we have an audience—that we're doing this *for* an audience.

The kiss ends and the king takes my hand, lifting it into the air. The motion swivels my body so that I'm now facing the audience. I focus on my breathing as I stare out at the crowd.

"May our marriage symbolize the peaceful joining of two hemispheres and the future prosperity of the world," the king says. His words grate on my nerves. Of course, he's marrying me because it's the easiest, most secure way of controlling the entire world and snuffing out potential rebellions. A political alliance based on matrimony. What bothers me more than this realization is that the king's motives make a difference to me.

The crowd's cheers seem even louder now than they did before, and I force out what I hope sounds like a giddy laugh as I gaze at the king. His eyes stare back at me with that intensity I've come to recognize. And in this moment, I realize my mind is a small thing. Much smaller than the tide we're being swept along, smaller than the king's empire, smaller than the number of people who have fought and died to lead us to this moment.

But most of all, it's smaller than the heart, and that's the cruelest irony of all.

IT'S LATE BY the time we finally return to the king's palace, and by then I'd shaken hands with hundreds of people, smiled until it felt like my face must've broken, and withstood the flash of dozens and dozens of cameras. Tonight I got my first taste of what it will be like as the king's marionette. It made me want to shoot someone—preferably the king.

King Lazuli met my seething looks and barely contained anger with uncharacteristic patience, which only pissed me off further.

Our shoes click on the marble floor as Montes escorts me back to my room.

"Why are you still making an effort with me?" I ask,

breaking the silence between us. "We have always been enemies, and we will always be enemies. Why try to force together puzzle pieces that will never fit?" I ask.

The king's hands slide into the pockets of his suit, and he bows his head, like he's actually thinking deeply on my question.

Finally, he speaks. "That first moment I saw you," Montes says, "I felt a jolt right here," Montes places a hand over his heart, "and I knew with certainty that you were mine."

"I'm not a possession, something you repeatedly seem to forget."

"Your heart is, and I wish to own it—I will own it."

I give him a curious look. "So confident."

We walk a few more paces in silence. "What is it that interests you?" Montes asks, glancing at me. "Apart from slaying, that is."

I ignore the barb and don't hesitate when I respond. "World affairs."

I glance at Montes to gauge his reaction, but he seems unsurprised. I was an emissary before I was his fiancée, after all. "Any areas in particular?" he asks.

Perhaps he means regions of the globe, but I interpret the question differently. An image of burned skin and patchy hair comes to mind. Another of the palsy a former soldier developed. All were the result of radiation poisoning and biological warfare. Not to mention that strange things are occurring in the king's labs, things he's kept quiet on. I want to know what those secrets are.

"Health," I say. "Innovations that will help people's

quality of life."

He watches me for a long time. "You will make a great queen."

I press my lips together to keep my upper lip from curling at the title.

"The people need a leader who listens to their needs," the king continues as we come to a stop in front of my door. "Cares about them."

At his words, I close my eyes. I'm not sure I want to hear what he has to say. It means committing to my role as the king's wife, as the queen. I'm not ready for that.

His hand cups my chin. "Open your eyes, Serenity."

I do.

"If you are genuinely interested in health and technology as it relates to world affairs, I will give you access to that information."

I raise my eyebrows. "Really?" Excitement creeps into my voice.

His smile is sly. He knows I've taken his bait. "As soon as we're married and you've proven that you're not planning on killing me or yourself, then absolutely."

And there's the catch.

I scowl at him. "I already told you, I'm not going to do anything."

He touches a finger to my lips, and I pretend his touch does nothing to me. "I need more than just your word," he says. "I need proof."

I DON'T SEE the king again until the next evening. He's

been busy all day with ruling the world, and I imagine that he will be especially busy for many months—hell, many years—to come.

When he knocks on my door, I just about bound out to meet him. Sure he's a slimy bastard, but men and women have been in and out of my room all day taking my measurements, asking questions about my personal preferences, and abusing my skin, nails, and hair in the name of beauty. There are forms of torture less painful than that.

"Someone seems happy to see me," he says.

"You are a sadistic bastard." I brush past him and out the door, glancing both ways just to make sure no one else is about to ambush me into picking out a color scheme for God-knows-what.

Somehow the king knows exactly what I'm referring to. I can see the laughter in his eyes. "I thought all women liked getting pampered?"

I narrow my eyes at him. "Do I look like the kind of woman who enjoys that?"

The king places a hand on my back and leans down to whisper in my ear. "You look like the kind of woman who shoots and asks questions later, and it's a turn-on."

My head whips back to look at King Lazuli. He's gazing at me hungrily. "You are a twisted son of a gun."

"Look who's talking."

I open my mouth to retort when the king cuts me off. "I want to show you something." He takes my hand and pulls me down the hall.

"Where's your little henchman, Marco?"

The king's hand tightens on mine. "He's around, but

I've asked him to keep his distance."

"So, he's still working for you?"

"Yes." King Montes doesn't look at me when he says it.

I pull my hand out of his. "That's it? He kills my father and he goes unpunished?"

"Watch your words." Now the king turns to face me, and his eyes flash. "You and your men killed and injured some of my best men, and you got a peace treaty and a promotion out of it."

I stop in my tracks. "A *promotion?*" My voice only gets quiet like this before I do terrible things. "You consider this a promotion?"

My hands clench and unclench. The king eyes them before he speaks. "From emissary of a dying nation to queen of the entire world? Of course it is."

I pull my fist back and slam it into his face. My knuckles split as they connect with the king's cheek. It's the most pleasant sting I've ever endured.

His head whips to the side, and I hear the click of his teeth as his jaw snaps together. Montes staggers, but only for a moment. I hear the pounding of several footsteps as some of the nearby palace guards run to help the king. He waves them off and rubs his jaw while he watches me, his eyes sparkling dangerously. Blood trickles out the side of his mouth. He must've cut himself with his teeth.

"So the king bleeds—I wasn't sure," I say.

He smiles. That's all the warning I get. Then he's on me. He swipes my feet out from under me, and I slam to the ground. The king follows, straddling me. He grabs my hands and holds them over my head. "Are you finished with your tantrum?"

"Not even close," I growl.

I try to buck him off my body, but it only serves to tighten his grip on me. The king's legs press into my sides, and he squeezes my hands. It takes me a few seconds and a couple deep breaths to realize that we're in a compromising position.

As if reading my mind, the king's eyes flick to my lips, a wicked grin forming along his own. I want to scream, but instead I force my strained muscles to relax. It's even harder to swallow my pride.

"Are you going to get off of me and show me this surprise of yours?" I ask, trying to sound exasperated. It's not very convincing, considering the series of events that led up to now.

"Hmm, I'm not sure," King Lazuli says, pretending to ponder my words. "It's not very often that I get my blood-thirsty wife-to-be on her back."

My face heats both with anger and embarrassment. He removes one of his hands from where they grip mine to brush his thumb over my lower lip. Heat ripples through my stomach. I don't want to react this way, not in the middle of some hall in the king's palace in front of palace guards. Not with him, and not after he's just tackled me to the ground.

I lie there, watching, waiting for what he'll do next. He gazes at my lips, and then he leans in.

He's a hair's breadth away from my mouth when I speak. "Don't," I say.

"Why not?" The king's breath fans against my lips. He's

smiling down at me rapaciously.

I don't speak. There are a hundred reasons why this shouldn't happen right now, but my mouth can't form a single one.

"I'll tell you what," he says, his voice low. "I won't kiss you if you can offer me something better."

"I'm not your fucking employee, and this is not a business transaction," I snap.

His grin deepens. "You're right, it isn't." His mouth presses against mine, and my stomach clenches. His tongue strokes my lips, encouraging them to part. Caught up in the moment, I let them. I'd forgotten how much I enjoyed kissing and how good the king's, in particular, are.

His tongue brushes against mine, and I relish the heady taste of him. With Will, my mind had loved him while my body had remained unmoved. In this situation, it's the exact opposite. I hate the king, yet I crave him. I want him to suffer, but I also want this.

Love and hate really aren't so very different.

He bites my lower lip, sucks on it, and I all but moan at the sensation. The king pulls away from me, and I lazily open my eyes, not realizing I'd closed them to begin with.

I just got owned, and the king knows it. I can tell by the way he bites his lip. He releases me and stands up.

I push myself up on my forearms and watch him. He reaches out a hand to help me up.

When I don't take it, he says, "Do you want to see my surprise, or would you rather I get back on top of you?" he asks.

I run my tongue along my teeth and take his hand, giving it a hard yank as I get up. He doesn't flinch.

I follow the king out of the palace. The cool night air raises goose bumps along my skin, but it's the sound of crashing waves that captures my attention. This is the first time I've been outside the palace since I arrived, and it's ecstasy.

I take a deep breath, relishing the smell of the salty sea breeze and let myself forget my past. The sea and the sky can do that—make me feel like an ageless thing.

This is the surprise, I realize. I'd like to be snarky about it, since it's so simple, but instead I feel a little unnerved. This is the best thing he could've surprised me with: escape.

I lift the skirt of the dress I'm wearing and run towards the waves, kicking my shoes off in the process. Behind me I can hear the king jogging, and I wonder if he's worried that I'm going to throw myself into the water like some tragic Greek maiden. 'Cause he should be. That's exactly what I'm going to do.

I yip as my feet hit the water and then I dive in, ruining my outfit and my hair and my makeup. Good riddance.

When I come up for air, I'm laughing. A moment later I feel hands wrap around me and haul me to my feet. It takes the king a moment to realize I'm fine.

He swipes the wet strands of my hair away from my face. "Jesus," he says, "you scared the shit out of me!"

I can't see him in the dark, but if I could, I bet I'd see that vein in his temple throbbing. "If I didn't know better, I'd say you were concerned."

"Why would you think otherwise?"

Water laps around us, swirling with the tide. My dress tangles itself around the king as he holds me to him. I taste saltwater on my lips and try to ignore the way Montes's dress shirt clings to his chest.

"Oh, I don't know," I say, "maybe because you killed my parents, destroyed my homeland, and are now forcing me into marrying you." My voice comes out flinty.

Rather than responding, the king releases me. He walks out of the water and back onto the beach, leaving me staring after him.

"Oh, *now* you walk away!" I yell at his back, mostly just to rile him up.

It works.

He comes stalking back into the water. "What do I have to do to prove myself? I've already moved mountains—an entire half of the world will prosper because you wanted it to be so. What more do you want me to do?"

"I want you to leave me the hell alone."

He grasps my jaw and holds it firmly, and in the dim moonlight I can just barely make out the shine of his eyes. "That is the one thing I cannot do."

He lets me go and leaves, this time for good.

CHAPTER 16

Serenity

THE DAY OF the wedding I sleep in. Normally I'm loathe to waste away the first hours of the morning, but not today. Today I want to forget that I have to get married. To the king. I make a face in my pillow.

People have been knocking on my door for the last two hours, and up until now I've done a pretty good job of ignoring them. But the pounding on my door right now is louder and more insistent than the others.

When I don't answer, the pounding stops. I smile into my pillow until I hear the click of my lock being thrown back. The door opens and footsteps cross the room.

My bed dips as someone sits down on it, and then I feel the feathery touch of fingertips on the bare skin of my shoulder. "You need to get up now."

My eyes snap open at that voice. "I thought you were

ignoring me?" I say to King Montes. He's leaning over me, and his nearness is doing strange things to my body. I haven't seen him since that night in the ocean.

"When it comes to you, that's impossible."

I bury my face in my pillow. "I want to sleep in."

"We're getting married in two hours."

"Don't care," I say, my voice muffled.

"Fine. We'll skip the wedding part and go straight to the honeymoon." He pulls back the covers and begins to slide in next to me. I yelp and jump out of bed.

The king steps away and sticks his hands into his pockets. He's wearing a uniform with a sash, and it takes me a minute to realize that's what he'll be wearing today when we get married.

I rub the sleep from my eyes and give him my best glare.

"Just so you know, you're not frightening at all in the morning," he says, smirking. "You look like a pissed-off kitten."

"Say that again, and I'll castrate you with a butter knife."

His lips quirk. "Ah, lucky me to have such a blushing bride."

"Isn't it bad luck to see me before the wedding?" I ask, folding my arms over my chest.

"What, you think our luck can get any worse?" the king says, raising an eyebrow. He has a point.

Before I can formulate a response, he walks to the door and ushers in a group of women who carry bags of makeup and hair supplies. I grimace at the sight.

"I'll see you in a couple of hours, Serenity," the king says, and then he's gone.

By the time I'm sitting in a small room waiting to be ushered down the aisle, a cold emptiness has settled in me. I'm wearing a dress I didn't pick out, holding flowers I don't care for, wearing makeup and hair someone else has styled, and I'm waiting to be married to a man I don't love because of orders someone else gave.

There's a rap on the door, and it opens after a moment. A young guard sticks his head in. "We're ready for you."

I shake out my arms and crack my neck. I'm supposed to be gathering my courage, not falling apart. I nod and follow him out, bringing the bouquet up to my chest.

Flashes go off, and cameras pan in on me. The photographers press against the velvet rope they're prohibited from crossing.

All I need to do is march down this hallway, then the aisle.

Easy, I tell myself.

I'm a horrible liar. I might as well be walking the plank. I'm just as frightened as I would be if my life were on the line. I have no one to hold my arm, and even though I don't believe in giving someone away (my current situation case in point), it'd be nice to not face this alone. That thought makes me think of my father and how unhappy he'd be if he could see me now.

Time's up, regardless. I turn the corner and stare at two large oak doors guarded by two of the king's men. Inside is the royal chapel, where hundreds of guests and dozens of camera crews eagerly wait. I can hear music softly playing from inside.

When the tune abruptly changes, the guard at my side

nods to the two men in front of me, and they grasp the door handles. "Congratulations," he says, stepping aside as the doors swing open.

I stand there blinking as I take in the foreign faces that watch me from the pews. I'm too terrified to smile, so I simply stare straight ahead. My eyes meet the king's, and strangely, in this moment, the sight of him grounds me.

He stands with his hands clasped, smiling at me. I can't help it, between my nerves and his smile, my mouth curves up. I don't look away as I walk towards him; ironically, he's the only thing that's keeping me from running out of here screaming. And I don't want that—not if this is somehow supposed to symbolize future peace and unity.

It seems like an eternity before I get to him. Once I do, relief washes over me that I'm no longer doing this alone. I pass my flowers to someone standing nearby, and the king takes my hands. I know he can feel them shaking by the way he squeezes them reassuringly.

The priest officiating drones on in Latin, and my pulse calms down a bit. At some point he reverts to English and asks King Lazuli to present me with the token of his commitment.

Montes reaches into his breast pocket and procures a ring. Giving me a soft smile, he slides it onto the finger where the engagement band already rests.

The stone of this new ring is dark blue, and flecks of gold are caught in its matrix. It looks for all the world like I'm wearing the night sky on my finger. Because what I love most about the sky are the stars.

He remembered.

It's also not lost on me that the stone is lapis lazuli; I'm wearing the king's namesake on my finger.

Someone passes me a ring, and with trembling hands I slip it onto the king's finger.

I gaze into his eyes as the priest speaks. They shine, and right then I feel beloved—by the man in front of me and the world that's looking to me.

Then I remember my father, and why it is that I'm up here. The lives the king has taken because of his selfishness. The façade is gone just as the priest says, "You may now kiss the bride."

My movements are jerky and automated. I kiss the king, but I'm not really present. My skin crawls as his lips caress mine. When he pulls away he smiles, but I can see something like uncertainty there. I want to laugh that I can make someone like the king feel vulnerable, but I'm too consumed by my own personal pain.

The priest announces us to the chapel, and I feel a tear drip down my cheek. I just married the monster under the bed.

THE KING AND I stand outside the palace, on the grassy lawn that overlooks the water. From the ice sculptures to the overabundance of flowers, it's clear the king's spared no expense on our reception. It had to cost a fortune of money better spent elsewhere.

A constant stream of people approaches us and congratulates the king and me on our union. I give most of them flinty looks. I know it's not fair of me to be hostile to people I don't know, but I'm insulted that anyone could assume I'm happy about what's happening to me.

"Congratulations my friend. You deserve all the happiness in the world," says the politician in front of us. He looks frighteningly similar to a walrus, and he eyes me like the object I'm supposed to be.

Montes nods and shakes his hand, "Thank you," he murmurs.

When the man reaches for my hand, I level a glare at him. He gets it.

Bowing, he says, "Congratulations again," and backs away.

The king watches him as he leaves. "I don't like the way he looked at you," he says quietly.

"That makes two of us."

The king nods to himself. "Then I'll take care of the situation."

I blink a few times. "Are you psychotic?" I hiss at him under my breath. "You can't just punish everyone who slights you."

"Of course I can," he says.

Before I can respond, the next guest approaches, this one a crusty old man who spews praise at the king. Once he moves along, I lean into the king. "Brownnoser, that one."

The king snickers, and I cringe that, at the moment, we are coconspirators. For the king, this seems to elicit the opposite reaction. He wraps a hand around my waist and rubs my side affectionately. I think I'm going to be sick.

A couple approaches us, and thankfully King Lazuli has

to drop his hand from my side in order to greet them.

"We are so happy for you," the woman says, "and we hope that this union brings prosperity to your home—and lots of children," she throws in, flashing me a sly smile. Like what every woman wants is a snotty baby.

I sway on my feet at the thought. "That won't ever happen," I say before I can help it. The idea of carrying the king's child is just too much for me to process at the moment.

The woman glances at me sharply, and the king stiffens at my side. "Er ... I can't have children." It's not even necessarily a lie, considering all the radiation I've been exposed to.

"You poor thing," the woman says.

"The queen doesn't know what she's saying," King Lazuli says. "She *can* have children."

I try to hide my swallow at the way the king looks at me, like my reproductive system is now at the forefront of his mind.

"Oh." Now the woman glances back and forth between us in confusion.

"Great to see you Claudette—Roger." The king nods to both of them and they take the cue to move on.

I watch their retreating forms. "Do you even have any real friends?" I say. "These people make me want to blow my brains out."

"What the hell was that about, Serenity?" King Lazuli says.

"Nothing," I say quickly.

The king studies me. "This discussion isn't over."

An older, regal woman greets us next.

"I'm so glad to see you settle down," she says to King Lazuli.

The king smiles back at her. "Thank you, Margot."

She squeezes his hand with her wrinkled one. I eye her withered beauty. She wears strings of pearls and gaudy gold jewelry. My upper lip curls. It changes into a grimace of a smile when she focuses on me.

Her eyes widen when she sees the scar that trails down the side of my face. I've gotten this reaction all day. And just like the others, I get the feeling that the woman in front of me has never seen violence firsthand. She's never killed a man, never watched his blood slowly seep out of him and the light fade from his eyes. I'd wager that she came from a nation that either allied with the king, or surrendered before war broke out.

She recovers from her shock and pats the side of my face. "My, my, what a pretty thing you are." My smile slips at her words, and she must see the killer in me because she recoils.

The woman clears her throat. "Congratulations again you two," she says, nodding at the king and trying hard not to look at me. I watch her as she walks away, and just as I suspected, she throws a final, spooked glance over her shoulder, like she can't help herself.

I narrow my eyes and give her a slow, predatory smile. Her eyes widen and she hurries away from us.

"Stop scaring our guests," King Lazuli says next to me.

"You mean your guests," I retort.

The king's eyes drift to my bare arm and move down.

The sight is possessive, hungry, and it makes my stomach churn.

I won't think about later tonight. I won't.

"They are our guests now, my queen," King Lazuli says.

"Don't call me that." I rub my shoulder against my neck, as if to wipe off the stain of his words from my skin.

"You better get used to it. That's what you'll be known as from now on." The king seems satisfied by the thought.

I snag a champagne flute from a passing waiter. The waiter looks between me and the king, mortified. The caterers are controlling the amount of alcohol I'm consuming, probably on behalf of the king's orders. It's a clever move too, since if I had it my way, I'd already be twelve drinks deep and unwilling to stop until the liquor killed me.

Before the king can take the glass from me, I throw it back. It's only my third drink of the night, but I can already feel the warm, tingly sensation of the alcohol sliding through my veins. King Lazuli scowls at me as I remove the now empty glass from my lips and flash him a triumphant smile.

The waiter snatches the champagne flute from my hands the first chance he gets, as though his attentiveness now can make up for the fact that he blew it.

The boy stutters apologies at the king, who waves him off. I watch longingly as the tray carrying champagne is whisked away.

I can feel the king's eyes on me, and I'm strangely interested in what he's thinking—not because I care about him, but because I want to know what his motives are for marrying me, a woman who loathes him.

The only answer that comes to mind is the obvious one: that this is some archaic form of a political alliance—marrying into power. Not that I have any power in my own right. But ideology is the most powerful currency in the world—it can start wars, and it can end them—and to the citizens of the nation, the king of the eastern empire and the emissary of the WUN symbolize two hemispheres tonight made whole.

However, feeling the king's eyes on me, I can't help but wonder if the marriage might be more than just a power play. I know the king finds me attractive and that he enjoys verbally sparring with me, but could something more be there?

The king waves Marco over. Marco, who's just as responsible for my father's death as the king is. Perhaps more so, if the king really didn't order my father killed.

This is the first time I've seen him, and I give him my most lethal look. The fact that Marco is not rotting in a jail cell or a coffin, but instead attending my wedding, has me seeing red.

He flinches, but that doesn't stop him from approaching King Lazuli.

"The queen is tired," the king says to Marco.

"No, I'm not."

Marco flicks me an annoyed look. I get perverse satisfaction knowing that it bothers him that I undermine the king.

The king ignores me. "We're going to head to our suite now. Think you can handle the rest of the wedding without us?"

"Absolutely. Go enjoy your wedding night," Marco says, smiling at me as he does so. It's his underhanded form of payback.

I work my jaw, then let my gaze flick back to the king. "I'm not tired. Please." I've resorted to begging. Anything to put off the inevitable for a little longer.

The king's eyes move over my face. "You want to stay now? I could've sworn that you said you wanted to blow your brains out at the thought of being around *our* guests."

I slit my eyes at him and he smiles. He places his hand at the small of my back and leads me towards the palace. I can feel the mounting stares of smiling guests. Why are they so happy? Why is anyone happy? They still have a tyrant ruler who's now married to a strange girl from the last conquered land.

The looming palace looks like my prison, and in some ways it is. Here I will always be watched, assessed, guarded. But I will stick to my decision. I'll leverage my new status for my people, I'll figure out the king's secrets, and when the time is right, I will kill the Undying King.

We pass into the palace. In here it's quiet, too quiet. The king and I ascend the stairs, and I follow him down the hall to a room I've never been in before. Our room.

He cracks the door open and turns back to me. "I think this calls for tradition." He bends and wraps one arm behind my knees and another across my back, then lifts me.

I yelp, and before I can think about what I'm doing, I wrap my arms around his neck. "Put me down, Montes."

Instead of putting me down, he pushes the door further

open with his foot and carries me inside. The large canopy bed is the first thing that catches my eye. And we're moving towards it. Next I notice a wall of windows that open up to a balcony. Beyond them I can see the starry sky and the dark ocean.

The king places me gently on the bed, and gazes at me like I'm his next meal. I scramble off the mattress.

"I-I need to use the restroom." I bolt for the gleaming bathroom before he has a chance to respond.

I close the door behind me and lock it. Then I lean against the wall and let myself slide down. I rest my head between my knees.

This is no worse than death I try to tell myself. But in some ways it is. I'm protecting a nation by following through with this wedding, but I'm dishonoring my parents. What I despise most is that, beneath all that anger and hate, I actually feel something else for the king. Sometimes desire—he is beautiful, after all—sometimes camaraderie, sometimes amusement, and sometimes ... compassion.

I get to my feet, my legs shaky, and lean over the counter. When I glance at my reflection I see a strong woman, one who's had to skirt right and wrong her entire life. I can do this.

I leave the bathroom without pretending to flush the toilet or wash my hands—the king's not a fool. He knows I'm scared as hell of what lies ahead.

When I enter the bedroom, Montes lounges on a side chair. His tie is loosened and his jacket has already been removed. He doesn't move for a moment, just takes me in.

Then, ever so slowly he gets up and makes his way to me. "I'm not a nice man," he says.

"I couldn't agree more," I say.

"This is happening tonight."

My throat works. "I know."

"Good." Then he closes the remaining distance between us and kisses me. At first, all I do is stand there, unresponsive. But eventually, I give in and move my lips. I wonder if this is how royalty felt when they were forced to marry one another. The repulsion, the nervousness, the sense of duty—all of it. I wonder if any of them felt perversely excited, as I do. Perhaps in this I am well and truly alone.

The king backs us up until I fall against the bed. He kneels between my legs to remove my shoes. First one comes off, then the other. But he doesn't remove his hands. Instead he slides them up my leg until they brush the lace of my panties.

I gasp, and struggle against the urge to rip his hands away. A second later his hands are gone, but only so that he can remove his tie. Once he's discarded the garment, he begins unbuttoning his shirt.

I squeeze my eyes shut. When I open them, he's shirtless. His body is all sculpted muscle. I appreciate the sight on a physical level, but it bothers me that he can care so much about his body and so little for entire nations.

Then again, perhaps he has to keep himself in shape in case he ever needs to use his physical strength. It's not like he doesn't have enemies. With that thought, I scour his body for bullet wounds. He's been shot before.

I reach out to his chest and run a hand over the smooth skin that covers his heart. "Where is it?" There should be scar tissue where he'd been shot. It was filmed on live T.V. I've seen him bleed in front of my eyes.

He closes his eyes slowly, as though he's relishing the feel of my skin on his. "Don't you know, my queen?" he says, opening his eyes. "I can't be killed."

I frown. "Stop calling me that."

"No."

I drop my hand and the king resumes undressing himself. I scoot further back on the bed as I watch him remove his shoes, then his socks, and then his pants. I fist the comforter beneath me to give my hands something to do.

When he stands in just his boxer briefs, his stomach muscles rippling, he returns his attention to me. "Come here."

I don't move.

He sighs. "You need to take your dress off, Serenity, and you need my help to do so." He says it like he's the most reasonable person in the world. As though I'm being ridiculous by wanting to keep on the dress I despised so much earlier. What he doesn't realize—or maybe he does— is that it's my last defense before we get intimate.

Reluctantly I scoot myself off the bed and pad over to him. I feel like the world's most wretched person that my eyes linger on all the sculpted lines of his body. He turns me around and begins unfastening the buttons that trail down my back. I can feel the brush of his fingers along my skin. They draw out goose bumps.

190

Slowly my dress peels away from me. Montes removes the last of the buttons, and the gown glides over my hips and pools at my feet. Instinctively I cover myself. I'm still wearing lingerie, but it hardly leaves anything to the imagination.

Montes pulls my arms down from where they hide my chest. He gives me a surprisingly gentle look, and I close my eyes.

"Open your eyes, Serenity."

"Then stop looking at me like that."

"I can't."

I press my eyelids shut harder. "You're heartless."

"Most of the time. But sometimes ... sometimes I'm not when I'm around you."

I open my eyes at that. He's being genuine. And this is the worst. A bad guy with a change of heart. I'm not his redemption; I'm going to be his executioner.

He kisses me, and this time I don't fight it. My lips move against his, and I tangle my fingers in his hair, relishing the fact that I'm ruining it. He makes an approving sound in my mouth and lifts me so that my legs are forced to wrap around his hips.

The king moves us to the bed and then places me on top of it. He reaches under my back and unsnaps my bra. I wince as he tosses the flimsy garment aside.

And then he's touching me, kneading my breasts, moving his thumbs over my nipples, and I can't figure out whether this situation disturbs me or turns me on. Both, I think.

Montes's mouth replaces his fingers, and his teeth skim

the tender flesh. I shiver at the sensation, and he flashes me a smile.

"Still a virgin?" he asks.

"That's none of your business."

"I'll take that as a yes," he says, "which means it's my job to make sure you enjoy yourself tonight."

"That's not going to happen."

"We'll see what you say after all is said and done."

His fingers hook under the thin fabric of my panties and he pulls them off me before removing his boxer briefs. When he returns to the bed, he lays his body over mine. I've never experienced so much skin-on-skin contact, and I'm surprised to find that it feels good.

Really good.

He rolls to my side and moves his hand until it's touching the most intimate part of me.

"*Montes.*" I jerk away from him before I remember myself.

He pushes me back down against the mattress and kisses my collarbone. His fingers slip inside me, and I jerk again.

"You're already wet," his whispers in my ear.

I get the logistics of female anatomy, but not how it works when expert fingers strum it. Judging by the king's smug tone, I can piece together what I'm missing. The way he touches me has me throwing my head back and closing my eyes.

My breath catches and picks up as his fingers rhythmically stroke me. Sensation is building up inside of me, and my eyes flutter closed to better experience this.

The king lets out a satisfied chuckle under his breath, then removes his fingers. I'm left bereft only for a moment before he rolls back onto me and positions himself. My eyes snap open and gaze into his. Oh God, it's happening.

"This might hurt," he says.

And it does, briefly. Then I feel him fully inside me.

Montes's hands brush back the hair of my face, and he presses a kiss along my cheek as he withdraws.

The optimist in me wonders if this is it. Show's over. Then Montes glides back into me, and I suck in a breath at the pleasant throb. The man who ruined my world, killed my parents and most of my people, is now my husband, and he's making love to me. And I'm enjoying it. It's so wrong it makes my skin crawl.

A stray tear streaks down my cheek. "I hate you," I say to him.

"You won't always feel that way," he says, thrusting into me.

"I will. I swear it."

"Give it up," he growls, pushing into me harder. "The war is over."

"Not for me. It won't ever be over for me."

CHaPTER 17

SERENITY

I LIE AWAKE for a long time afterwards, staring at the ceiling. Next to me the king's breathing is steady and even. He fell asleep a while ago. When I can't take it anymore, I push his arm off of my waist. The king makes a noise in his sleep and rearranges himself.

I slip out of bed and grab the silk robe that someone had set out for me earlier. The smooth material makes me want to shrug the garment off. After wearing rough fatigues for most of my life, such soft fabric feels unnatural against my skin. Instead I cinch the robe around my waist and walk outside.

I grip the stone railing. Here, wherever here is, the night is pleasant. I can smell the seawater carried along the breeze.

Now that no one is watching, I bow my head and allow myself to weep. Weep for my life, for all those who've killed or died because of the war, and for the uncertain future of the world.

When I've cried myself out, I lie down on the cool floor of the balcony and stare at the stars. I make out the Pleiades, a constellation my mother taught me years ago. *Make a wish upon the seven sisters,* she'd whisper to me when we'd catch sight of them.

And I do so now. *I wish I could be up there with you.* I gaze at them until my eyes drift closed.

Sometime later I feel my body lifted off the ground and the warm press of skin against mine as I'm tucked back into my bed.

I'm pulled from sleep once more when I feel a light kiss on my lips, and the sensation of hands caressing my skin. I make an approving sound at the back of my throat and stretch like a contented cat.

Then my situation comes rushing back to me. My eyes snap open, and I stare into Montes's deep brown ones. His hair hangs down around his face, and I can't help but notice that the ruffled look suits him well.

The sky outside has a predawn glow. It's not morning yet, which means ...

"Again?" I widen my eyes. Of course we weren't going to do this only once. I'd just hoped that it wouldn't happen again so soon. I enjoyed it far too much the first time.

"I plan on acquainting myself with you many times."

I feel his erection press against me, and my breath catches. Just like last night, his fingers touch the soft skin between my legs. His thumb dances circles around my sensitive flesh until I moan. I bite back the sound, but it's too late.

Montes wears a knowing grin, and his finger moves faster. "Like that?" he whispers against my ear.

"This changes nothing," I gasp out.

"I think it does." I can feel myself getting slick against him, and the bastard's fully aware of this as well. He removes his hand, and I feel the hard press of him against my opening.

I'm still sore from last night, so when he pushes himself inside me, air whistles through my teeth as I inhale. And just like last night, the soreness is soon replaced by the first stirrings of pleasure. The whole thing is wrong, wrong, wrong. Then again, I'm not the most morally righteous person; war hasn't afforded me that luxury. So instead of retreating into my mind, I tentatively begin to touch the king.

First my hands glide over his shoulders and arms, stroking the bunched muscles beneath the skin. Above me the king stills, and I meet his gaze.

"What are you doing?" he asks.

"Discovering my . . . husband." It's hard for me to call him that—to think of him like that, but some wars are won by surrendering certain, doomed battles, and this is one of them.

He watches me, unmoving, and I squirm against him. "Why have you stopped?"

Something a whole lot like affection—or maybe victory—brightens his eyes. He leans in and kisses me, and the feeling of being joined in two places nearly throws me over the edge. Who knew that beneath my tough exterior was a sex-starved woman?

When the kiss ends, he begins moving again. "Does that feel better?" he whispers.

I close my eyes and hum in response. We continue like that, enjoying extremely sinful and morally questionable sex for a while, before I open my eyes again and run my fingers down his cheek. His large, dark eyes shutter at my touch and his tempo increases.

Heat builds at my core, and finally I cry out and clutch him as my orgasm lashes through me. His strokes become harder and deeper, and I feel him throb inside me as he finds his own release.

He collapses against me, and we're both slick with sweat. In some ways sex is a lot like the lifestyle I'm used to, and that surprises me. I'd always imagined that it was something purely soft and sweet, but what we've done tonight proves otherwise. That there's something primal in the act—some strange combo of pain and pleasure, an adrenaline rush, exertion—just like there is in war.

I'D NEVER REALLY thought through marrying the king. The horror of it eclipsed any curiosity I might've had at being someone's partner. I'm greatly surprised to find that in private the king can be gentle and—dare I think it—caring.

I watch him as morning sunlight streams through our balcony windows and find I want to touch him again. His tan skin dips and rises over corded muscles. I see a solitary freckle just below his shoulder blade.

He's human.

It's the stupid freckle that reminds me. He may be broken and wicked and narcissistic, but he's human. He bleeds, he feels.

Thinking like this is risky, particularly when I still plan on killing him. I don't want to grow close to this man, but I can't seem to help myself, even after all he's done. Maybe he doesn't need to die. Maybe he can be changed.

I scoff at my own ridiculous thought. If nothing has swayed the king into growing a conscience before now, I doubt I'll be what does.

His thick hair dusts his cheekbones, hiding his features. Before I can think twice, I reach out and push the dark locks away from his face. In sleep, he's lovely. At my touch, he stirs but doesn't wake.

I didn't quite realize humans could savor each other the way we did last night. In the bunker, people didn't talk about these things, and if they did them, they kept their business private.

The bed shifts next to me, and when I refocus my attention on the king, his eyes open. "What is my queen doing up?" Sleep roughens his voice, and again, I'm reminded that at the end of the day—or the beginning of it, rather—the king is just a man.

He scoops me to him when I don't respond, and we spend a minute staring at each other. "Sore?" he finally asks.

I feel my cheeks flush. I hate that this subject still makes me uncomfortable. "I'm fine."

His fingers brush across my face. "Hmm. I thought we

were past the lies."

Lying and discussing this with the king seem like two very different things. My eyes move between his. "Are you happy now that you finally have me?"

The king shakes his head. "I don't have you—yet. But I will."

SOMEONE BRINGS IN strawberries and champagne shortly after we wake up, and now it's clear that not only can one enjoy good food and good sex, but also enjoy the two together. It seems outrageously gluttonous, but it doesn't stop me from reaching over to the platter and picking up a strawberry while the king pours champagne.

Just as I open my mouth, the king catches my hand and makes a *tsk*-ing sound. "This, I believe, is my job."

He takes the strawberry from me and presses a champagne flute into my hand.

"So now I'm permitted to drink?"

"As long as I'm the one pouring, you are."

"You're a control freak."

The king scoops cream onto the strawberry from a nearby bowl. "This surprises you?" he asks.

"No, but you could try loosening up for once in your life."

He raises an eyebrow. "What, exactly, do you think I've been doing for the last twelve hours?"

"Punishing me," I say without missing a beat.

He sighs. "You keep lying. Hasn't anyone told you the key to a healthy marriage is trust and honesty?"

I scoff at him. "There are so many things I could say to that statement."

The king smirks and lifts the strawberry like he wants to feed me.

"Do that, and I'll bite your fingers off."

"You like my fingers too much to do them harm. Now, open your mouth."

I eye him like a wary creature even as I part my lips and he feeds the berry to me. My annoyance with him is less compelling than my desire to eat the fruit.

My eyes close as I bite down on it and enjoy the taste. I can't remember the last time I had a strawberry.

When my eyelids lift, Montes is watching me with fascination, like he craves these reactions.

That sense of wrongness comes back. I shouldn't be doing this with the king while the world toils on. I feel like the traitor everyone made me out to be.

I flash him a cautious look, and never taking my eyes off of him, down the champagne.

Bad idea. Whether it's my empty stomach, all the alcohol I've imbibed, or the rich palace food, something's not sitting well.

"Serenity?"

I scramble out of bed. I don't bother grabbing the silk robe on my way to the bathroom. I barely make it in time. The water's tinged red, and I can't tell if it's from the berry or the blood.

Behind me, the king swears. What's he doing in here?

"Get out," I say weakly.

"Last I checked, I'm the king, not you."

I flush the toilet and rise to my feet. I'm more fatigued than I should be. I fear that just when I decided I had the will to live, my body decided it didn't.

Montes presses a button built into the wall of the bathroom. "Marco, get me a doctor—"

"No." My voice is sharper than I intend it. "Please," I add, leaning against the counter, "the alcohol didn't sit well. That's all."

"Your Majesty?" Marco's static-y voice blares into the room. Just the sound of it makes my trigger finger itch.

The king scrutinizes me for a long time before he turns back to the intercom. "Scratch that, Marco. Just bring some broth, crackers, and something with electrolytes in it. Oh, and I believe it's time to put the queen on my pills."

My ears perk up at this.

"Consider it done," Marco says, and the line clicks off.

"Pills?" I inquire. "Trying to poison me?" I fish.

Montes's gaze lands meaningfully on the toilet. "Seems like you're doing a perfectly good job of that on your own."

"Then what are they for?"

"Your long-term health," he says cryptically, and that's the last he'll say on the subject.

EVEN ON THE king's honeymoon he has to work; it's one of the drawbacks of being the leader of the entire globe.

"I'm coming with you," I say, as he buttons his cufflinks.

The king assesses me. "You're fatigued. You should

201

spend the day resting. One of the servants can give you a massage if you'd like."

I yank a dress from a hanger in our closet. "I wasn't asking."

"Nor was I."

Today I'll discover what happens when two stubborn people reach an impasse.

"You're going to have to physically stop me from leaving, then." I've been cooped up for too long. I need to get back to the world of the living.

"Don't tempt me. I can get creative." The look Montes is giving me makes me flush. I wouldn't mind his methods one bit, and I've made peace with this disturbing realization.

His words, however, don't stop me from getting dressed. When he's about to leave, I block his exit. "I'm coming with you."

"No, you're not."

I reach up and trickle my fingers over his jaw. I've learned that the king enjoys any casual affection I give him—likely because I have so little to offer. "Find something for me to do, Montes. Surely you have more than enough work to keep the both of us occupied."

I'm more than ready to begin healing the damaged lands of the world. I need to prove to myself and to my people that I haven't turned my back on my past.

He scrutinizes me, then sighs. He must have figured out what I already know: if he leaves me alone, I'm going to get myself in more trouble than if he simply drags me along.

"Aw," I give him a fake pout, "is someone having buyer's remorse?" The king's finally realizing just what a handful I can be.

He catches my jaw. "You believe you can push me without repercussions. You can't, and you will be repaying me for this later."

The king should know by now that threats don't scare me. I hope he can see in my eyes that I don't give a flying fuck about his words.

When I don't back down, Montes drops his hold so that he can reach around me and open the door.

I turn to go, but he catches my wrist, reeling me back in. "Serenity?" he says, his lips brushing against my ear. "I'm glad you're not frightened by my words, but you should be."

FIVE HOURS LATER, I'm sitting in a conference room, trying to keep my lunch down. The king flashes me a concerned glance, like he has been all day. Perhaps part of the reason he's come to rule the world is because he misses nothing.

I finger the document in front of me and focus on evening my breaths. It helps with the nausea. If I concentrate long enough, I can ride this out. I shouldn't have let myself go following my father's death. My body's paying for it now and making it painfully obvious that I'm not okay.

"Reports suggest the Resistance is growing in unprecedented numbers," one of the king's political advisors says. "They've raided the Toulouse research facility and bombed the Department of Defense in Berlin. There have also been threats to air footage of the queen."

I suck in air too quickly and choke on my own saliva. I begin to cough, and once I start, I can't seem to stop.

Next to me Montes stands. "Bringing you along was a bad idea." He's been waiting for an excuse to say this. "You should go back to the room and rest."

I wave him off but continue to cough. My lungs seem to rattle with the effort, and my whole body shakes. Finally I manage to clear my throat. As I draw my fist away from my mouth, I notice the bright red speckles.

Blood.

I drop my hand before the king can see what I have. "I think I will."

The king's brow crinkles. If anything, my easy agreement only worries him more.

I stand to leave, hiding my hand in the folds of my dress. The king's eyes dart to the action, then up to me. He doesn't say anything, instead waving his royal guards over. "Escort the queen back to our rooms," he commands.

"I'll be back in a few hours," he says to me. "If you need anything, you only need to ask the staff."

Without waiting for further direction, I nod and leave the room. Behind me the guards scurry to catch up. My heels click as I cross the halls. I should be wondering what the king thinks about my behavior, or what will happen if the footage of me leaks.

Instead I think of my dwindling health. I've never coughed up blood before, but I've known people who have. This is the moment of truth, the one I've ignored for so long.

It's starting. The beginning of the end.

CHAPTER 18

SERENITY

A HAND GLIDES through my hair, and I blink my eyes open. Montes sits on the edge of the bed. He's fully dressed, while I'm only clad in skimpy lingerie. I pull the sheets a little tighter around me before I realize that he's already seen it all, touched it all.

His lips quirk when he sees what I'm doing. "You have an appointment," he says.

"What are you talking about?" I ask, edging away from him. Outside the sky is dark. I can't imagine any appointment occurring this late in the day.

Instead of answering, Montes crosses the room, opens a drawer in a nearby dresser, and pulls out a pair of stretchy-looking pants and a cotton shirt. I almost cry out with joy when I see that the outfit is, one, not a dress, and two, made out of something that's neither too soft nor too itchy.

"I need a shower," I say. I already took one, but between Montes's news, and the determined set of his jaw, I'm pretty sure I want to avoid whatever it is he's arranged.

"It's going to have to wait," he says. "We need to go right now."

This can't be good.

I SHAKE MY head. "No. No, no—"

"Yes," Montes says to the doctor that's trying to hand me a hospital gown.

I fold my arms. "You're going to have to force that thing on me."

A doctor's appointment, that's what Montes had in mind this evening. The king was right not to say anything earlier. I'm practically shaking from nervousness. Most people don't fear the doctor; they have no reason to. I do. War has given me plenty of reasons to.

"If I must." Montes casts a lazy glance at the two guards who stand on either side of the doorway. "Guards, why don't you help your queen remove her clothing?"

I flash them a heated look. "You touch me, you die."

Five minutes later, I'm screaming as Montes and his guards hold me down. The doctor has a pair of scissors poised over the thin cotton of my shirt.

"Fine, *fine*! I'll put on the goddamn robe, just get your hands off of me!"

I will say this for Montes, his methods may be inhumane, but they are effective.

Montes nods to his soldiers, and they back off immediately. He flashes me a victorious smile as he pushes himself off the ground and holds out a hand to help me up.

I ignore his hand and snatch the robe from the doctor. "Where's the bathroom?"

"Uh-uh, Serenity," the king says. "It doesn't work like that. Not after that little demonstration. You're going to have to change right here."

My nostrils flare as I stare him down. I'm the first to break eye contact. I shake my head and strip off my shirt. Instead of looking at the king, I smile at one of his guards while I take off my pants.

The king glances between the stoic guard and me. Just as I reach back to unclasp my bra, the king steps in front of my line of sight, his eyes narrowed. I smirk at him and finish sliding off my bra.

Montes's eyes draw down to my breasts. For a moment his look is hungry. Then he shutters the expression. He takes the thin cotton hospital gown from me, shakes it out, and holds it open for me to step into.

I thread my arms into the gown while the king ties the strings in the back. Once Montes is done, I move to the sole hospital bed in the room and lie down. A strange device arches over it.

"This is for yesterday's comment, isn't it?" I ask, remembering the way Montes looked at me after I stated that I couldn't have children.

"I want an heir ... eventually," he says, coming to stand next to me.

I snort at this. "As if you'd ever give up the throne," I

208

say.

"All good things must end at some point." His fingers press against the bare skin of my leg.

"That they do," I agree.

"More importantly," he says, "I want to make sure you're in good health."

He knows. Somehow, after only spending a full day in my presence, he's figured out what no one else has: that something other than grief has weakened me.

I'm struck that he cares. Something uncomfortable catches in my throat at the thought. Right when I assumed I was the loneliest creature in the world, I find out I might matter to someone.

The doctor comes over and starts up the machine that's centered over my lower abdomen. I'm beginning to guess it is some type of scanner.

Montes sits in a chair next to me and takes my hand. The whole situation should be ridiculous. It's not.

The scanner thrums to life and begins to travel over my abdomen and up my body.

Behind the doctor a wall of computer screens come to life. The main one catches my eye. On it I can see my skeleton, and fainter but no less clear, I spot my reproductive organs, then my intestines, then my heart and lungs, and lastly my head.

The doctor scrutinizes the computer screens for a long time, looking over the images and the readouts. "There are no cysts, no apparent scarring or obvious swelling. I don't see anything that might indicate you're infertile, Queen Lazuli."

209

The king's hold on my hand loosens with his relief.

"Great," I say, lifting my torso off of the bed. "That means I can go, right?" I ask, trying to rush this along.

The doctor hasn't looked away from the main screen. "Hmm," he says.

Montes's grip tightens again, and he pushes my chest back down. "What is it?" the king asks.

The doctor sucks in a breath, and the king's hand begins to crush mine.

"Ow." I pull my hand out of his.

"Sorry," Montes says, distracted. He recaptures my hand and watches the doctor.

My heart thumps. Montes actually apologized. For squeezing my hand too tightly. The man who apologizes to no one.

"What is it?" King Lazuli asks the doctor.

The doctor pauses. "The queen has cancer."

CHAPTER 19

SERENITY

THERE IT IS, the burden I've been hiding for a year now. Radiation-borne cancer. It was common in the WUN, especially in and around big cities where the king deployed the nukes.

Montes stands up and drops my hand. "Cancer?" I've never heard that tone in his voice. Like devastation and disbelief wrapped into one. Surely I'm not the source of that anguish.

"We'll have to do a biopsy to be safe, but judging from the imaging here," the doctor says, returning his attention to the screen, "it's overwhelmingly likely that what I'm seeing is cancer. It looks like it's metastasized."

And that's the other discovery I made earlier today when I coughed up blood. I've had stomach problems for the last year, not lung problems. However, I'd seen several bunker residents suffer through the various stages of cancer. I know this is the tail end of the process.

The Pleiades granted me my wish. I'm going to join them soon.

Montes glances down at me, and I see true fear in his eyes. "What can we do?" he asks the doctor.

"It depends on the particulars. The queen will need to be placed in the Sleeper to remove the cancerous tissue where possible."

The Sleeper?

"She'll also need to be put on the same medication as you, Your Majesty." The doctor gives Montes a meaningful look.

"It's already done," Montes says, and there's something fierce in his voice now.

I glance at him, my heart constricting. I've fantasized about killing the king—there have been times in my life where I wanted nothing more than to see him suffer and die for all the pain he caused me. And yet now that the tables are turned and my life is in danger, the king seems to want to do everything in his power to keep me alive.

I can't stand that my ethics might be more corrupt than the king's.

The doctor comes over to us. "Have you experienced any unusual symptoms up until now?"

I give him a long look. "I've lived most of my life in wartime conditions. I have no idea what 'unusual symptoms' might be."

The doctor's eyebrows dart up. "Were you exposed to radiation during that time?"

"Of course." It was everywhere—in the soil, the drinking water, the crops. No one living in the western hemisphere could totally avoid it, but especially not me, who lived so close to D.C.

The king's hand squeezes mine, and I glance at him. His expression is carefully blank, but that vein is pulsing in his temple.

War tears down everything. Morals, loyalties, lives. Its aftershocks can ripple long after it ends. This is merely one more way that it's ripped my life apart. And now, maybe for the first time, it's affecting the king's life on a personal level.

"We will fix this," the king says in that commanding voice of his, like this is just another minor obstacle.

Suddenly, I pity him, because some things simply cannot be conquered, and this might be one of them.

THE NEXT EVENING we sit on a jet flying to what was once Austria. Next to me, Montes drums his fingers on his armrest, his leg jiggling. His eyes keep returning to my stomach.

"Cancer," he murmurs. He's said that word several times today. Stomach cancer, to be precise. It's one of several types of cancer caused by radiation.

I can't help my next words. "Ironic that you caused the cancer you're now trying to stop from killing me." There's poetic justice in that, though only the king gets the luxury of justice. The rest of us just pointlessly suffer.

He rubs his eyes. "We—*we* are trying to stop it from killing you." I notice that he doesn't address the other part of my statement. I guess he has to pretend it all away, otherwise he might actually realize what a despicable human being he's been.

"Have you taken your medication?" he asks.

I shake my head. It's the same mystery drug the king takes. Neither he nor the doctor told me what it does, but it leaves me wondering what exactly an undying king would need a prescription for.

Montes digs through a bag at his feet and pulls out water and a bottle of pills.

I take them with me into the small restroom and shake one of the small white pills into my hand. Staring down at it, I try to divine its use. Perhaps I'll turn into the same douchey prick the king is. The thought makes me smirk, despite my circumstances. I unscrew the bottle of water and toss the medication into my mouth before taking a long drink.

Almost immediately my stomach clenches. I'm sure even a healthy stomach might rebel against this medication if it were as empty as mine.

I lean against the counter and take slow, steady breaths. The jet chooses that moment to hit a patch of turbulence. I barely have time to turn my body to the toilet before I start to retch. Hot tears roll down my cheeks as my stomach tries to force its contents out of me.

I'm still bent over the toilet when the bathroom door bangs open, and the king strides in. He pulls back my hair while I dry heave, and once I'm done, he gathers me to him and strokes my face as I shake.

"How did you manage to hide this from everyone?" he asks, his voice soft.

I'm still too nauseous to answer. I curl up into him and bury my face in his shirt. "Don't leave me," I whisper. I don't know why I say it; I don't know why I'm giving or receiving compassion from this man. But I do know this: only compassion can redeem someone. Even the king. Even me.

THE KING CARRIES me out of the bathroom and lays me out on one of the jet's couches. I won't let him go, and the feeling seems to be mutual by the way he cradles my torso in his arms.

He pulls one of his arms out from under me and brushes my hair away from my face. "You're okay," he whispers over and over again. His eyes look frightened, like I might die right here and now.

Gradually my stomach settles, and I feel a bit better. The king kisses the skin along my hairline, and I continue to cling to him. "I'm supposed to hate you," I whisper.

He laughs humorlessly. "Are you finally admitting that you don't?" he asks, his throat catching.

"Never," I whisper.

"Liar."

I curl up against him, forgetting for a while that he's the culprit behind every bad memory I possess, and eventually I fall asleep in his arms.

OVER THE NEXT two days, a biopsy is taken, and it's confirmed that I have cancer. Then come the X-rays. By the end of my second day, I'm scheduled for surgery.

The hospital allows me to stay with the king for the evening. As soon as I see the fluffy bed in our room, I collapse onto it. The mattress dips as the king joins me.

We're in yet another one of his estates. I'm no longer surprised at the excess of it all.

I feel Montes tug off one of my shoes, then the other. Next he rolls me over and begins removing my pants. I raise my eyebrows but say nothing; I'm not completely opposed to sex.

But the king doesn't try to seduce me. Once I'm undressed, he strips down and joins me on the bed, gathering me to him. Our exposed skin presses together and it feels exquisite. Never in a million years did I think I'd enjoy casual intimacy with the king.

Since finding out that I have cancer, Montes has revealed this other side of him, one that's inexplicably compassionate. It's made me realize something else: the king is lonelier than even me, and he desperately doesn't want to be.

"Don't make me go in for surgery tomorrow," I whisper. I'd kept quiet about the cancer because everything about illness frightens me. Declining health, doctors, medications, surgery.

The king doesn't answer for a long time. So long, in fact, that I assume he won't.

"My father killed himself," the king finally says. "Died at the hand of his own gun. And like you, he was the last family I had."

I stiffen in the king's arms.

"Why are you telling me this?"

The king touches my temple. "You have that same look in your eyes he had. It's been there from the first moment I saw you. And I fear both he and you know a secret I don't."

I watch the king for a long time, my throat working.

"We do." Never had I imagined my life leading me here, to this moment. Yet now that I'm here, I wonder if there is a beautiful design to things.

"Then tell me what it is," the king says. Those intense eyes are fully focused on me.

He doesn't know; he really has no clue when it's quite obvious. It's the secret he continually hides from.

"Everything that lives must eventually die."

THE SURGERY HAPPENS the next day, and just like the last time I was in the presence of a doctor, soldiers have to hold me down while the doctor administers the sedative.

The ordeal is one that should be solely reserved for the worst inhabitants of hell.

"Why are you fighting this?" the king asks me as he holds down my shoulders.

It's a good question, especially since I want the cancer out. "That needle better not come any closer to me," I say. Like I wield any power in this situation.

"Serenity, you need to be put under. You know this," the king replies.

"No—please, no."

"Christ," the king says looking away, "Stop begging. I can't take it."

"Montes, please."

"I'll have to leave if you don't stop."

I lock eyes with him. *"Don't leave."*

He nods and I hold still. I squeeze my eyes shut when I feel the needle enter my skin. The doctor kneeling next to me begins to talk. "I'm going to count back from one hundred. Follow along with me. One hundred, ninety-nine, ninety-eight, ..."

I repeat the numbers in my head, focusing on his voice until my eyes drop and my mind drifts off.

CHAPTER 20

SERENITY

WHEN I WAKE up, the king is at the side of my bed. He's smiling and holding my hand. Almost reflexively I smile back at him. It's strange to feel this way about anyone. The fact that the king is the one who's opened my heart is just proof that fate is a cruel bitch.

"How long have I been out?" I ask.

"Not long, although now the entire hospital knows you snore."

I narrow my eyes. "I don't snore."

The king smiles slyly. "You're not the one who has to fall asleep next to you each evening."

"Most people bring their loved ones gifts; instead you bring your effortless charm."

He squeezes my hand tighter, and he leans in until his lips are barely an inch from mine. "How do you think I came to rule the world?"

"You're an asshole," I say, staring into his eyes, "and as an asshole, you've done a lot of asshole-ish things—including marrying me. *That's* how you came to rule the world."

The king touches my cheek. "Hmm. I think I like your dirty mouth better in the bedroom," he says, and then he closes the remaining distance between our lips.

My mouth moves against his, my tongue enjoying the taste of him. It's frightening how right he feels pressed this close to me. He has the same dark soul I do; he knows and embraces my sins, and I'm learning to accept his. I know he is dangerous to be around—dangerous to love— but my heart doesn't seem to care.

I lift a hand and run it through his hair, my fingers rubbing a strand of it together. This thing of my nightmares is just as human as I am.

Finally, he pulls away. "I have a meeting I've been putting off until you awakened." He glances at the clock hanging in the room. I can't put it off too much longer, but ..."

My hand slides from his hair to his cheek. "Go. I'll be waiting here for you to return."

He stands, looking reluctant to leave.

"The sooner you leave, the sooner I'll be out of this god-forsaken place," I say. The shudder that ripples through me is very real. My skin crawls even now at the smell of disinfectants and sickness that lingers in the room. An epidemic tore through this land years ago. I'm sure many people filed through these doors only to perish.

The king bends down and kisses my forehead. "Promise me you won't shoot anyone until I get back," he says.

My lips waver before they tug up at the corners. "I won't make a promise I can't keep."

IT'S NOT UNTIL the door to Serenity's room clicks shut that I let the façade slip. I run a hand over my mouth and jaw, feeling my age even if I don't look it. If my guards notice, they don't say anything. Not if they want to continue getting their cushy paychecks.

She's dying. The phrase repeats over and over in my head. That's what the doctors here seem to think. They aren't the only ones to think this, either. The royal physician had also pulled me aside, shook his head, and murmured his fears. Nothing official—it was a concern, not a diagnosis.

But several of the world's best doctors sharing the same fears? I'd be a damn fool not to take their words seriously.

I grapple with emotions I've never fully experienced before. I hadn't realized the depth of them—hadn't realized I even could feel this way about someone.

I'd wanted Serenity's affection, her fire, even her love—I just hadn't realized I'd give anything back in the process.

I rub the skin over my heart. The thought of losing her after I've only just gotten her makes it twinge.

Marco meets me at the end of the hall. "Your Majesty," he says in Basque, as he often does when he wants privacy, "how's the queen doing?"

"Fine."

Marco peers at me. We've known each other—trusted each other—since we were kids. The man can read me like a book.

"You talked to the doctor then?" Marco guesses.

Of course Marco would piece it together. I nod.

"And?"

I rub my eyes. "Doctor said the cancer had spread. The Sleeper reversed the damage, but ..." I take a deep breath. My hands tremble slightly, "we don't have the knowledge to stop the mutated cells from continuing to replicate." Which means the cancer is still, at this moment, producing more malignant tissue inside Serenity.

The Sleeper can fend it off so long as it doesn't move to her brain. But it inevitably will, and as soon as it does, it was game over. Not even the Sleeper has the ability to replicate the intricacies of the mind.

"So she's ... ?"

"Yes, I believe so," I say, before Marco can finish his thought. We'd bought Serenity time, but not much.

"Have you considered keeping our queen in the Sleeper until a cure's been discovered?"

I hiss in a breath. That's months—maybe even years—away.

My gaze snaps to him. "Of course I have. That's a last resort."

I've spent all this time pouring money into destroying healthy bodies and perfecting a body that isn't broken. Scant few of my efforts have focused on fixing sick ones.

"Hasn't it gotten to that point?" Marco asks. "She's dying. This could halt the damage."

Something thick lodges itself in my throat. It comes down to the Sleeper or death, and either option still takes her away from me. It's been hard enough waiting out her recovery during the last few weeks.

"Since when do you care?" I give Marco a sharp look.

"Since you started to."

Just like that, his words deflate my rising anger. I rub a hand over my mouth. "She might spend years asleep in it before we have the technology to remove the cancer forever." My voice comes out strong and smooth; I can't let even Marco, my oldest, closest friend, see how vulnerable I feel.

"Your Majesty," Marco pauses, picking his words carefully, "if you want her to live for as long as you will, this might be the only way. "

I WATCH THE door for several minutes after the king leaves, making sure that he's not going to double back to my room. When nothing happens, I fling the hospital sheets off of me, more than a little surprised that my body doesn't scream at the movement. In fact, I feel fine—not at all like I've just woken from an operation.

I'm right in the middle of an Eastern Empire hospital, one of the most coveted and secretive places under the king's control. It's where cutting edge medical research takes place.

Now is my chance to find out what exactly that research is.

Before I leave my bed to go explore, I gather up my gown to take a look at the extent of my surgery. I don't want to accidently reopen the wound and find myself a patient here for longer than absolutely necessary.

I lift the thin cotton fabric and reveal inch after inch of skin. I unveil my stomach, and a strange sort of disbelief twists inside my core. Just to be sure I'm seeing correctly, I run a hand over the smooth skin.

There are no surgical marks, no scars. Nothing. The only indication that something's happened to me is that a dark freckle that should've lingered near my bellybutton has now vanished as though it never existed in the first place.

So what did they do?

I PEER OUT the door of my room.

"What are you doing, my queen?"

I yelp at the sound of the voice. A guard stands off to the side of the door. Of course the king left a guard outside my room. Now I'm going to have to figure out how to shake him.

"I need to talk to a nurse," I say, slipping out the door and walking past him. Now that I'm up and about, I can feel my exhaustion after all. I'm not quite as fine as I assumed I was.

"Wait—my queen!" the guard calls from behind me. "You should not be out of bed."

I ignore him and continue towards the main desk on this floor concocting a quick plan to ditch my extra shadow.

The nurse manning the desk glances up when she hears my guard and me coming. Her face lights with surprise—I'm now that recognizable—before falling back into a careful mask.

"Do you need anything, my queen?" She doesn't demand to know why I'm out of bed, nor does she rush to get me back in my room.

Whatever operation was performed on me, she seems to feel I'm in good enough health to walk around.

"Can I speak with you in private?"

The nurse nods, her brow wrinkling. My guard still stands behind me, and I shoot him a look.

"I've been commanded to not let you out of my sight if you leave your room," he explains.

I turn back to the nurse and lean in close. "I need to

use the bathroom and I'd like to not be shadowed like a prisoner."

The nurse's gaze moves from me to the guard.

"Is there anyway you can make sure he stays out here?" I whisper.

The nurse mulls this over, then finally nods. "I think that'll be just fine," she says, her voice low. "Need anything else?"

"Just directions to the bathroom."

"Down the hall and to your left." The nurse nods in the appropriate direction.

Perfect. I'll be out of the guard and the nurse's line of sight.

"Thanks," I say, flashing her a genuine smile.

I push away from the counter. My guard is now looking at me suspiciously. I brush past him. When he begins to follow me, the nurse clears her throat. "Sir, sir—yes *you*," I hear from behind me.

I don't wait to listen to the rest. I move down the corridor and turn left, just so that it looks like I'm going to the bathroom. At the end of this hall is a stairwell, and right before it, a storage closet hangs slightly open. I stop by it and peek in. Medical supplies and a spare pair of scrubs rest on the shelves. I grab the scrubs and change into them quickly, just in case whoever left the door open is about to come back.

As I unfold the soft material, a keycard slips out. I pick it up and glance at the face of the male nurse whom these scrubs belong to. On it is a barcode, probably to allow him access into restricted areas.

The whole thing could not have gone better had I planned it.

I finish changing and palm the keycard. Slipping out of the closet, I enter the stairwell and take it down. It takes me ten minutes to locate where the research labs are, and I'm sure I only have minutes before the guard sounds the alarm that I'm missing.

I enter the lowest basement of the hospital. My first glimpses of this subterranean floor aren't promising. Paint peels from the walls and the exposed metal pipes I see. It smells like mildew and rot down here—not exactly the ideal atmosphere for cutting edge medical research.

Despite my misgivings, I begin to scrutinize the hall. The floor is abandoned.

A shiver races down my back. An epidemic preceded the king's war, culling the Eastern Hemisphere's population to little over a third of what it once was. I'd never noticed what exactly that looked like until this moment, when I stood in one of their understaffed hospitals.

I go for the first door I see. Locked. Damn. I place my head next to it; I can hear lugging noises on the other side. It must be a boiler room. The next door I come to is the morgue. I wrinkle my nose at the thought. As curious as I am to see if any of the research occurring in these hospitals has landed test subjects in here, I decide against it. Who knows if victims of biological warfare are in there? It would be a damn shame to survive cancer only to die of a virus.

The next door is unmarked. I try the handle. Just like the boiler room, this one is locked. Next to the handle, however, is a scanner. I lift the plastic card in my hand and hold it in front of the device. It beeps and a light flashes green next to it. I try the handle again and the door opens.

I slip into the room and flip on the lights. Whoever normally works here is gone for the time being. I glance around, almost afraid to touch anything. The counters are covered with racks of vials, strange machines, and data readouts.

I don't know where to start or what I'm looking for. I never thought my problem would be making sense of the research I came across. Hell, I don't even know if I'm in the right place.

I begin moving, my eyes scanning the papers strewn across the counters. I see numbers and percentages, but nothing that I recognize. Moving further into the room, I scan the counters, the machines, the spines of books that are sitting out.

I want to scream. Nothing here corroborates the Resistance's sparse findings.

I'm about to leave when the title of a document catches my eye: "Recent Medical Advances in Memory Recall and Suppression." It looks like an article from a medical journal, and the publication date printed below it is from a month ago. Recent. I read the abstract at the top of the page, which summarizes the content of the article.

There are more scientific terms than normal jargon, but from what I read, the topic seems to have to do with repressing long term and short term memories as well as reversing memory loss.

Those dazed technicians the Resistance had reported

on when I'd been back in the WUN... they'd been in the king's research labs. Could their predicament be related to this?

The very non-scientific wheels of my mind whir. Why *would* anyone want to repress a person's memories? The answer is so simple that I'm embarrassed I asked the question in the first place.

Control.

THE LAST THINGS I read are the news articles someone's taped to the wall. They all have to do with biological warfare. Some discuss the pathogens involved, and some go over the cures the king doled out once a region fell.

Death and health were the stick and carrot the king regularly used to gain control of a new land on the eastern hemisphere. He still doesn't seem to understand that repairing that which he broke doesn't make it new again. It makes it scarred.

I try the other doors in the basement. All are locked, and none will open with the key card in my hand. It makes me think that I never entered the room where the real research is occurring. A simple nurse might not have that kind of clearance.

I'd like to explore the rest of the hospital, but I've already been gone too long. So I walk back to the closet, change into my hospital gown, and place the scrubs where I found them.

"Last time I checked, the bathroom was across the hall."

I spin, only to come face-to-face with my guard. Despite

his soft-spoken words, he's angry.

My first instinct is to become defensive. So I do the opposite. "What does it matter to you? I'm the queen."

He grabs my upper arm. "You need to get back to your room, now." He begins leading me down the hall.

"I'm going to tell the king that you're manhandling me," I say, as I yank futilely against his grip. "He's not going to like that."

My guard chooses to ignore me. He opens the door to my room and pushes me inside.

"Hey—!" The door slams shut behind me.

What an ass.

I lean against the wall, not ready to get back in bed, and let my eyes drift around the room. They land on a calendar that hangs across from me.

I still. It says it is May, but it should still be April. I'm about to shrug it off when my hand goes to the smooth skin of my stomach.

What if some new technology was used on me—the same one that removed all traces of the king's bullet wounds from his body?

Perhaps I'm being paranoid, reading into things that aren't there, but that thought doesn't stop me from reaching for the door handle next to me and slipping back out into the hall.

"Your Majesty," the guard growls, blocking my exit. I feint to the right and duck under his arm, hurrying to the main desk.

"Can you tell me what day it is?" I ask, breathlessly to the nurse behind the desk, the same nurse who helped me earlier.

A moment later my guard comes to stand beside me, but he doesn't drag me off like I worried he might. I guess threatening to narc on him was effective after all.

The nurse across from me looks baffled by my request—or maybe just the fact that I'm out here again. "Of course, my queen," she says. She turns to the screen in front of her. "It's May tenth."

I do the math in my head. That would mean that it's been almost three weeks since I married the king and over two weeks since I came here for the operation.

"Is something the matter, Your Majesty?" the nurse asks.

I shake my head, my mind still far away. The surgery should've taken hours, not days, and definitely not weeks. I'm not being paranoid after all. Something did happen to me.

"You're sure that's today's date?" I ask.

The nurse glances from me to her screen again, looking uncomfortable. "Yep. May tenth." She smiles warmly at me, but it falters a bit when she takes in my expression. "Would you like me to escort you back to your room?" The nurse eyes me and the guard at my side, missing nothing.

"I'm fine." I back away from the main desk.

"I'll have someone check in on you in five minutes," the nurse says. She says it to comfort me, but I know her true motives are to make sure I'm okay before the king returns.

I walk back in a daze. Why would Montes not mention that I'd been out for weeks? And, more importantly, why *was* I out for that long?

THIRTY MINUTES LATER, I hear the click of expensive shoes on the hospital linoleum. The king is coming back to my room, and I'm ready for him.

As soon as the king takes up the doorway, his eyebrows raise. I'm sitting on top of my bed in my hospital gown, my forearms slung over my knees. In one of my hands I'm playing with a scalpel that I lifted from the nurse that checked on me.

"Where'd you get that?"

I narrow my eyes at the king. "You don't seriously expect me to answer that question, do you?"

He smirks, totally at ease with the fact that I'm playing with a scalpel in his presence.

Behind him I see Marco and some of the king's bodyguards flank the doorway. "He," I jut my chin at Marco, "better make himself scarce, or else this scalpel is going to find itself lodged into his chest."

King Lazuli saunters into the room. "There is no need for threats, my queen."

My eyes shoot daggers at Marco.

"Marco and his guards are going to wait outside while I spend time with my recovering wife." The king's mouth curves up at the last word.

Marco opens his mouth to speak. As soon as he does so, my hand tightens around the knife, and I rearrange my grip for throwing it. Marco's eyes flick to my hand, and his mouth closes. Without a further word, he slips out of the room.

"You need to stop threatening my men," the king says.

"Or else what?" I ask insolently. "You'll divorce me?"

He sighs. "Is that what you're trying to do? Make me regret my decision to marry you?"

"Absolutely." Gone for the moment are my blossoming feelings for the king. Instead I can't help but feel deeply disturbed once more by the king and his science.

The king leans in close—close enough for me to stab him if I desire it. He knows this too. I can see him daring me with his eyes.

"If I wanted to punish you for threatening my men, I'd find something infinitely more creative than divorce."

I flip the scalpel around in my hand several times, a small smile forming on my lips. "You're right. Divorce would hardly be punishment."

Montes's fingers touch my jaw, angling it to better face him. "Why are you so angry?"

"What have you done to me?"

The king's brows lift. "This is about your surgery?"

"See, there's where you've got it wrong," I say. "Surgeries require this—" I raise the scalpel, "—and they leave scars. Most importantly of all, they don't take *two weeks*."

"My doctors have access to the latest technology. You were placed in a device called the Sleeper. It removed the cancer and regenerated healthy tissue."

The king has equipment that can do that?

Before I can respond, the king wraps his hand around the base of the knife and tries to pull it from me.

"Hey—" I can tell I'm about to lose the scalpel, so I give

234

it a good yank and slide it against the king's skin.

The king curses as the knife cuts into the flesh between his thumb and forefinger and blood pools.

I let go of the scalpel just as the door to my room is thrown open. Marco comes in, gun drawn, a group of guards spreading out behind him.

I roll my eyes at Marco and very slowly relax my coiled muscles. Despite appearing indifferent, I'm not. I'm staring down the same gun barrel that my father had. The one that might've killed him.

"Your Majesty," Marco says, taking in the scene, "is everything alright?" His eyes flick to the king's bloody hand. "You're bleeding."

The king holds out the scalpel for Marco to take while studying me. "I'm fine," he says as Marco takes the knife from him. "I just cut myself while I took the scalpel from the queen." The king's giving me a strange look. I get the impression he's trying to figure me out.

"Your Majesty?" Marco says, not buying the story.

"That's all Marco," the king says.

"But sir, your hand ..."

"Later Marco," the king says, his eyes never straying from mine. "Leave us."

Marco hesitates, piercing me with a look that says just what he'll do to me if more harm befalls the king. I flash him my most nefarious grin as he backs out of the room.

"Must you terrify everyone you meet?" The king asks, grabbing some paper towels out of a dispenser to cauterize the flow of blood.

"Yes."

The king comes back to me, and that strange look is back in his eyes. "Why did you cut me?"

My skin prickles, not because of his question, but because he's not angry at all. He's *curious*. It's the wrong reaction, and it makes me worry that there indeed is something very, very wrong with the man I married.

"I wanted to see if you could bleed," I say. My words sound cruel and calculating even to my own ears. There is also something very wrong with me.

"No, you didn't," the king says. "You've already seen me bleed." He comes closer to my bed. "You want to know how I heal, don't you?" he says, his eyes ever so inquisitive.

My heart thumps. "Yes," I admit.

The king nods slowly. "You thought because I refused to tell you how I died before, I'd always refuse to tell you."

"How you *died* before?" I go completely still. Already he's admitted so much more than I expected.

"Perhaps 'died' is the wrong word." He sits on my bed and cups the side of my face. In his eyes I see something I hoped not to. I don't know what love is, and I doubt the king does either, but the expression he wears seems awfully near the mark.

"You really want to know?" he asks.

I nod.

He lets out a breath, then making a decision, he says, "All right. I'll tell you the whole sordid story—it's a long one."

This moment strikes me as terribly anticlimactic. King Lazuli, the feared ruler of the entire globe, is about to tell me his biggest and most well kept secret. A secret men

236

have killed and died for. A secret that used to bring goose bumps to my skin.

He presses his mouth to my ear, exhales, and breathes the first line. "But not here—"

The sound of shots ring out.

The king pulls back, and we stare at each other for a moment. Then we're moving.

Ambushed. Someone knows we're at this hospital, and we're being ambushed.

On the other side of the door, I hear Marco's voice. "Montes, Serenity," he shouts, dropping our titles, "stay inside." Then his footfalls move away from us.

He expects us to hide in this room like sitting ducks, but I've had too much military training to ever act like a civilian again. Oddly enough, Montes seems to have the same idea. He tries to push me behind him as he approaches the door. Instead I brush past him.

The king catches my hand. "Serenity—"

I turn and look at him. "I know what I'm doing."

He opens his mouth, then closes it. Montes tugs me to him and kisses me.

"I'll follow your lead," he says when he breaks away. "Just don't get hurt—that's an order."

I pull away from him. "I won't." I just hope I'm right.

CHAPTER 21

SERENITY

I CRACK THE door open and peek out. Just as I do so, my guard, who has been stationed at the door, turns toward us.

"Get back inside," he commands.

"You and I both know we're outnumbered," I say. That's the only way a group would be ballsy enough to infiltrate the hospital. "We need to leave this place."

The guard hesitates, and in that span of time, a series of shots punctuates the silence.

Now is the perfect time to kill the king or, at the very least, severely injure him. It's an unpleasant realization that I don't want him to meet his end here.

"Can you help me get the king out?" I ask.

I can feel Montes press in behind me.

The guard's eyes flick from me to the king. "There's a

back way out of the hospital where a car should be waiting," the guard says. "I can get him to it so long as the enemy isn't waiting there to ambush us."

Having been in communication with the Resistance for so long, I know how these groups work. They probably jumped on the unusual opportunity to attack the king while he was in a vulnerable position. It's a toss up whether they know the layout of the place or not.

"I'll go first," I say to the guard. "You'll have to navigate."

"No." Montes's hand falls heavily on my shoulder, like he's considering physically restraining me.

"My queen," the guard says, "it's my job to protect you too."

The sound of gunfire is getting closer.

"If the king dies, the world will be leaderless when we need one the most." I shouldn't be worrying about the king's death. He can't be killed. But I've seen him bleed just as easily as I do and watched him take medications like any other person might. I am beginning to think the Undying King isn't quite so resilient as he might have me believe.

"Serenity—" Montes begins.

I swivel to face him. "I'll be fi—"

The king shoves a gun into my hand, and for a beat I stare dumbly at it. I hadn't even realized the king was carrying.

"Don't hesitate to use it," he says.

My fingers curl around the weapon, and I nod. I open the door wider and pull Montes out with me.

To the king and the guard I'm sure I look resolute. That's not how I feel. Inside I'm battling years of conditioning. Two months ago, I would've used this opportunity to assist those who are attacking us. Now I am protecting the very person I once hated.

"Where do we go?" I ask.

The guard points down the hall, and we begin to trot. We pass the nurses' station, which is now abandoned.

The sound of gunfire is moving, but I can't tell where it's coming from.

At some point the guard yells, "Stop!"

I halt and turn to him and the king. The guard pulls out a key and inserts it into a door that blends into the wall.

My eyes move to Montes. He looks surprisingly calm, and I have to wonder how often he's been in this situation. As for me, I'm breathing heavily, but I feel exhilarated.

The guard opens the door and beckons us through. I enter first and glance around. It's a stairwell.

"The car is down two floors," the guard says.

I begin moving, ignoring the chill that seeps into my bare feet. The gunfire has died down, which means that someone's soldiers have been dealt with. I hope it's theirs rather than ours, then cringe when I realize just how quickly I changed sides.

The silence that follows has my heart pounding. This isn't a good situation, us being here in this stairwell with only a single guard to protect the king.

I descend the second flight of stairs. A narrow hallway

branches off of it, leading to a door that exits to the back of the hospital. Through the narrow window a nondescript van stands out against the inky black night.

"Is that the getaway car?" I ask.

"It is," Montes responds from behind me.

I turn to gaze at him. "I'm going out there first."

"No, you're not," Montes responds.

I glance at the guard.

"I take my orders from the king," he says.

I work my jaw but nod. I have to assume that everyone here can take care of themselves.

"Jose," the king says to the guard, "you'll go first, I'll go second, the queen will go last."

I open my mouth to protest, but Jose is already moving. I jog to keep up. Once Jose reaches the exit, my stomach clenches. If someone's waiting for us, we're either going to meet our maker or be in a whole lot of pain in the next few seconds.

Jose pushes open the door and sprints to the van. The king's right behind him, and then I'm out the door moving, gun in hand, my skin prickling at the cold night air.

The shot takes us all by surprise. I see Jose and the king flinch in front of me at the same time my body jerks. I already know whose been hit before the pain sets in.

I stumble and fall forward, clutching my side. Dark liquid seeps under my hand, and then the fiery sting of the wound explodes across my skin. I grind my teeth together at the lacerating pain.

The king shouts, and Jose muscles him into the car. Above that I can hear the pound of footsteps coming closer.

"Go!" I scream at them. I want to say so much more, but I can't seem to formulate my feelings into words. Not now when the pain is pushing every other thought to the wayside.

More shots blast my eardrums, and I jump at each one. Bullet holes dent the van frighteningly close to the wheels. Luckily the night makes the shooters' aim less accurate.

I lift the gun in my hand and fire in the vague direction of our attackers, but it's no use when I can't see them.

I hear the van's engine turn over. The king will make it. My sight blurs, but I can still see Montes struggling to leave the vehicle, and Jose's hand pushing him down so that he's not in the shooter's line of sight.

The pounding footsteps get closer and I glance behind me. A man and a woman wearing black fatigues jog towards us, their guns raised.

I aim my weapon and fire off three more shots—all misses due to my trembling hand—then the gun clicks empty.

Tires screech and the van peels out. Several more shots ring out, and bullet holes puncture the side of the van. The last thing I see before rough hands grab me is Montes's face.

It's a mask of despair, and that, more than anything frightens me. If the king is already in mourning, then I am as good as dead.

"WE GOT THE queen," the man radios to his accomplices. I guess I know which side survived the gunfire. "We're going to load her and take her back to the warehouse."

That can't be good.

Rough hands lift me from where I'm crumpled against the ground. I scream at the sensation. The woman grabs my arms and the man grabs my legs.

I shriek as they lift me, and salty tears sting my eyes. My wound feels like it's ripping me in two; warm liquid exits it and slides across my skin.

They carry me to a nearby ambulance and load me on a stretcher. I'm already starting to shiver.

"She's losing a lot of blood. Think she'll survive the ride?" the man asks the woman.

"Nadia will make sure she does."

I groan from the pain and squeeze my eyes shut, trying to forget just how my life led me here. Given the situation, I hope the wound takes me. Chances are good that if I live through it, I'm going to die a much more painful death.

The door to the ambulance opens, and I see the nurse I talked to earlier. "So you're the traitor?" I wheeze.

"I'd say the same thing to you." She glances at the man hovering over me. "Get the car started. The rest of the team is leaving."

She turns her attention back to me. "Let's get you fixed up." This must be Nadia.

They shot me only to stitch me back together. "This is why I hate doctors," I whisper.

"I'm a nurse," Nadia says, snapping on gloves. And then she touches the wound.

I scream. What she is, is a sadist.

I BLINK OPEN my eyes, confused about where I am. I twist my body to look around, and pain lacerates me everywhere. I yelp and still. My side throbs long after I stop moving, and I quickly fill in the gaps of my memory.

The king and I were ambushed. He escaped. I didn't. I'd been operated on and passed out at some point, either from the pain or the blood loss. And now I'm here.

I no longer side with the Resistance. That realization leaves a bitter taste in my mouth. They'd been my allies for so long. But I'd made the choice to defend the king—my husband—when I could've let him die. I find I don't regret it, either. *And now the Resistance and I are enemies.*

I'm still wearing the hospital gown, and crusted blood and bits of tissue cake it. I run my hands over my ribcage and waist and feel layers of gauze encircling the bullet wound. They've done a good job dressing my injury.

I sit up slowly, careful not to jostle anything. The glimpse of my room isn't promising. Cement walls and floor, a cot—which I'm resting on—a table and two chairs, a T.V. mounted near the ceiling. But my absolute favorite two details are the one-way mirror and the stainless steel toilet. If I need to go to the bathroom, I'll have an audience.

Someone must be watching me because the knob to my room twists and the door opens. I watch it, my face carefully arranged to look disinterested.

But the mask slips when I see exactly who steps through the door.

CHAPTER 22

SERENITY

"WILL?" I'M NOT sure whether to be horrified or elated that he's the one entering my cell. I do know that I'm shocked.

He's wearing the same black fatigues as everyone else, and I notice that he's carrying his weapons on him. Either he's planning to use force, or he hopes to intimidate me.

He crosses the room in three long strides and then I'm gathered in his arms. I wince from the pain.

"What are you doing here?" I ask, standing. "What's going on?"

"I'm now the head of the western chapter of the Resistance. And I'm here to help you kill the king." He lets me go long enough to cup my face. I swear for a moment he considers leaning in and kissing me, and I can't help but rear back. His hands drop, looking confused at my reaction.

"Will, you're still a part of the Resistance? What were you thinking? If the king finds out, he'll kill you." My heart pounds at the thought. Then the implications of Will's new position sink in. My eyes widen. "*You* ordered your men to shoot me?"

He cocks his head, like he doesn't understand me. "It needed to be believable."

"Believable for what?"

He leans in, his voice hushed. "Everyone thinks you're with the king except for me."

I give him a disbelieving look. "Will, I *am* with the king." That was why the representatives made me marry Montes—to glue together two warring hemispheres.

Will stares at me long and hard, like I might really be the traitor everyone else claims I am.

Surprise morphs to anger. I sacrificed so much for the good of my friends and my nation, and Will still wants to play soldier, to gamble with lives like this is a game.

"Does your father know of your actions?" I ask.

"Leave him out of this."

"He doesn't," I state.

Will shakes his head. "That's not the point, and that's not why we dragged you here." He grips my upper arms. "The king can be killed," he says, shaking me slightly.

His words catch my attention, temporarily distracting me from my current situation.

"How?" I ask.

Will releases me. "He hasn't told you?" He actually sounds surprised.

I hesitate. "The king was going to tell me once I recovered," I finally say.

Will's head tilted. "Is it true then? Do you have cancer?"

"If I answer your question, will you tell me how you know the king can be killed?"

He gives me a sharp nod, and I exhale, glancing down at my soiled gown. "It's true," I say quietly. "All that radiation ... I have stomach cancer."

As I speak, Will's brows draw together, and in the silence that follows, he glances away. One might think that he was overcome with emotion, but I know what he's really thinking—it's the same thing that plagued my thoughts for a while. He's wondering why the hell the king is trying to save my life.

"Did they get the cancer?" Will asks.

I fold my arms over my chest. "I wouldn't know. I was shot and kidnapped before I heard the prognosis." Voicing this only throws the absurdity of the whole situation in sharp relief: Will allowed Resistance members to shoot me even though he knew I might be sick. Right now his heartlessness is giving the king a run for his money.

Will grunts, and that's the closest he'll come to saying, *point taken.*

"I shared my news," I say. "Your turn."

"One of our members found out that the king takes a certain prescription," Will begins.

My mouth dries, and my fingers grip the skin of my arms tightly.

"We were able to get ahold of a sample of it and study what it does," Will continues.

I wait with bated breath.

"The thing's the fucking fountain of youth in a pill. Test subjects reported that their sunspots vanished, their wrinkles disappeared, and their hair regenerated—and that's only what they noticed. The truth is that daily doses of this drug lead to denser bones, stronger muscles, better eyesight—you name it."

I swallow. A pill that could effectively make you immortal. And I was now taking it. "Are there any side effects?" I ask.

"Don't know. However, this is the kicker: we found medical journals on this drug from almost thirty years ago."

I purse my lips. That was more than a little odd.

"Want to know who funded the bulk of the research?" Will asks.

I raise my eyebrows and nod for him to continue.

Will smiles grimly. "Your husband, Montes Lazuli."

I'M REELING FROM this revelation, though I shouldn't be too surprised, given the king's nature. Sometime in the shadowy bowels of history, Montes had come across this wonder pill. He could've been taking it that entire time—no, not could've, he *must've.*

I marvel at the thought that his real age might be close to sixty. Montes always struck me as ageless—not twenty, not sixty, not a hundred. There simply wasn't a number I could ascribe to him. I find that even now, even knowing he's as old as he is, my opinion of him doesn't change.

I'm still pondering this discovery when Will turns my

chin to face him. "The king is not immortal." He enunciates each word.

"If he's mortal," I say, playing devil's advocate, "then how do you explain him surviving getting shot? Or the explosion?"

Will shakes his head. "Another one of his medical discoveries—that must be at least part of the reason why he took over the hospitals first."

I admit, it makes sense, especially after being healed by the Sleeper. I've seen firsthand what the king's medical devices can accomplish. And it makes more sense than the king actually being immortal.

Strange, I preferred him an unnatural thing. It made who he was and what we had more okay in my mind.

"You can find out the rest." Will still holds my chin in his hand, and his eyes move to my lips. "Find out what makes the king supposedly indestructible and kill him."

"No."

"What?" Wills looks genuinely surprised.

"What makes you think I'm willing to work with you and the Resistance?"

He drops his grip on my jaw. "Why wouldn't you? Serenity, I'm trying to make things right."

I laugh at that. "This is you making things right? *Wow*."

He crowds me. "I'm not giving you a choice. We can torture you until you agree to this, if you want to be difficult. We also have enough damning material to blackmail you into following through should you get cold feet."

His words are a slap in the face, and at first I think he's joking, being hotheaded and speaking before he's thought through his words. But one glance at his eyes tells me that he's serious.

"You'd do that?" I ask, incredulous. "Blackmail me? Torture me? All just to get what you want?"

Will's jaw clenches.

God, he *would*. I suppose I shouldn't be surprised; this is the role he's trained for. To be a general, one has to make hard choices, to set one's feelings aside for the good of the people. Still, I can't wrap my mind around this side of him. This is not the Will I remember.

"What happened to you?" I ask, peering at him.

"What happened to me? What happened to *you*?" he retorts. "If I didn't know better, I'd say you were in love with the king."

I fist my hands. "Fuck you, Will," I whisper. "You don't have to lie with your parents' killer every night. You don't have to live with the guilt and disgust that comes with trying to make that situation work, because as queen you have the opportunity to benefit the world."

There's a flicker of remorse in his eyes, but I'm not done.

"I've given *every* ounce of myself," I say. "How dare you question my motives."

Will reaches up and touches a lock of hair. "I love you Serenity, you know that," he says. "But this is larger than us—we're talking about millions of lives here. Millions of lives that we can save."

"What do you think I'm trying to do right now?" I ask.

He shakes his head. "Whatever it is, it's not good enough."

250

I lift my chin. "What happens if the king dies? Who leads the world then?"

"You would, Serenity, along with whoever you appointed."

My breath catches. The Resistance's plans are all so painfully simple. If I came into power, I'd push the agenda I'd been raised with, and I'd likely employ those trusted few people I'd worked and fought alongside. Will would be one of them. Hell, he and the Resistance might've taken this a step further and assumed Will would replace the king.

A little piece of me dies; it's been dying since the moment I realized my friend allowed me to get shot.

I'm surrounded by bad men.

"You are blinded by power, Will." When had this happened, and how had I never noticed this metamorphosis?

Will raises his eyebrows and barks out a disbelieving laugh. "You think *I* am blinded by power?" He leans in, his lip curling. From his expression, I can see that my lack of cooperation has fermented into some more poisonous emotion. "The king has you under his thumb, just where he wants you. Who knew all it took was a little romance and a little dick?"

In one smooth motion I cock my fist back and slam it into his face. I can feel the agonizing movement across my entire body, and I bite the inside of my cheek to smother my cry. Still, hitting him is incredibly satisfying.

Will reels back, holding his nose, but I know it's not broken. I'm too weak at the moment to put much force behind the punch.

A moment later the door to my cell opens up, and a Resistance soldier steps a foot into the room. Will waves him away. "I'm fine," he says.

The man's eyes dart between us, but he steps back and closes the door, leaving us alone once more.

I step in close to him. "You and the rest of the WUN traded me for peace," I say, my voice rising. "If the king brainwashed me, that is your fault. If I'm falling for the king, it's only because you forced me to marry him." I'm shaking I'm so angry. "You don't have the right to use me anymore. *You already gave me away.*"

Will reels back, and I see genuine emotion in his eyes. Remorse. Regret.

I square my jaw. "I won't do what you ask," I say, my body still burning with fury. "You will have to torture me."

"Serenity." Will's voice drops low. "Please."

"Screw you, asshole. No."

Will exhales. "Fine." He looks over his shoulder at the one-way mirror beyond. "Omar, can we run that clip of the queen?"

A few seconds later the screen in the interrogation room winks on. It glows white for a moment, and then footage appears. I suck in a breath at the sight.

I watch myself step into the doorway of a jet. The short dress I wear is in tatters, and it flaps in the breeze. But it's not what flares my nostrils as I watch myself descend the stairs to the ground. Maroon blood is caked all over my body, and strange dark flecks of what must have once been flesh are splattered across me. I want to puke at the sight of myself.

"That's what will hit the Internet," Will says. "The king won't be able to sweep that under the rug—and if he does, we'll start posting the recordings and emails from the Resistance meetings that incriminate you until he is forced to do something about it. He will kill you. And he'll enjoy it. Still want to refuse my offer?"

I close my eyes and swallow. "I never thought you'd be the one to betray me, Will," I say.

"That's not an answer."

I open my eyes. "If you want to sentence me to death, so be it. You already received my answer."

Will's nostrils flare. He strides to the table, grasps a chair, and flings it at the one-way mirror. "Goddamnit Serenity, stop being an idiot!"

I watch him. "Is that supposed to scare me?"

His chest heaves. "You will be imprisoned, tortured, killed if you don't agree to do this. Do you care so little for your life?"

"I live with the devil. I've already died and gone to hell. So no, I don't care." The truth is, I don't want to die, and torture scares the shit out of me. But I've already bent to the will of too many men. I'm done compromising.

Will stands motionless. I can tell he doesn't know what to do. He probably assumed that I'd willingly agree to his plan, and that if I didn't, pain would sway me. He hadn't counted on me folding out altogether.

An alarm in the corner of the room sounds, and then someone radios Will. "The king's men have found us. The warehouse has been infiltrated."

For a split second, Will's distracted. This is my chance

to escape. I don't want to be the Resistance's pawn any-more than I'd wanted to be the WUN's or the king's. I lunge at him, my hand reaching for his weapon.

In one smooth move I flick open his holster and pull the gun out. I see a flash of betrayal in Will's eyes when I point the weapon at him, but I feel no remorse.

"So what, you're going to shoot me?" he asks.

"I'm seriously considering it, you fucker." My words burn like acid.

Will tilts his head. "You really are a traitor queen."

I pull my arm back and slam the gun into his temple. He crumples to the ground in front of me, unmoving.

I crouch next to him and avoid looking at his face. It's hard to reconcile this discontent man with the strong, kind friend I grew up alongside. Of all the ways I thought war would affect me, this is one I hadn't predicted. I never imagined that I could lose one of my closest companions.

Beneath my fingers I can feel Will's pulse. It's a little sluggish, but he'll be fine. For now.

Shots ring out somewhere around me, and I can't help feeling like a sitting duck in this room, even though the king's men have come for me. *They've come for me.*

I search Will's pockets for a key or a card—something that will get me out of this room. But he has nothing on him, and judging by the look of the door handle, there isn't a keyhole nor is there a keypad. It seems the interro-gation room has been designed to only unlock from the outside. Just my luck.

Five minutes later the door bursts open. I already have Will's gun trained on the door, ready to blow away anyone who considers using me as their ticket out of the warehouse. But instead of a Resistance soldier, one of the king's men surges into the room.

We make eye contact and I can see the relief soften the expression on his face and loosen his taut muscles. I drop the gun in my hand and kick it away.

The guard grabs a radio from his belt and calls in. "The queen is alive and secure. Repeat, the queen is alive and secure."

Will moans on the floor at my feet, and the guard's eyes snap to him. The guard glances down at my bloodied hospital gown and sucks in a breath. He cocks his gun and points it at Will.

"It wasn't him," I say. "This wound was from when I was shot outside the hospital."

The guard radios in a second time. "The queen is injured. Repeat, the queen is injured. Requesting a stretcher."

"I am *not* leaving this building on a stretcher," I growl out.

Over my dead body would that happen.

I GLARE UP at the hallway's florescent bulbs as I'm wheeled out. Around me several guards push the gurney, and I swear they're suppressing smiles. Pricks.

Somewhere ahead of me, one of the king's soldiers leads a handcuffed Will. But most of them surround me.

From the brief glimpses I get as I'm rolled out, I see bodies littering the floor, most lying in pools of their own blood. One of them is Nadia, the nurse that stitched up my gunshot wound, her eyes glazed and empty. The Resistance members here have been massacred.

My throat works. I shouldn't feel anything for them—not after they were so willing to hurt me. But these were once people I worked with. People whose courage I admired. Sorrow wells within me. Wrong is right, and right is wrong.

Somewhere ahead of me doors open, and early morning light pours in. I squint at the sunlight shining down on me.

Above me several helicopters circle the warehouse. I can't see my surroundings well, but by the looks of it, the king has brought most of his army here.

I hear a cheer rise through the air, but I can't tell who's watching.

Suddenly a head eclipses the light, and I make out the dark eyes of the king. My stretcher stops as the guards halt. The king cups my face and bends over me.

I feel a drop of water against my cheek. A tear—the king is crying. Over me.

He presses his lips to mine, and I feel the brush of his wet eyelashes against me. I've never seen the king cry—no footage has ever captured this side of him.

"I thought I'd lost you," he says, his voice choked.

My heart thumps painfully in my chest. It should never have been this way. My comrades turning on me, my enemies saving me. But worst of all, I should never have felt anything other than hatred for this man, the king. Definitely not this, this warmth that thaws my soul.

I stare into the king's eyes. I am Isolde, I am Juliet, I am Guinevere.

I am every one of those idiots because I've fallen for the king.

CHAPTER 23

THE KING

I WILL MURDER every last one of them. I will rip every last survivor from limb to limb, I will torture them for days for what they did to Serenity. For what they tried to do to me.

I can feel small pricks of pain behind my eyes, but I hold back my tears. She's safe now.

I thread my hands behind my head and pace outside Serenity's hospital room, where she's been resting since she returned.

Henry, the lead investigator of my secret service unit, approaches me. "Your Majesty, the prisoner who was found with Serenity in the interrogation room—we have reason to believe that he's the leader of the western division of the Resistance."

This is news. What is the leader of the western division doing here? And why was he the one in Serenity's room?

Cold dread settles in my stomach, but I keep my resolve steely.

"We're trying to figure that out at the moment." Henry's lips thin. "That's not all, Your Majesty."

I wait for him to go on.

"The prisoner is William Kline, the son of the former general of the WUN, Chris Kline."

HE KNEW HER. He knew her. He knew her.

And he betrayed her. He betrayed me. Hell, he probably betrayed his father.

There's nothing I hate worse than a traitor.

I watch him through the one-way mirrors as he's being tortured for information. Funny how quickly he's gone from being interrogator to interrogated.

Usually I stay far away from these sessions. They're a little too gruesome for my taste. But while Serenity is still sleeping off her latest surgery to undo the mediocre medical attention her bullet wound received, I'm savoring justice in its most savage form.

"Why did you kidnap Queen Serenity Lazuli?" the interrogator asks.

The general's son is silent.

"Still not going to talk?" the interrogator asks.

When William, the general's son, doesn't reply, the interrogator grabs the metal pliers and moves it over to an untouched finger. The table he sits in front of is already slick with blood.

"Stop!" William shrieks as another fingernail goes. This

isn't even the worst part yet.

"Do you want to talk?" the interrogator asks calmly. Civilly.

William is sobbing, and sweat drips down his pale face.

"Perhaps I should move to chopping off fingers ... or other things," the interrogator says.

The Resistance leader's jaw clenches.

"No? Then perhaps we'll just have to drag your father into it."

William's face pales further. "I—I'll talk." I can hear the defeat in his voice.

What the boy doesn't know is that my men are already on their way to execute his father. It's long overdue.

WHEN I WAKE up, my golden hair fanned out around me, I'm alone in the hospital room. The monitors beep and whirr.

I throw my legs over the side of the bed, the pads of my feet touching the cool linoleum. Not surprisingly, I feel like I've been rolled over by a tank. It doesn't matter. I can't take it in here. Not one second more. I've been either injured or recovering for the last few weeks in the hospital; I'm done being sick.

I rip out the IV drip taped to my wrist, only wincing slightly when I feel the momentary pain. A monitor next to me goes off.

Out of curiosity I lift up my hospital gown to look at my wound. Unlike the last time I was here, my body shows evidence of surgery. Clean bandages wrap around my torso. Relief floods me at the sight of it; it means that I haven't lost days or weeks.

I pull the cloth gown back down and exit my room.

In the hallway a swarm of guards keep watch outside my door. I guess the king didn't want to chance an attack again. As soon as they see me leaving, they try to coerce me back into the room.

"My queen, you need to—"

"The first person who tells me to rest will find themselves castrated," I say, piercing each guard with a glare.

The guards go silent, and I smile. "I want to see the

king," I say.

"But—"

I narrow my eyes on the guard who spoke and whatever he was going to say dies in his throat. "Take me to him— that's an order."

I FINGER MY spare clothes as I follow the guards through the secret service building. My arms shake; they've been doing that since I was told the king was extracting information from Will.

The guards glance nervously at one another. "You have my word you will not get in trouble for this," I promise.

I can tell which interrogation room Montes is in by the cluster of officials standing around it.

A couple of them see me and try to cut me off. "My queen, you can't—"

"I am fucking tired of hearing I can't do things today," I say. "Let me through or I will force my way through."

One tries to grab me. My fist snaps out, but he blocks it with his forearm. Another closes in, pressing a finger to his ear and speaking in low tones. I know what this is—containment.

"*Montes!*" I shriek.

Hands are on me, and the guards that led me here are nowhere to be seen. Pansies.

"Let me *go*," I snap, yanking at my arms. They won't release me. My anger spikes; there is nothing so infuriating as being physically helpless against another human being.

The door opens and Montes walks out. "What is going

on?" The moment he processes that I'm being detained against my will, his face hardens. "Let the queen go." His voice is steel.

Hands release me, and I glare at the guards.

"Serenity, what are you doing out of bed?"

"I want to see Will."

The king's jaw works. "You can't."

There's that command again. That I can't. And now I've heard it one time too many.

I push past the king and dart for the door he's come out of. I've barely managed to open the door when arms wrap around my midsection and pry me away. But not before I catch a glimpse of the viewing room, and beyond it, the interrogation.

All I see is crimson blood and all I hear are Will's screams. The outer walls must be thick to silence such agonized cries. The king's wrath is just as frightening as I'd always feared.

My mouth parts as I'm dragged away. "Oh God." My words croak out. "Stop," I whisper.

"Serenity—" The king's voice comes from behind me. He's the one restraining me.

"*Stop!*" I scream.

The king's hand rubs my skin, as if I am a child needing soothing from a nightmare. "We need information from him," he says.

"I don't care." I'm shaking all over. I've seen and done many horrifying things, but it's this one that undoes me. "This needs to stop." I'm no longer just talking about Will's interrogation. I'm talking about war—about being a woman raised on a diet of pain and punishment. Where evil is avenged with more evil. It will never be enough to remedy the world.

The king feels me trembling beneath his hands. "You need to rest."

"I'll do whatever you want, Montes, just please, stop torturing him." A tear leaks out. It's Will, after all. I might hate what he's become, but torture ... I don't wish that on my worst enemy.

The king sighs. "If we don't get information out of him, then your life might still be in danger. I can't allow that."

"Montes," I say, my hands clutching his arms. "*Please*."

That vein near his temple throbs, and I'm sure he's going to say no.

His hold on me drops. "Get the queen out of here." The king eyes each one of his soldiers. "And I don't care what threats the queen made to get here, the next time you defy my direct orders—it will be your head."

He raises an eyebrow at me—the warning is for me as well—then he turns on his heel and re-enters the interrogation room.

"*Montes!*" I yell after him. The door clicks shut; the bastard ignored me.

I stare at the room as I'm dragged away. My world is completely falling apart.

The walls of this place might be thick, but they don't muffle everything. I'm halfway down the hall when I hear a bang. My body jumps at the sound, and a tear leaks out.

Gone. Will is gone.

I'M GETTING TOO soft. That sentiment is running on repeat as my men drag the Resistance leader's body out of the interrogation room.

I've been the master of strategy and power plays since the beginning of my career. I don't compromise, ever. Yet here I am, watching the cleanup crew wipe up the boy's spilled blood. I did as Serenity asked—I put the traitor out of his misery. Thanks to listening to my bloody fucking heart instead of my brain, I threw away the opportunity to learn the locations of dozens of Resistance cells.

Deep in my gut, unease pools. Killing him was a mistake, one I can't correct. And it's one I might repeat if I become too compassionate. I rub my mouth.

"Your Majesty," Henry, the lead investigator, enters the room.

"Hmm?" I glance up at him.

"There's something you need to see, and it concerns the queen."

"THE RESISTANCE RECORDED the queen's interrogation," Henry explains as he leads me to one of the station's conference rooms.

That horrible rage that I've kept in check since we retrieved Serenity now rears its ugly head once more. That anyone would dare harm my wife. No one crosses me and gets away with it.

"Show me the footage." I know Henry doesn't miss the flinty edge to my voice.

Henry grabs a remote control sitting on the conference table and points it at the large screen that dominates one of the walls.

A grainy black and white image of a cinderblock cell flickers on. I lean my knuckles heavily on the desk, and I lean forward. My blood pressure rises as several Resistance members drag an unconscious Serenity into the room and dump her onto a cot.

Henry's time lapsed the footage so that it fast forwards several hours. During all that time, my wife's form barely moves. The sight of her looking so fragile does something to me.

The tape slows; several seconds later, Serenity's eyes open. After taking in the room, she sits up. I only have to wait a minute more before the door to her cell opens and William Kline joins her.

The sound is even grainer than the video, but I can still make out the words. I grit my teeth as William cups my wife's face. He touches her like he has a right to. Now I doubly regret my decision to end his life.

As I watch and listen to the entire interrogation—which really isn't an interrogation at all—my breathing slows. The Resistance knows so much more about me than I believed. I thought this might be the most worrisome aspect of it, until William threatens my queen.

"She's associated with the Resistance," Henry says.

"I can damn well see that," I snap.

I glare at the man on the screen. I should've gotten

more information out of this piece of shit. They've set their sights on the throne, and they plan on using my wife to usurp me. This needs to be suppressed stat.

I'm a cold-blooded bastard. I know this, the world knows this, and most of all, the queen knows this. Yet as I watch her, my heart pounds madly. She's vicious and frank, and she's not giving into their demands.

If I didn't understand her, I might've worried that she was some sort of double agent. But Serenity doesn't hide her violence and anger. No, she puts the worst parts of herself out on display and hides the best aspects of herself. Even that she's not so good at because she's risking torture and death by defending me.

She's the most fearless person I know.

My opinion of her only increases when she slugs Will, and again when she pulls his own gun on him.

It doesn't take a genius to know I married up.

CHAPTER 24

SERENITY

I'M RETURNED TO my hospital room where I languish until I'm questioned on my time spent in the warehouse. It's a sad day when giving a statement is preferable to the alternative—leaving me alone to my thoughts.

After the stunt I pulled with Will and the king, I have extra guards watching me throughout the day, none of whom want to make small talk. I burned that bridge either when I killed their comrades, or when the king threatened them with death for listening to me.

Hours tick by before I see Montes again. By then the officers are long gone, as are the painkillers I've been fed. Several sets of shoes click against the linoleum floor outside my room.

The king doesn't knock. He stalks inside, his men filing in behind him. My eyes flick to them.

Montes crosses the room, cups my face, and kisses me long and hard. It's over before I can react.

"Let's get the queen out of here," the king orders his men. There's shuffling.

"Does this mean I'm all better?"

He returns his attention to me, and he's looking at me funny. "I'm not making the same mistake twice," the king says, evading my question. "We'll be finishing your treatment in a more secure location."

That's when I know, I just know, I'm not all right. Not at all.

Things happen quickly after that. A nurse comes in with another round of pain pills, and I take them to distract myself from the king's unnerving expression. He's either deeply worried or deeply moved by me. Neither emotion is particularly welcome.

It's only as I'm moved to a stretcher and wheeled out that I realize something's amiss. My eyelids droop.

"What did you give me?" My voice slurs.

Montes is there, his brows pinched. "A mild sedative."

"Am I going to die?"

"No, Serenity, you're going to be fine."

THE KING

THE RESISTANCE MAKES good on their threat of blackmailing the queen. The first leaked file hits the Internet shortly before we land in Geneva.

Serenity's still unconscious, her body encased in the Sleeper, and she'll remain in there for the rest of the week. The machine is busy regenerating the muscle and skin destroyed by the gunshot wound and removing the cancerous tissue that's regrown since her last treatment. I could keep her in there like Marco suggested, but I'm a selfish prick and I want her out and by my side as soon as possible, cancer or no.

Marco himself is down in the hull of the aircraft with her, stashed away in another Sleeper. He also barely made it out of the hospital alive. The thought that I almost lost both Marco and Serenity to the Resistance has my fist curling in on itself. They're going to regret pissing me off.

So far the Resistance has released just a single audio file from one of their meetings, one where Serenity's taken an active role in the discussion. But even this small piece of evidence is damning. Serenity's promised the Japanese Resistance members weapons in return for information.

The leader in me admits she's good—shrewd, assertive, compelling, and empathetic when the conversation calls for it. Too bad she's on the wrong side of the conflict.

Already the Internet is blowing up with this. The audio has been compared to that from the peace talks here. It matches.

"I want those sites shut down," I say to the advisors onboard with me. "Have all the major search engines do a sweep for this audio file and have them block all the links they find. I want my top guys to trace the leak back to its source.

"Your Majesty," one replies, "it's likely encrypted."

"I don't fucking care. Have them find the source, or you're all out of jobs. I'm going to hunt these assholes down."

When I get my hands on them, I won't kill them.

They will wish I had.

I BLINK MY eyes open. An unfamiliar room stares back at me. My hands finger a velvety comforter, and around me a fresco covers the walls.

I push myself upright in bed, belatedly realizing there's no more pain. My eyes flutter shut as my hand brushes over my torso. Someone's removed the gauze, and where a bullet hole should be, there's only smooth skin.

The king's technology has cured me once more. The thought pisses me off, mostly because I got duped. Montes does what he wants when he wants to whomever he wants.

Flinging the sheets off, I begin to storm out of the room. Halfway to the door I realize I'm still in a hospital gown. I practically growl as I rip the thing off of me and search the dresser and closet for real clothes.

Five minutes later, wearing tight pants, a loose shirt, and ass-kicking boots, I stalk out of the room. My hair whips wildly around me. I couldn't care less how I look. In fact, the scarier the better.

Outside the room a guard intercepts me. "Your Majesty," he says, scurrying after me.

"Where's the king?" I demand.

"If you'll follow me, Your Majesty."

His acquiescence surprises me. I guess the king's learned that he can't keep me stationary unless he locks me up.

I trail after the guard. My body receives a shock when I

realize we're back in Geneva, inside the king's estate, and not the palace where I married him.

Why stop here and not there?

My thoughts are interrupted when the soldier halts in front of a door. Before he can politely knock on it, I push past him and throw the door open. Storming inside, I catch sight of over a dozen important people, including my husband. A tape recording immediately blares throughout the room.

I freeze as I hear a familiar voice—my own.

CHAPTER 25

Serenity

"Serenity," the king says, pushing his chair back and rising to his feet, "I wasn't informed you were awake."

I can hear the surprise—and happiness—in his voice. That's where the two of us are now. Caught between hate and love, between our grim reality and what might be.

Montes comes to my side while someone else clicks the recording off. He runs a hand through my hair, tilting my head to get a better look at me. "Are you feeling all right?"

"Don't baby me, Montes." I hear several of the king's men suck in air at that. I want to laugh. I've said so much worse to this man.

Montes's mouth curves at my words. He likes me best with my claws out.

I lift my chin a little as my gaze flicks beyond him to the other people in the room. Amongst them is Marco; guess he survived the hospital melee. Shame.

"What's going on?" I ask.

"The Resistance is blackmailing you," the king says.

My throat catches. "How bad is the situation?"

Montes lets out a breath. "People's opinion of you was already shaky since we were still at war with you only months ago. But you also participated in this terrorist group."

I don't deny it. I don't even try to.

"The Resistance is capitalizing on that. Over the last week they've begun a smear campaign, and they're targeting you."

I'm preoccupied with another portion of his statement. "A week?" I say. "Is that how long I've been unconscious?" I can't keep the accusation out of my voice.

"Yes." He's remorseless. Seems neither of us feel the need to defend our actions. I can respect that.

I turn my attention back to the situation at hand. The Resistance followed through with their threat; they'd already begun to disclose the incriminating files they had on me.

"How are people reacting?" I ask.

"Exactly how you'd think they might—they're getting worked up. Our statistics suggest that there's been a surge of new recruits in the Resistance."

All because of some audio files from when the king and I stood on opposite ends of the war. It's the ugly elephant in the room, this volatile history of ours. When we were more likely to kill than kiss. There will always be that looming shadow, and now it might mean more battles and more violence on the horizon.

I saunter towards the conference table. The rest of the room's been quietly watching the king and me up until now. I can tell by the glares of some of the king's men—and they're all men—that my presence isn't welcome. They could go screw themselves for all I care.

"I'm going to need to make a statement," I say, swiveling back to face the king.

He shakes his head, following me to the table. "They're waiting for that. As soon as you do so, they'll release the footage of your bloody arrival into the WUN. It'll undermine your credibility."

"We could release the footage first," I say. It would still be a shitshow, but at least we'd control the chaos somewhat.

Again the king shakes his head. "Better to let my team attempt to delete it from the Internet before it catches on."

I press my fingertips onto the conference table and nod. "Well, now you all know I've worked with the Resistance." When I look up, I give each one of the men in the room a piercing look, then turn back to the king. He's scrutinizing me, a small smile tugging at the corners of his mouth. I'm giving him a show, one that he seems to greatly enjoy.

"That means you might want to actually utilize me. I'm good for more than just staring at."

Next to me, the king's mouth tilts further up. "Yes, why don't we?" He places a hand on the small of my back and leads me to his seat while someone fetches him another chair. Finally, for the first time since we've met, I can tell the king doesn't just see me as a distraction.

He sees me as an equal.

"THE RESISTANCE HAS moles everywhere," I say to the men in the room. "And I do mean everywhere. When I was with them, they'd infiltrated many of your research labs. Now, however, they seem to have focused their attention on King Lazuli and me, which means they'll focus on the king's homes as well as those places we visit."

A muscle in Montes's jaw jumps. "You mean you believe there are Resistance members here right now?"

"Absolutely."

The king slams his fist into the table. "That should be impossible. We do intensive screening."

"Montes, tens of millions of people have died fighting this war. There are plenty of identities one can take on, and the Resistance excels at scrubbing them down. You'd never know."

This causes the king to pace, his hands clasped behind his back. He pauses and scrutinizes the men in the room. Suspicion flares in his eyes.

"Usually Resistance fighters take on positions that allow them to disappear," I say. "Maids, drivers, cooks, and so on. It's unlikely that any of the men in this room are in the Resistance's pocket ... though not impossible."

One of the king's advisors, who's been staring at me with intense vitriol, now speaks. "Your Majesty, how do we know the queen's not still working with them?"

The king stops pacing.

I tense, and not from the accusation itself. I couldn't care less what the king or his men think of my loyalties. I owe no one an explanation.

No, my muscles coil up the moment the king's shoes stop clicking against the floor because something bad is about to happen.

My eyes move over the men at the table. Like me, everyone's frozen in their seats.

I hear the squeak of the king's shoe soles as he swivels to face the man who spoke. "Are you questioning your queen's loyalty?" I can hear the dangerous edge in his voice.

Don't speak, I want to tell him.

I can see the man's body shaking. "N-no, merely—"

"You said 'how do we know the queen's not still working with them?' didn't you?"

"Yes, but—"

"How do we, indeed?" the king says. "Perhaps, you know something I don't about the queen's loyalties? I'm sure she's had plenty of time to deceive us between getting shot and fighting cancer."

The man's gone pale. The officers sitting at his sides are scooting away from him, like being too close might make them guilty by association.

When I glance at Montes, a smile is playing on his lips. He's a cat that's caught a mouse and is now toying with his food. "Or maybe it was when the Resistance kidnapped your queen and threatened her with torture?" Montes snaps his fingers. "Oh wait, she never gave into their demands."

My breath catches when I realize that my interrogation must've been recorded. Somehow the king got his hands on it.

Montes's voice goes cold. "How do we know you're not working with the Resistance, Ronaldo?"

The man, Ronaldo, shakes his head furiously, a sheen of sweat coating his forehead. "I'd never do such a thing. Please, Your Majesty, forgive me."

I and every other person in this room—including Ronaldo—know there's nothing he can say that will save him. This is a witch-hunt, and guilty or innocent, Montes has found his first suspect.

The king nods to Marco, who's seated to my right. I'd managed to ignore the asshole so far, but now my eyes move to him. Marco pushes out of his chair and approaches the man who spoke, the king's guards leaving their stations to flank him.

Now I understand why these men have kept so quiet. Speaking means catching the king's attention. Defeated nations everywhere can testify that garnering his attention is never a good thing. Hell, I can testify to that.

Montes has murder in his eyes. I stand abruptly, my chair scraping back. When his gaze meets mine, I shake my head. "I will not sit by and watch this."

The room's fallen silent, save for Ronaldo's quiet sobs as Marco and the guards drag him out. The king's just proved how he responds to challenges of any kind.

I, however, don't give two shits.

The king's arms are folded and he pinches his lower lip as he studies me. "You don't get a choice."

"I do if you want my help."

The king takes two ominous steps towards me, until he towers over me. "You might be my queen, but I am the leader, Serenity, and I make the decisions. And fuck it if I'll let you make demands of me."

So much for being equals.

I push past him, and he grabs my wrist. "I haven't dismissed you," he growls.

I laugh. "I don't answer to you, Montes. You better fucking remember who you married." There are millions of demure ladies who would've done his bidding in a heartbeat, who would've carved out their own identities to become whoever they thought he wanted. And yet he chose me, the one woman who won't do that, the one woman who's as likely to explode as he is.

Yanking my wrist out of his grip, I stalk out of the room, and no one stops me.

I don't know where I'm going, but it's a good thing I'm unarmed or else someone might get hurt. As it is, I'm eyeing the coat of arms that's on display ahead of me, and I'm seriously considering maiming the thing.

Behind me the door opens.

"*Serenity.*"

I rotate and see Montes headed towards me, his eyes angry. When he gets to me he wraps a hand around my throat and pushes me up against the wall. A knee slides between mine.

"You really shouldn't have left the room."

I should be pissing my pants at the look in his eye and the way he presses himself against me, but I'm not. I'm no longer frightened of this man. I don't know when that happened. The king has always been my nightmare. But he's not anymore. It's just further proof that I'm maladaptive.

I lift my chin. "Are you going to cart me away like you did Ronaldo?"

"I'm considering it."

I don't get the chance to reply.

Montes captures my mouth with his. Fear, anger, lust—they must all function on the same wavelength because one moment I'm pissed at the king, and the next I'm twining my tongue with his, my breaths coming in short, heavy pants.

His free hand grabs my hip and pulls me even closer to him. Close enough that I can tell he wants me. I find it curious that insubordination—and the resulting anger—could turn him on. Do people get intimate when they really just want to throttle each other? If so, I believe I'd excel at it.

"I think I will cart you away after all," Montes murmurs. He bends to pick me up. I'm slammed back into reality.

I rip my mouth from his. "We can't do this right now."

The king's eyebrows rise, and he smirks like I'm funny. "We're the rulers of the entire world; we can do whatever it is we want."

"But I still want to punch you in the face."

The king clucks his tongue. "My queen has never heard of angry sex. I think a woman like you would enjoy it."

The door we exited from opens. "Your Majesty, the Resistance just raided one of the warehouses of our weapons supplier. They took most of the armaments stored inside, including technology that hasn't officially hit the market."

Montes curses. His hold tightens on me before he releases me—though not completely. His hand slides down my arm and clasps my hand. He begins walking, tugging me along behind him.

I halt in my tracks, causing Montes to glance back at me. "I don't want you to hurt Ronaldo."

If I'm conceding something by returning to the king's conference room, then he's going to have to concede something, his earlier words be damned.

Montes narrows his eyes. "That man was the one who coordinated the atomic blasts that destroyed your nation all those years ago."

The news is a slap in the face.

"Still want to save him?" the king presses.

My throat constricts, but I force my words out. "Killing him will not resurrect my people."

The king tilts his head, like he has all the time in the world to ponder my request. "I know what you're doing, Serenity," he says, finally. "He'll return unharmed if you come with me and assist us with intel on the Resistance. If you don't, I can promise you that you'll never see Ronaldo again." I can see it in his eyes too; he'll end that man's life.

Bastard. Now look who's blackmailing whom.

"Deal?" He smiles like the devil he is.

I run my tongue over my teeth and nod. "Deal."

I SPEND THE rest of the day and well into the evening discussing what I know of the inner workings of the Resistance. My words will jeopardize hundreds of Resistance members, people I once worked with. The thought leaves a bad taste at the back of my mouth, but it doesn't stop me from telling Montes and his men everything they need to know.

The war's over. We should be focusing on healing communities, not more violence. Yet we can't. Not when stolen military weapons are in the hands of a terrorist organization. Because that's what the Resistance is and what it's always been, a terrorist organization. Vigilantes that use intimidation and coercion to fight for a cause they believe in.

When I stood with the WUN, I never minded their activities. It was enough that we were fighting a common enemy. Now that the war is over, the violence is no longer excusable. No matter where my allegiance once lay, I can't risk more innocent lives lost by staying quiet.

By the time Montes and I head back to our room, the mansion has a stillness to it that only comes with the deep night.

The king's hands are shoved into his pockets, and there's a vertical crease between his brows.

Once again my opinion of the king subtly shifts. Worries plague him. Another weakness. Another sign that he has a conscience.

He catches me looking, and the edge of his mouth tips up. He reaches for my hand.

We are the epitome of dysfunction. Our marriage won't work—it shouldn't. We are miserable human beings. And yet, when he laces his fingers through mine and I feel the thrill of contact, that tiny flame of hope I carry around flares up.

Anything's possible. From darkness to light, war to peace—hate to love.

The king brings the back of my hand to his lips and presses a kiss to it. The entire time he stares at me like we're sharing a secret. We are. We're two monsters that might not be quite so monstrous after all.

Anything's possible.

CHAPTER 26

SERENITY

BEFORE WE LEAVE Geneva, there's something of great importance to me here. A visit I've been anticipating and dreading. I come to find out it's the reason the king stopped here instead of his Mediterranean palace.

I enter the morgue alone—well, as alone as I'm allowed outside the king's estate. Today that means two guards flank me. Montes has wisely made himself scarce.

My eyes fall on the body in the middle of the room. He's already laid out, and suddenly, he's the only thing I have eyes for.

In four quick strides I cross the room. The medical examiner stands off to the side, and my guards fall away. It's just me and him.

My father.

Before I can think twice about it, I take his hand. It's

cold and the texture is somehow all wrong. He's been gone long enough that, even embalmed, there is no pretending that he's a living thing. Still, I can't seem to let him go.

My gaze travels to his face. The blood has been washed from him, and the bullet hole in his forehead's been sealed up.

A tear drips onto the metal table beside my father's head. "I was supposed to die with you," I whisper to him.

The loneliness of my situation slams into me. How am I supposed to live if the one person who mattered most to me is now dead?

Killed by my husband's people. How could I forgive Montes for this? What kind of weak woman would that make me?

"I'm so sorry, Dad." For a moment I wait for him to respond. I know what he would say: *Don't be. I'm so proud of you.*

A memory from two years ago floats in. I'd been so angry at the king, angry at all the senseless death.

My father placed a hand on my shoulder.

"Do you know why your mother and I named you 'Serenity'?" he'd asked me.

I shook my head; I had no idea where he was going with this.

"Serenity means to be at peace," he explained. "When your mother was pregnant, she said the thought of you gave her that—peace."

Ironic that my life had known so very little of it.

"You'll never live up to your namesake if you don't forgive, Serenity."

"Dad—" He managed to use my one weakness, my mother,

286

against me.

"No," he shook his head, "this is not an argument. What you choose to do with all that anger is your business. But you can't control the world; someone will always be there to wrong you. It's your choice to let it go. Only you can decide the woman you want to be."

It's finally time to let it go. I'm not excusing Montes's atrocities, nor all the monstrous acts that his war brought with it. No, I'm releasing my bitterness so that I can find peace within myself. I want to be that woman my father spoke of, the woman my mother might've imagined I'd become.

Perhaps my father was against my current circumstance. It doesn't change the fact that he always wanted the best for me. He'd want this, serenity.

BY THE TIME we arrive back at the king's palace by the sea, my father's remains are on their way to becoming ash. I didn't think he'd want to be buried in the ground after spending so many years down in the bunker.

Once he's cremated, I intend to scatter his ashes over our homeland, just like we did my mother's.

I walk into Montes's room—our room—and see the bed I lost my virginity in. I have mixed feelings about this place, but it's definitely better than Geneva, where memories of my father haunt the halls.

Montes comes in behind me. His arms weave around my torso and across my stomach. It's clear what feelings this room stirs in him.

He places a kiss along my neck. This hasn't happened in awhile—angry hallway encounter not withstanding. Surgeries, kidnapping, and healing wounds have kept us apart. But as the king's hands glide down my torso, I can tell that's all about to change.

I turn my head to face him. The look he gives me commands attention—demands I quiet my thoughts so that I can be filled with his. I see his charisma, his charm. It's what everyone notices, but below all those hardened layers is a shred of the man he must have been long ago. Someone who wasn't nearly so cruel. Perhaps it isn't just me who's capable of becoming a better person.

His fingers hook under my shirt, and he peels it off me.

"I hate you," I say quietly, without any of my usual venom.

Montes tosses my shirt aside. "I know—you've told me many times." He doesn't stop undressing me.

"But."

The king's hands still on the button of my pants. "But?" he repeats calmly. I know his cool demeanor is a ruse, especially when his eyes slowly travel up to mine.

I press the palm of my hand to the side of his face. "But it is not the only thing I feel for you."

The king's eyes smolder at my words. He understands what I'm saying even if I can't really put words to it.

He threads a hand behind my neck and pulls me to him, and I catch sight of it: a flicker of something vulnerable and compassionate on the king's face. His lips press hard against mine, kissing me like I'm his oxygen. This is magic, this is heaven, this is everything my life has denied me.

We begin tugging off our clothes. My hands grasp the collar of Montes's shirt, and I yank it open, popping buttons as I go. He growls low in this throat. The sound makes me pause until I realize that this is an approving sound.

The king pushes me up against the wall, and my back hits hard.

"Fuck," the king swears quietly, "did that hurt?"

There's that shred of humanity again in his eyes. Too bad it's misplaced. I am most comfortable with pain.

I tunnel my fingers into his hair and drag his head back harshly. "Don't stop."

The king's eyes hood, and he recaptures my mouth, his tongue forcing its way in.

For all his rough ministrations, his hands and his gaze are gentle. While his chest pins me to the wall and his mouth pillages mine, his fingers trail down the skin of my arms and my torso. They come to a halt low on my belly, and there they linger.

It's the area where a woman carries a child and just below the epicenter of my cancer.

The king falls to his knees and kisses it. I lean my head back and close my eyes at the tender gesture. We both know the king's plans for an heir will be put on hold indefinitely—at least if he wants one that shares my blood. It's one of the many things that go unsaid between the two of us because we can't seem to acknowledge things that waken our cold, charred hearts. Like the fact that I'm still dying.

He unzips my pants, tugs them off, leaving me in only

my lingerie. That's what I wear now—scraps of lace. I only tolerate them because I'm obviously not wasting material.

Montes stares at them, and I can see his thoughts turning wicked. "I wouldn't have guessed my wife would go for these." His eyes move to mine. "I always assumed you were more of a cotton panties lady."

"Better be careful what you say when my knee is that close to your face."

A wolfish smile breaks out on his face. His lips skim over the material, and then he drags them off of my legs.

Suddenly I feel far too exposed. I've only done this with Montes a handful of times, and before that, never. I'm not used to baring myself, and the king is at face-level with the most intimate parts of me. I reach down to cover myself, and the king catches my hands.

"I don't think so." He pins them to my side.

When he moves his mouth to my core, I yelp. "Montes!"

I'm scandalized; I wasn't aware that anything could still shock me.

The king lets out a husky laugh, then his lips return to the sensitive flesh. I don't last long. My legs buckle, and Montes is there to catch me. He stands and picks me up.

He quiets me with another kiss, and carries me to our bed. When he lays me out on it and removes the last of his clothes, I swear his eyes shine in the dim glow of the room's light.

Where I'm modest with nudity, the king isn't. Once he's fully unclothed, he approaches me, completely unselfconscious. My eyes stray to all the pleasing lines of his body. He is mesmerizing to look at.

He prowls over to me, his hands stroking my legs as he watches me, a slight smile playing along his lips. I can't stand just laying here, so I push myself to my knees.

Reaching out, I stroke the king's chest for no other reason than I want to. After all, he's clearly put his fingers—and lips—everywhere that pleases him.

The king's eyes close, and he covers my hands with his own. They're warm and they dwarf mine.

"Don't stop," he murmurs.

I blink. I hadn't realized that his touch had stilled my own. I move our hands down, over the ridges of his abs, across his obliques, to the hard, lean muscle of his thighs. Here the king's hands tighten over mine.

He releases his hold and softly pushes me back against the bed and follows me on, his body blanketing me.

There's something to be said about physical touch. I've gone so long without it that the sensation is better than the sweetest of the king's liquors. I don't believe I'm the only one that feels this way. Montes is stroking my skin.

It hits me: he's been with far more people than I have—he told me so himself—yet he's acting as though I'm something coveted.

One of the king's knees slink between my legs, spreading them apart. His hips settle heavily over me, and I can feel him right at my entrance. He shifts his pelvis, and then he's pushing into me.

The king enters slowly, watching me the entire time. This isn't the rough sex I expected. Somewhere along the way our frenzied movements have turned into this.

My lifelong enemy is now the person who's physically closest to me. And I don't mind. The remorse I felt on our wedding night is gone.

Montes thrusts into me, and the sensation is overwhelming. He's overwhelming—over me, inside me.

Something about the languid way he moves and the way his eyes track mine makes me think this is more than just physical for him. That I might now consume the thoughts of the man who consumes mine.

A small smile tugs at the corners of my lips.

Montes stills. "That's a first," he breathes.

I'm finally giving into whatever it is I feel for this man and forgiving myself for circumstances beyond my control. I'm drawing a new beginning. One where not everything is a battle.

LONG AFTER WE'VE finished, Montes clasps me to him. A light and fizzy emotion surges through me. Hope.

If not war, then love.

I don't know the first thing about it—love. I don't know if I'm even capable of it. But I also know that I have a limited time to learn. I'm still dying. If I hope to help the world before my time's up, then I'll have to work with the king to achieve it.

That's asking a lot of the two of us—working together. We're the last people for any of this. But it will happen. I'll make sure of it.

"Weeks ago you promised I could get involved with medical relief," I murmur.

Montes's fingers trail my back. "I did."

"I want to start tomorrow."

His fingers halt. They tap against my skin once, twice. "Then I'll put you in touch with the advisor on global health and wellness first thing," he says. Whether the king is actually doting on me or just interested in keeping me busy doesn't matter. I'll get to work immediately.

Neither of us speaks again for several minutes.

Eventually, Montes breaks the silence. "What do you fear above all else, Serenity?" he asks quietly.

It's a strange question, given our circumstances.

"You," I say automatically.

I glance up at him, but he's not looking at me. He's staring at the ceiling, a faraway expression on his face.

His thumb strokes my shoulder. "Is this another one of your 'facts'?" Now his eyes do travel to mine.

I give him a shove, even as my lips curve up. He has me there. One doesn't make love with one's fears. Not willingly. Then again ... perhaps I am the poster child for immersion therapy.

"Aside from me, is there anything you fear?"

My brows furrow.

When I don't respond, Montes says, "You can't answer my question."

I can't. Death doesn't scare me. Nor does pain. I might've said I feared losing the things that I love ... but I've already lost them all.

"What do *you* fear?" I ask.

He's silent. "I don't know," he finally says.

"You do," I accuse.

He sits up, the action causing the blanket to draw down and expose my breasts. I push myself up as well, dragging the sheet back over my chest.

"They kept blood and oxygen flowing to my brain," Montes says, rubbing his jaw. "That's how they did it—how they kept me alive even after I'd been shot. You can replace everything but the brain. If that goes, a person is well and truly dead."

My hands tighten on the cloth. I don't know why he's decided to confide in me now, but I don't stop him. People have killed and died to learn what he's telling me. And he's telling *me*, the woman who's threatened to kill him to his face.

He knows things have changed between us.

"The origins of this war began decades ago, when I was just a successful businessman trying my hand at politics. I'd caught wind of a company developing an Alzheimer's drug with unusual side effects. It could turn back the clock—it could return a patient to their brain's peak performance, reverse baldness and bone loss, increase skin's elasticity, repair torn tissue.

"I took a chance and bought the majority shareholding of the company, and gave it the capital needed to continue testing. The drug was further tweaked, and we found a way to prevent aging completely."

Will had been right; Montes had stumbled upon the fountain of youth.

"The company's shares skyrocketed, and for a while, there was real concern in the medical field that the drug had just made tens of thousands of health related jobs obsolete." The king gives a dry laugh. "It probably would've too."

That sounded ominous.

"A super-virus swept through the Eastern Hemisphere. It spread rapidly, killing seventy to eighty percent of its victims. People panicked. The world hadn't seen something like this in centuries."

Apprehension skitters through my veins.

"Then one of my researchers discovered that my drug could cure the illness—if taken in the right dosage for the right amount of time. "

The king stares down at his palms. "People demanded I mass produce it and hand it out for free."

It dawns on me, how these long ago events affected the present. "You didn't?"

"No," he says quietly. "I didn't. I sold it for profit instead. And as the world got sicker, I became richer."

Montes shoves a hand through his hair. "In the beginning, I didn't want power, I just didn't want to lose everything I'd built. But somewhere along the way the line between money and power blurred, until I became king of it all."

All those people that died when they could've been saved.

I cover my mouth with my hand and scramble out of bed, no longer caring that I'm exposing myself. My entire body is shaking.

"I should never have saved you," I whisper.

A muscle in Montes's cheek ticks. It's the only sign that my words affect him.

He pushes himself out of bed and stalks towards me. "You wanted to know what I fear most? Here it is: I fear I will always be alone. That no one who truly knows me will love me. Not even my wife."

I balk at this. "You've made piss poor life choices, and you want me to love you in spite of it? You're insane."

I swivel to grab my robe and get the fuck out of here when Montes catches me around the waist.

He tugs me to him, pulling me in close. "I'm not insane, Serenity," he whispers into my ear. "And you and I both know why you saved my life. It doesn't matter that you think I'm an evil bastard. You love me."

CHAPTER 27

SERENITY

"HERE THEY ARE," Nigel Hall, the king's head advisor on Global Health and Wellness, sets a crate of papers down on the desk between us, "the regional reports you requested. All two hundred and fifty-seven of them."

Montes made good on his promise to put me in touch with Nigel. That was three days ago, and it takes the king's advisor that long to collect and deliver all the information on the state of affairs in every corner of the world.

Tossing aside the cardboard top that covers the box, I pull out a handful of folders and begin flipping through them. There are hundreds of locations in need of medical relief. Places where the crime rate is exorbitantly high and the death rate is even higher.

This isn't just a medical issue; it was simple of me to assume so. I'll have to take a holistic approach: education, shelter, basic amenities, regional justice systems, health—they all need to be addressed if I want to do this right.

I thumb over the pages. "Who wrote up these reports?"

"The committees on health and wellness, environmental sustainability, regional economic ..."

I tune him out after that. I've heard enough. These reports were all written in-house, which means they're skewed to please the king.

Just to test my theory, I interrupt him. "Where are the WUN's?"

He flips through the files still in the box and pulls several out. I open them up. The regions are strangely divided here. I realize why when I delve into the reports.

The Midwest is sectioned off from the surrounding land. The committees involved decided that it was the region in the most dire need of relief, and here measures will be taken to rid the earth and water of radiation, repair the economy, and get people back to health.

It's laughable. The Midwest was one of the most unscathed areas of the WUN's land. Our former representatives figured that the king had plans to make use of the miles and miles of farmable land. This analysis only seems to support our theory.

"Interesting," I say, snapping the folder shut.

"What is?"

"The data gathered. It's inaccurate."

Nigel balks at my words. "Your Majesty, I assure you, these are the most comprehensive reports out there."

"Oh, I have no doubt of that. They're the *only* ones out there. But they're still inaccurate. I will not be following your committees' recommendations."

Nigel looks scandalized.

"Has anyone gone into these communities and asked the people themselves what they need?" I ask.

"Your Majesty," he says my title disparagingly, like how an adult might talk to a small child, "most of these areas are far too dangerous to enter."

"All the more reason to find out how to change the situation. I want you to pull together a team and begin plans for us to visit these places."

"'Us'? No, no, no. I'm afraid that's not possible. The king will have my head."

"You'll do this or *I'll* have yours."

"But the king—"

"I don't give a shit about the king's opinion on this." I talk over him. "I vow on my life I will offer you protection from him, Nigel, but this *will* be done." Montes owes the world that much.

Someone raps on the door. "Your Majesty." It's Marco. Abominable, douchelord Marco.

"I'm busy," I say, staring down a panicked Nigel.

"Not for this," he says. "The video has leaked."

WHEN I ENTER the king's conference room, I find him pacing. Behind him, footage of my entrance into the WUN plays in loops across the screen. When Will had showed the tape for me, I couldn't see all the meaningful details. Now I can. My face is alarmingly calm.

Marco shifts uncomfortably next to me as he catches

sight of the footage. In fact, most of the king's advisors sitting in on this meeting stare at me with a mixture of anger and horror.

"We've been deleting various uploads of the video all morning, but it keeps surfacing," Montes says.

"Why now?" I ask, my eyes traveling over him.

Three days ago, this man admitted to me how he stayed ageless and how the war came to be. I still can't wrap my mind around how he can look at himself in the mirror every day, or why my heart hasn't stopped aching for him.

Montes turns to look back at the screen. "We've destroyed numerous cells over the last several days."

The cells I'd told the king about. So this was a direct result of my efforts.

"How bad is it?"

That vein in Montes's temple pulses.

"You haven't been able to completely stop the leak, have you?" I say. He'd been so sure.

That's how kings fall. Hubris.

Montes glances away from the screen, piercing me with his gaze. It's an explosive look, one full of vicious protectiveness. For all his wicked deeds, he doesn't just care about himself. No, he cares fiercely about me too.

"It'll be taken care of," the king says. The edge in his voice makes me think more people will die.

I back out of the room and leave the king to his collusions. This isn't my battle. It once was, but no longer. I've already surrendered.

OVER THE NEXT week, Bedlam breaks out across the globe. The king isn't able to suppress the footage of me, and it's done exactly what the Resistance intended: sparked rebellion.

Uprisings pop up across continents, some more organized than others. The Resistance spearheads many of them, and they're the most destructive. Provincial governments are demolished, the king's research labs burned, armories ambushed. Reports suggest the group's numbers have nearly doubled since the video leaked, and membership was already in the hundreds of thousands.

I rub my forehead, trying to focus on the files Nigel gave me a week ago. I sit out in front of the palace soaking up the morning sun as I flip through them.

I've never been more unsure of myself than I am now. A year ago, I knew exactly who I was and what I stood for. The king was the enemy. He was evil and he wreaked death and destruction.

Now I'm married to that very man, and he's no longer so easily compartmentalized. The Resistance, whom I'd sided with for so long, is now the one perpetuating violence when the world's finally found peace. Right and wrong are lovers; I can't have one without the other.

I lean back against my chair and try to discern fact from fiction in these reports. I could be sifting through this inside, in the fancy new office I've been given, but I haven't had the luxury of lingering out in the sun for some time, and feeling the warm rays on my skin is better than even the king's most luxurious rooms.

I glance up from the report when I hear the distant

sound of a car coming up the drive.

I squint my eyes. Not one car. A battalion of them. And not just cars. Armored vehicles.

I stand, dropping the file on the stone bench beside me.

I hear a familiar whine; my mind sharpens at the sound. That ransacked warehouse, those missing weapons. I'm now facing them down.

The whine turns into a hiss as a rocket arcs across the sky from the bed of one of the cars. It's headed straight for the palace.

So today's the day I die.

CHAPTER 28

The King

My men get the call while I'm setting up provincial governments in South America. I see their fingers go to their earpieces one moment, and in the next, they're surrounding me.

"Your Majesty," one says, "we need to get you out of the palace. Now."

"What's going on?"

The explosion knocks me over the desk, the sound a roar in my ears. The walls shake as dust and plaster rain down on me.

Someone bombed my palace. *Someone bombed my palace.* Anger and incredulity war for dominance.

"Security breach! Front gate!" a guard yells, and then my soldiers are pulling me to my feet and dragging me out of the room.

The front gate? Serenity's out there. A bolt of panic flares through my veins.

I yank the hands off of me. "I'm not leaving without the queen." I need to see her now.

"Our men are already on it."

I hesitate, forcing my guards to drag me out of my room and propel me towards the map room, where escape waits.

Oh God, what if something already happened to her?

THE MISSILE SLAMS into the west wing of the palace, and the building erupts in a plume of fire and stone. I barely have time to cover my face before the wave of heat slams into me.

After all their years of planning, the Resistance is finally making their big move, and now I'm on the wrong side of the fight.

Go figure.

"Your Majesty!" The guards who've shadowed me all morning now sprint towards me as I rise to my feet.

When they reach me, I don't think. I grab the gun from one of the guard's holsters.

For a split second he looks at me like I've betrayed them. No, I have something much stupider in mind. "We need to cut them off."

The words are barely out of my mouth when one of my guards lays a hand on my shoulder. "We need to get you out of here. Now."

Perhaps if I'd grown up in a world without violence, I would've readily agreed to this. Instead I duck under the guard's arms and begin running for the front gate. I pump my arms; I can hear the king's men behind me.

I fall to one knee and line up the gun's sights, and then I fire, aiming at the leading car's front window.

A miss.

I correct my aim and try again.

Another miss.

I can see the line of vehicles a little better. Someone's reloading the rocket launcher in the bed of that truck. I bite my lip and pull the trigger. I miss my target—I am too far away for much accuracy—but my bullet punctures the driver's side window.

That's all it takes for the car to swerve, sending some of the men in the back over the tailgate.

A pair of arms wrap around my midsection, and I'm lifted off my feet. One of the king's vehicles cuts across the expansive lawn and lurches to a stop behind us. More of Montes's soldiers grab me and throw me into the car.

Fighting my guards' orders any longer will only get more people killed. This isn't a battle I'm equipped to fight in.

I right myself and glance out the window. Behind us I can see the Resistance's vehicles still barreling full speed ahead towards the gate. Other palace guards stationed near the palace entrance are already firing their weapons, but it's making no difference.

The gate lets out a sickening groan as the first car rams into it, and it's torn from its hinges. The palace has now been breached.

"Where are we going?" I ask.

"There's an escape route inside the palace that leads to a launch pad. The king's already on his way there."

Our car slams to a stop at the fancy courtyard in front of the palace's front doors.

"Move, move, move!" one of the soldiers shouts as we exit the vehicle. And now I understand; wherever this exit is, we're not nearly close enough to it.

A black cloud of smoke rises to my left, where a third of the palace lies in smoldering ruins.

I sprint towards the entrance of the palace, shielded by a cluster of guards. Behind us I can hear gunfire. The soldier next to me grunts and grabs his arm. A man to my left goes down.

This all has an eerie sense of déjà vu to it. There's even a good possibility that those shooting at us will avoid hitting me. Political figures tend to have higher currency alive rather than dead.

Though I doubt it'll do me any good surviving this if the enemy captures me. Torture, humiliation, and a slow death likely wait at their hands.

We burst through the front door. Inside, plumes of smoke and dust hover in the air.

At our backs a car screeches to a halt and car doors slam. They're practically nipping at our heels.

I still have the guard's gun, and I can't help swinging around and firing off a shot. My bullet hits a Resistance fighter square in the chest.

Finally made one goddamn mark.

"Come on, my queen." Hands are on me, dragging me back.

I rotate around and begin running again. "Where to?" I shout.

"Montes's map room."

"Is the king still alive?" I ask. I hate the way my pulse jumps when I ask the question. I've been trying to shove him out of my mind. Worrying can sabotage a soldier so quickly. In my experience, the harder you think about your fears, the likelier they are to manifest themselves.

"Aye," one of them says.

Relief courses through me. I've gone from wanting the man to die in the worst possible way to fearing for his safety. I'm sure there's some unhealthy explanation for this, but I am also far beyond caring. I'm a recovering monster that cares about another soulless creature.

Behind us I hear shouts, gunshots, and the sound of shattering objects. Anything that the king once held sacred is likely getting desecrated.

"There she is! I see the queen!" someone yells on the other end of the hall.

The soldiers tighten their guard around me. "Keep moving!" one of them shouts even as bullets begin to spray. "We're almost there!" I sense rather than see the soldier at my back go down. The tight circle around me shifts to close the space.

We take a sharp turn and the firing stops. The silence is a welcome relief until I hear the sickeningly familiar sound of an object clattering against the floor behind us.

"Grenade!" I shout.

My men shove me to the ground. I split my lip at the impact, but I don't register the pain before the grenade goes off. I feel the heat on my back, hear the yells and groans of the men who've taken the hit, breathe in the smoldering air.

My leg burns, but that's it.

The Resistance soldiers are already moving—I can hear their footfalls—and most of the soldiers that surround me are still.

I can tell the men above me are dead. I roll their blood-ied bodies off me. Something sharp lodges itself in my throat at their instantaneous decision to cover me; they surely knew they were sacrificing themselves.

"Anyone alive?" I shout.

"Aye," comes a pained voice beside me. Someone else grunts.

The survivors—two currently—are working their way out of the dog pile. None of us have any hope of escape unless we can get to that launch pad.

Pulling a gun out of one of the unquestionably dead men, I rise to a knee.

The Resistance fighters are already closing in on me, but all I see are targets—heads, hearts. I aim, fire, and move on to the next target. Rinse and repeat.

I'm in my element. Anger and aggression flood through my veins. I hit four soldiers before they get wise to my ways, and one shoots my arm. I scream as the bullet rips through skin and muscle.

Fuck that hurts.

I fire back before the shooter can clip me again. My aim's off, and the slug buries itself into the wall instead of his heart. Behind me I hear another gun go off and a Resistance soldier falls.

I can't turn, but I know it's one of my surviving guards. I rise to my feet and back up towards him. Before I reach him, his head whips back. I see blood and bone spray onto the walls and floor around him. He's gone.

I empty my gun and two of the three remaining men go down. The final man left standing reaches for his radio as

I grope around for another weapon.

I feel like a grave robber as I lift a gun off a dead body. People who've never seen action think there's something honorable in this—giving your life for a higher cause. This moment is proof that the human spirit is capable of nothing baser than war. The indignity of death. The desperation and apathy. I've been raised on it, but even I grasp the horror of it all.

I swivel and point the gun, but the Resistance member is gone, likely getting backup before he comes at me again. I push myself to my feet, hissing in a breath as I put weight on my scorched leg.

"Anyone alive?" I call out.

No one answers back. The second soldier who'd called out to me earlier must've died during the shootout.

I waste several seconds grabbing another gun and shoving it down the small of my back.

Move, I command my broken body. I have no idea where the king's map room is in this palace of his. I only saw the one in Geneva. And without a clear destination, I'm essentially a fly caught in the spider's web.

I limp down the hall, towards the first door I see. I doubt it leads to some promising destination, but I open it anyway and peek inside. Guest room. Not promising. I continue on.

I can hear shouting in the distance and those damn footfalls that herald another wave of Resistance fighters.

Hitting the end of the hall, I glance to my left and to my right. The walls have caved in one direction. I've hit the edge of the destruction. In the other direction dust is still settling from the blast.

One of the soldiers had said we were close, and this hall looks vaguely familiar. I might be able to find the exit on my own.

A moment later as I move down the remaining corridor, I spot the door to the king's conference room. The king's map room must be close by. Hope flares up in me. I hurry down the hall until I come across a door that looks like it leads to an important room. I try the door. Locked.

The footsteps are getting closer. No time to waste at this point. This is my only option. As soon as I step back to gun down the door, I hear voices on the other side.

I think I've found the map room. And here I thought I had the world's worst luck.

"Help!" I scream and begin to pound on the door. "It's the queen!"

I've got seconds left to get inside; otherwise, I'm as good as dead.

The door opens just as Resistance fighters turn down onto the hall. I level my gun and begin firing at them.

"Your Majesty!"

"Serenity!" The king's voice rises above the fray. What is he still doing in the palace? He should be gone by now.

Someone grabs me around the waist and drags me inside the room, and I suck in air through my teeth as my injured arm is jostled. The door slams shut, and I'm surrounded by the king's soldiers.

"Can you walk?" one asks.

I groan. "Yeah, but not quickly."

The king pushes through his men and comes to my

side. His hands don't know where to touch me, so he settles on my face.

No words are exchanged. They're not needed. I can see relief mingling with panic. And then he kisses me.

It's cut short by banging on the door. The door shudders. Several of the king's soldiers hang back to watch the room's entrance. It won't hold for long now that the Resistance saw me enter.

I'm assisted to a blast door propped open at the back of the room. I've seen these before, I know that once this door closes, there will be no getting it back open. Beyond it I can see a sleek passageway; I'm sure this is the escape route the soldier mentioned earlier.

Outside the room, the muffled pounding of footsteps lessens. Not a good sign.

The king's men lead him through the escape passage first. Marco stands to the side, waiting to follow us in. I notice something in his hand, but I never get a good look at it. Behind me I hear a muffled clink of a heavy object out in the hallway.

"Grena—!" My words are cut off by the explosion.

My body's thrown forward, right into Marco. The two of us fall in a tangle of limbs just outside the passage entrance. A plume of ash and dust obscures the room, but I can hear the tread of feet.

"Close the door!" Marco shouts.

The king roars something in response, but it's cut off by the slam of the blast door. The sound is a death knell; there will be no escaping now. Once again, the king's been shuffled away while I remain in the fray, this time with Marco, one of the men I revile most in the world.

I scramble to get up when Marco's hand presses me back down into the floor.

My gaze flicks to his. "Get the fuck off of—"

The side of Marco's fist slams down against my chest, and I choke on my words. A sharp, burning pain punctures my heart. I can't make sense of it until Marco withdraws his fist, and with it, an empty syringe.

"What've you done?" I ask, drawing in a ragged breath and touching my chest.

Shots are fired on the other end of the room, and I have no idea who's killing whom.

"It's a serum to make you forget."

My eyes widen in surprise. Those dazed technicians, that article on memory suppression—I'm staring down the terrible invention behind it all.

"The king's told you his secrets," Marco explains. "They'll torture them out of you unless they're not there."

"You bastard," I whisper. My memory is all I have left. I'll forget who I am, where I came from. I'll forget my father, my mother, my entire life.

I want to scratch the liquid out of me.

"The king possesses an antidote. It's reversible."

I huff at that. "Like that's going to do me a lot of good if I can't remember the king."

The sounds of gunfire are getting closer.

"He'll find you. Trust me, he will."

Marco rolls off me and pulls out a gun.

My breath catches. "What are you doing?" I ask, scrambling to sit up.

He clicks off the safety. "I only had one vial."

Marco doesn't hesitate. He places the gun barrel against his temple and fires. Blood and viscous things hit me.

And that is the end of Marco. For only a moment I find it strangely poetic that my father and my father's killer both died from the same wound. Then the thought is whisked away from me.

I try to snatch it again, but it's somewhere beyond my reach.

The serum is already working.

I press the back of my bloodied hand to my mouth. Whatever he gave me, it's puncturing holes in my memory almost at random. I remember entering this room, but not how I got here.

In the next breath I can't remember the name of the dead man in front of me, only that I hated him. The memory should scare me, but it just serves to piss me off.

I grab the dead man's gun and the one shoved down the small of my back and begin to shoot the encroaching militants. I'm not even positive who they are, or what they want, but they're approaching me like an enemy would.

My guns click empty, and I throw them as hard as I can at some of my attackers. I clip one and miss another.

Now I'm weaponless and I can't remember how I got here.

A handful of guns are trained on me, but they're not shooting. *Death is better than whatever they have in store.* I know this on some deep, instinctual level.

As soon as they come within range, I kick out at one and slam my fist into another. A man tackles me to the ground and yanks my wrists behind me. The movement tugs at my injuries and I scream out.

"Shut up," he growls.

"Fuck you."

He takes a fistful of my hair and smashes my head into the ground.

Once my wrists are bound, a black bag is dragged over my head, and the world goes dark.

I'm pulled up to my feet and led out of the room, and the men who've captured me start barking out questions I don't have answers for. Questions they expect answers to.

"*Where is the king?*"

"*Why did you betray your country?*"

"*How do you kill the king?*"

When I don't respond, they begin hitting my injuries until my body simply gives out and they have to drag me away.

I'm bound and blinded, but those are not nearly so constricting as the confusion running rampant in my head.

There are only a handful of things I understand with complete clarity at the moment: I'm a woman without a past, and these people need to access it. And if I can't remember it soon, I'm going to die a very painful death.

I know I'm someone powerful, someone dangerous. A grim smile tugs at my lips despite my current circumstances. I know I'm not afraid of pain or death. And these men and women? They should be afraid of me. Because whoever I am, I am violent, and I will be having my revenge.

Keep a lookout for the sequel:

The Queen of Traitors

Coming January 2016

Be sure to check out the Laura Thalassa's new adult
science fiction series

The Vanishing Girl

Out now!

Be sure to check out the Laura Thalassa's young adult
paranormal romance series

The Unearthly

Out now!

Acknowledgements

Dan Rix, you will always hold the place of honor in every one of my novels because, simply speaking, they wouldn't exist without you. Thank you for always encouraging me to write, for our ridiculous discussions on books, for designing my beautiful covers and formatting my manuscripts. But more than anything else, thank you for your unconditional love and unfailing support through thick and thin.

A huge thank you to Sunniva Dee, who edited this novel while juggling the release of not one, but three books of her own. Your comments and edits were, as usual, not only helpful, but also insightful and warmhearted.

To all the writer friends I've made along this journey, thank you for the laughs and encouragement. I'm ridiculously lucky to call you all my friends and colleagues.

I'm not sure what the fate of this book would be without the support of some of my most dedicated readers. Your emails, tweets, Facebook and Goodreads messages made me realize that Serenity's story was one that you wanted to read. Your excitement and your patience truly touched me.

Lastly, this book is dedicated to my mother, one of the strongest women I know. Mom, I hope that one day you'll truly grasp just how intensely I love you and how much I look up to you. Your life hasn't always been easy, and there were some times that were downright awful, but you braved on. Thank you for being such a light in my life and for being not just an amazing parent but also my best friend.

LAURA THALASSA LIVES in Santa Barbara, California with her husband, Dan Rix. When not writing, you can find her at www.laurathalassa.blogspot.com

Made in the USA
Middletown, DE
21 February 2015